D0007537

The Prodigal Son

Also by Kimberla Lawson Roby

The Reverend Curtis Black Series

A House Divided
The Reverend's Wife
Love, Honor, and Betray
Be Careful What You Pray For
The Best of Everything
Sin No More
Love & Lies
The Best-Kept Secret
Too Much of a Good Thing
Casting the First Stone

Standalone Titles

The Perfect Marriage
Secret Obsession
A Deep Dark Secret
One in a Million
Changing Faces
A Taste of Reality
It's a Thin Line
Here & Now
Behind Closed Doors

The Prodigal Son

KIMBERLA LAWSON ROBY

GRAND CENTRAL PUBLISHING

NEW YORK BOSTON

The characters and events in this book are fictitious. Any similarity to real persons, living or dead, is coincidental and not intended by the author.

Grand Central Publishing
Hachette Book Group
237 Park Avenue
New York, NY 10017

HachetteBookGroup.com

Printed in the United States of America

RRD-C

First Edition: May 2014
10 9 8 7 6 5 4 3 2 1

Grand Central Publishing is a division of Hachette Book Group, Inc.
The Grand Central Publishing name and logo is a trademark of Hachette Book Group, Inc.

The Hachette Speakers Bureau provides a wide range of authors for speaking events. To find out more, go to www.hachettespeakersbureau.com or call (866) 376-6591.

The publisher is not responsible for websites (or their content) that are not owned by the publisher.

Library of Congress Cataloging-in-Publication Data

Roby, Kimberla Lawson.
The prodigal son / Kimberla Lawson Roby.
pages cm.—(A Reverend Curtis Black novel)
ISBN 978-1-4555-2613-0 (hardback)—ISBN 978-1-4555-2612-3 (ebook)—ISBN 978-1-61969-466-8 (audio) 1. Black, Curtis (Fictitious character)—Fiction. 2. Fathers and sons—Fiction. 3. African American men—Fiction. 4. Domestic fiction. I. Title.
PS3568.O3189P76 2014
813'.54—dc23

2013034418

To the most loving and caring mom ever:
Arletha Tennin Stapleton.

After all these years, I still miss you every single day of my life, but I do know that you are with me eternally.

Thank you for everything, Mom.
I will love you always.

Acknowledgments

First and foremost, I thank God for absolutely everything. Without You, not a single blessing in my life would be possible. Your grace and mercy have sustained me since the day I was born, and I am beyond grateful. Thank You for allowing my twentieth title, *The Prodigal Son,* to be published.

To the most amazing husband in the world, my dearest Will. You have given me the best twenty-three years of marriage that any wife could hope for, and I will always love you from the bottom of my heart and soul. I so thank God for giving me you.

To my brothers, Willie Jr. and Michael (and my sister-in-law, Marilyn) Stapleton; my mother-in-law, Lillie Roby; my stepson and daughter-in-law, Trenod and Tasha Vines-Roby, and grandchildren, Alexander Lamont and Trenod Jr.; my sisters-in-law and brothers-in-law, Gloria, Ronald, Robert, Tammy, Terry, and Karen Roby; my nieces and nephews: Michael Jamaal, Malik, Ja'Mia, Ja'Mel, Shelia, William, Nakya, Kiera, Talia, Nyketa, Bianca, Lamont, Shamica, Brittany, DJ,

KaSondra, Kaprisha, and Kiara (our goddaughter); my aunts and uncles: Clifton Sr., Vernell, Fannie, Earl, Ada, Ben, Ollie, Mary Lou, Charlie, Shirley Jean, Ed, Ruby, Lehman, Thressia, Rosie B., Isaac, and Iris Jean; and all my many, many cousins—thank you for supporting me with every book I've written, and please know that I love you all so, so very much. This includes Tennins, Ballards, Lawsons, Stapletons, Youngs, Beasleys, Haleys, Romes, Greens, Robys, Garys, Shannons, Normans, and everyone else I'm so blessed to be related to!

To my late brother-in-law, James E. Roby. I love you, and you will never be forgotten.

To my girls/sisters for life: my first cousin and fellow author, Patricia Haley-Glass (who I spent just about every weekend with as a child at both our houses), Kelli Tunson Bullard (my best friend since age six), Lori Whitaker Thurman (my best friend since 1986), and Janell Green (my dear cousin)—I love each of you dearly. To the mothers of my nieces and nephews who are also like sisters: Karen Coleman, Danetta Taylor, and April Farris—I love you all; to my spiritual mother, Dr. Betty Price, for all your tremendous love, kindness, compassion, and support—I love you with all my heart; to everyone at the best publishing house ever—Grand Central Publishing: Jamie Raab, Beth de Guzman, Linda Duggins, Elizabeth Connor, Deb Futter, Emi Battaglia, Scott Rosenfeld, and the entire sales force and marketing departments—thank you all so much for everything and then some. To the best freelance team in the world: Connie Dettman, Shandra Hill Smith, Luke LeFevre, Pam Walker-Williams, and Ella Curry—thanks a million for all your talent, dedication and well . . . everything.

Then, to every bookseller who sells my work, every newspaper, magazine, radio station, TV station, and website or blog that supports me as an author year after year, and to every book club that continually chooses my work as your monthly selection—thank you so very much.

Finally, to the folks who have been the biggest blessing of all when it comes to my writing career—**my wonderfully kind, truly fabulous, and very supportive readers**. As I mentioned above, this is my twentieth novel, and I am forever grateful to **ALL** of you.

Much love and God bless you always,

Kimberla

E-Mail: kim@kimroby.com
Facebook: www.facebook.com/kimberlalawsonroby
Twitter: www.twitter.com/KimberlaLRoby

The Prodigal Son

Chapter 1

Matthew stared at his wife of ten months and shook his head.

Racquel, who was sitting at the opposite end of the chocolate brown leather sofa, looked over at him and frowned. "What?"

Matthew shook his head again. This time, his eyes screamed disappointment. But all Racquel did was purse her lips and turn her attention back to the flat-screen television. It was a noticeably warm Friday evening in May, and though Matthew was a bit tired from his long day at work, he would have loved nothing more than for the two of them to be out somewhere enjoying each other; maybe have a nice dinner and catch whatever new movie was playing. But, as usual, Racquel was contently curled up—like an unconcerned couch potato—doing what she did best: watching some awful, ungodly reality show.

Matthew leaned his head back on the sofa and closed his eyes. Not in his wildest imagination—not in a thousand lifetimes—would he have ever pictured himself being so miserable. But miserable he was, and worse, he now realized that getting married at the young age of nineteen had been a horrible mistake. He'd now turned twenty, but he could kick himself for giving up a full, four-year, academic scholarship to Harvard University, something he'd worked very hard for his entire childhood—and now *this* was all he had to show for it? *This*, a tiny, two-bedroom apartment, a twelve-dollar-an-hour job at a bank, and no love life of any kind to speak of? Not since the day he'd been born had he ever had to struggle financially. Even before he'd met his father, which hadn't happened until he was seven years old, Matthew had lived a pretty good life because his maternal grandparents had always seen to it. Then, of course, when his mom had married his dad, he hadn't gone without anything.

He must have been crazy in love or crazy out of his mind to think he was doing the right thing by getting married. He also couldn't deny how right his mother had been every time she'd warned him about having unprotected sex. He still hadn't spoken to either of his parents in more than a year—not even when they'd mailed him a ten-thousand-dollar check, and he'd torn it up—but his mom had been correct in her thinking. Matthew wasn't sure why he'd been so careless and irresponsible. However, he was proud of the fact that he'd immediately manned up as soon as he'd learned of Racquel's pregnancy and had decided to be there for both her and the baby. Then, as it had turned out, Racquel's parents had also told him that they would take care of little MJ until he and Racquel finished college—since Racquel had been scheduled to attend MIT a few months after the baby was born. So, off to Boston he had gone—and life had been great until that dreadful day in January when Racquel had gone into labor much too early. A huge blowup had ensued between his mother and Vanessa, the two grandmothers-to-be, at Racquel's baby shower, and Racquel had gotten herself all worked up over it. Next thing anyone had known, her water had broken and she'd been rushed to the hospital.

Matthew remembered how terrified he'd been that Racquel would lose the baby, but thank God, everything had turned out well. Little MJ had been born with a respiratory problem, but he'd ended up being released from the hospital just a few days later. Although, the more Matthew thought about all that had evolved, he was saddened further because none of what had occurred on the day of the baby shower could compare to any of what had happened a few weeks afterward. His mother had concocted the most outlandish scheme, and before long, the Division of Children and Family Services had come knocking at the front door of Racquel's parents', stating that they'd received two phone calls claiming child abuse. Of course, none of this had been true, and although in the end, the truth had been exposed and Charlotte had been arrested, the whole idea of little MJ being snatched away from her had been too much for Racquel to handle. It was the reason she now regularly obsessed over their one-year-old son, and she never felt comfortable leaving him with her own parents, let alone anyone else. She wasn't even okay with Matthew taking MJ to see his sister, Alicia, or his great-aunt Emma because she feared something might happen to him or that he might be kidnapped. That whole DCFS incident had ruined Racquel emotionally, and Matthew had a feeling things would never be normal for them again. As it was, she rarely left the house, and she no longer visited any of her friends when they came home from school for the weekend. She never invited anyone over to the apartment either.

Matthew opened his eyes and turned his head toward Racquel. At first she ignored him, even though he knew she saw him looking at her, but finally, she turned toward him in a huff.

"Why do you keep staring at me?"

Matthew gazed at her. "Because."

"Because what, Matt?"

"Look at you? All that long, beautiful hair. When was the last time you even bothered to comb it? Or put on a little makeup?"

"Excuse me? Well, in case you haven't noticed, I have a baby to take care of. So trying to look beautiful is the very *least* of my worries."

"Maybe. But have you taken a good look at this place?" Matthew scanned the living room and looked toward the kitchen. Her and MJ's dirty clothes were scattered everywhere. He also saw just about every toy MJ owned strewn across the floor. "It's a complete mess, Racquel. We're practically living in filth, and you stroll around here like it's clean as a whistle."

"Like I said, I have a baby to take care of."

"Is that also the reason we don't make love anymore?"

Racquel squinted her eyes. "Is that all you care about?"

"No, but I think it's a cryin' shame that I'm a married man, yet I haven't had sex in over two months. And even when we did it then, I had to nag you for three days about it."

Racquel rolled her eyes and turned back to the television.

Matthew snatched the remote control from the sofa and turned it off.

Racquel stood up. "Are you crazy? What's wrong with you?"

"Everything, Racquel! I'm sick of this. All you do is watch those mindless reality shows, eat a ton of junk food, and then you watch *more* stupid reality shows. And I'm not sure how much more I can take."

"Oh really? Well, why don't you leave then? Why don't you just file for a divorce, because nobody's forcing you to be here."

Matthew swallowed hard. He'd known for a while that they had major marital problems, but he hadn't expected her to suggest a breakup so quickly. "Wow. So that's how you feel about me?"

"You're the one complaining, Matt, so if you want out I won't try to stop you. If you're that miserable and unhappy, then what's the point?"

"Are you saying you don't love me anymore?"

"I'm not saying that at all, but your mother ruined everything for us. She had my child taken from me, Matt. She made false accusations about me and my mom, even though neither of us would ever do anything to hurt little MJ. I nearly had a nervous breakdown over that nonsense."

"I understand that, baby, but my mother hasn't been in the picture for a while. I cut her off because of what she did, and then I married you. I stuck by you, because I love you."

Racquel didn't respond and walked into the kitchen. Matthew wasn't sure whether to follow her or not. He knew she'd been traumatized, but he also didn't think it was fair for her to blame him for his mother's actions. He hadn't done anything to cause her pain, and actually, all he'd done was try to love her and be there for her. He'd given up Harvard, a close relationship with his parents, and a comfortable way of living—all of which he hadn't minded doing as long as he had his wife and son.

Racquel walked back into the living room with a can of orange soda and a package of cookies in her hands and dropped back down on the sofa. She sat as close to the arm of the couch as she could and as far away from Matthew as possible.

"Maybe we should see a counselor," he said.

Racquel picked up the selector and turned the TV back on, but she never looked at him. "I don't think so."

"Why?"

"Because there's nothing wrong with me."

"Maybe not, baby, but you just said yourself that you nearly had a nervous breakdown."

"That was then, but I'm fine now. I'm good."

"No, you're not, and neither are we as a couple."

Racquel sighed loudly and pulled her legs under her behind. She flipped through a few channels and finally settled on... another reality show.

Matthew wanted to protest—wanted to shut the TV off again—but instead, he got up and went into their bedroom. He dove face-first onto the bed and took a deep breath. A ton of thoughts gyrated through his mind but there was one thought that troubled him a great deal: he regretted ever marrying Racquel. He did still love her, he guessed, but he was starting not to like her very much and that wasn't good. As a matter of fact, to him, not liking the person you were married to was a lot worse than not being in love with them. If you didn't like someone, you almost hated having to be around them. Then, you eventually got to a point where you avoided them completely, and there was usually no turning back from that. Matthew hated the way he was feeling because something told him that his once happy marriage was only going to crumble even further—not just slightly but to the extreme.

Chapter 2

Dillon smiled at his stepmother, but silently he hated her. Charlotte was a real piece of work, one of the wickedest women he'd ever met, and he couldn't stand her. The only reason he pretended that he was genuinely fond of her was for his father's sake, because he could tell that this *relationship* between Dillon—his new son—and the wife he loved so much made Curtis happy. Dillon lived for the day when he would no longer have to deal with Charlotte, but for now he tolerated her. He did whatever was necessary to remain in his father's good graces.

Take this evening, for instance; he would have much rather been spending some one-on-one time with his father, but instead, he sat there laughing and chatting with that witch, Charlotte, his bratty baby sister, Curtina, his spoiled twenty-seven-year-old sister, Alicia, and her ex-husband, Phillip. Of course, his fiancée, Melissa, had also accompanied him to his dad's house, but to be honest, he didn't want her there either. Last year, when they'd first moved to Illinois—before Curtis had learned that Dillon was his son—Melissa had sneakily helped him get close to his dad. However, as far as Dillon was concerned, she had served her purpose and he no longer needed her. He had in fact given her an engagement ring, but that had only been so he could convince his father that they were about to be married and that they needed premarital counseling sessions with him. But Dillon certainly didn't love her—not even as tall and beautiful as she was. Still, Melissa wouldn't leave and move back to Atlanta the way he'd tried to persuade her. He'd even offered her a few thousand dollars as a way of saying "thank you"—something he could definitely afford since his father had gifted him with such a large chunk of money a year ago—a half million dollars to be exact. But Melissa had turned it down and then made it clear that all she wanted was to love him and be with him. Right now, though, his only priority was building the best father-son relationship he could with his dad, so for the most part he didn't have much time for Melissa. She was good to have around for sexual purposes and she took care of their condo pretty well, but she would never be his wife.

Dillon watched and listened as his father played with little Curtina, and for a moment a tinge of rage and resentment overtook him. Curtina had just turned six last month, and she was having the time of her life. She was by far one of the happiest children Dillon had ever seen, but what angered him was the fact that *he* was Curtis's child, too—his firstborn—yet Dillon hadn't been given the same opportunity to grow up in a loving environment the way his baby sister was. His dad had slept with Dillon's mom, denied that he was Dillon's father, and then he'd blackmailed Dillon's mom in such a cruel way that she'd taken her own life. Dillon had only been a newborn at the time, but fortunately, his aunt had been kind enough to take him in and raise him. Still, he hadn't lived the kind of life Curtina was living, because his aunt worked a lot of hours and had been forced to leave him with a lot of different babysitters; not to mention that most weeks she'd barely been able to make ends meet.

Which was the reason that even today there were times when Dillon felt like an abandoned orphan. He felt as though he were alone in this world, and that he would never fully know what it felt like to truly be loved by someone. He wasn't looking for the kind of love Melissa and other women had tried to offer him; no, what he wanted was unconditional love from a parent. Love from his biological father. Love from the man who was sitting a few feet away—the man whom everyone said Dillon looked like. Love from a father who was having a joyous time with the baby of the family and not paying much attention at all to his son. More than anything, what Dillon wanted to know was when it would be his turn. In the beginning, his father had seemingly gone out of his way trying to welcome him to the family and, yes, he'd also included Dillon in all their gatherings, but every time they seemed to be getting closer, Alicia or Curtina always interrupted them.

Two months ago, when Curtis and Dillon had planned a trip to downtown Chicago to see the car show, Charlotte and Curtina had decided at the last minute to join them. Then there was the time when Curtis had invited Dillon to drive up to a church in Milwaukee where he was scheduled to be the guest speaker, but Alicia and Phillip had met them there as well. Or like tonight, when they'd originally planned on ordering Mexican food for dinner—because Mexican was one of Dillon's favorites—they'd decided against it because Queen Curtina had wanted pizza. So, needless to say, Dillon was starting to realize that Curtina would always get what she wanted and that she would always be more special to Curtis than he was. Everything was always about Dillon's two sisters, and had his brother, Matthew, not ended his relationship with his parents, Dillon was sure he'd have to compete with him, too. So again, every time Dillon looked forward to spending good quality time alone with his father, someone always went out of their way to ruin it—and Dillon was becoming a little tired of it.

But then, maybe if he hadn't gone public on television about what his father had done to his mother, his father might work a bit harder at making him a priority. Dillon hadn't wanted to go that far, anyway, placing his father on blast on live television, but that was a whole other story, and now he had to live with his decision. Although, actually, what he'd done hadn't seemed to bother his father so much at the time, and to prove it Curtis had apologized profusely to Dillon for disowning him for so many years and he'd given Dillon that huge windfall. So now Dillon didn't know what to think or what he needed to do to become his father's most beloved child—the child he cared about more than he did any of the others.

"It's getting real close to your bedtime, little girl," Charlotte said to her daughter.

Curtina was still playing with her dad but said, "Can't I stay up just a little while longer, Mommy? I don't even have school tomorrow."

"I know, but around here curfews don't change just because it's the weekend. Little girls need all the sleep they can get."

Alicia got up, walked over, and tickled her baby sister out of the blue, and Curtina squealed with laughter.

"Stop it, Licia!"

Alicia tickled her more, and Curtina squealed louder. Curtis, Charlotte, Phillip, and Melissa laughed out loud, but Dillon wanted to slap that little brat. Once again, Curtina had stolen the show, and Dillon just sat there like a stranger.

Thankfully, Charlotte told Curtina again that it was time to head up to bed.

"We'll be up to kiss you good night," Curtis told her, and she ran on her way.

"Oh well," Charlotte said, scooting to the edge of the grained-leather loveseat that she and Curtis were sitting on. "I think I'll turn in myself. I have to be up pretty early for the women's breakfast."

"Me, too," Alicia said, "so I'll be right behind you."

"I'm so glad you're going," Charlotte said. "It's gonna be a great time."

"I'm glad you invited me."

Wait a minute. Was Alicia spending the night here? Dillon knew she still had her own bedroom there, but all this time he'd been sure she and Phillip were only visiting and that they would be heading back to Chicago tonight. But apparently not. Even more so, where was Phillip staying? His dad's house was nearly a mansion, but clearly Phillip wouldn't be shacking up in the same room with Alicia, because it wasn't like they were still married. Dillon shacked up with Melissa every night, but he would never do something like that in his father's house. He had better respect for him than that.

Charlotte looked over at her former son-in-law, and it was almost as if she'd been reading Dillon's mind. "Agnes freshened up one of the guest rooms for you, Phillip. The one toward the end of the hall and around the corner."

"I really appreciate that," he said. "Especially since your *husband* and I will be getting up much earlier than you and Alicia."

"Isn't that the truth," Curtis said, laughing. "I can't believe I let you talk me into goin' fishin' at the crack of dawn."

"Best time to go," Phillip said, chuckling.

Dillon looked at his father and Phillip, as they laughed together like father and son, and his heart dropped. A part of him wanted to burst into tears, but he would never give any of them the satisfaction of seeing how hurt he was. Not only were his sisters sucking up all his father's time, but now some ex-son-in-law was going to spend an entire Saturday with him? This was dead wrong on so many levels, and Dillon could barely think straight.

"It was good seeing you again, Melissa," Charlotte said, hugging her and staring coldly at Dillon. Charlotte was so slick with her dirty ways, and Dillon knew no one else had seen the way she'd looked at him. She did this all the time, even at church on Sunday mornings, and she always got away with it.

"Thanks for having us over," Melissa said, smiling.

Alicia hugged Melissa, too. "Maybe one day my brother will step up and make you my sister-in-law... isn't that right, Dillon?"

What? Alicia couldn't have been serious? And what gave her the right to meddle in Dillon's affairs, anyway? She had better be glad they were at their father's because what he wanted to tell her was, "I'll marry Melissa just as soon as Phillip makes the stupid decision to marry you again." But Dillon kept his mouth shut. Instead, he sat for a few seconds thinking about how badly Alicia wanted to remarry Phillip, even though she'd messed around on him with a drug dealer. That was how she'd lost Phillip in the first place. The reason Dillon knew this was because she'd shared that pathetic story with Melissa, and Melissa had told him everything. For some reason, Alicia had taken a liking to Melissa, so maybe she hadn't seen anything wrong with fessing up about her indiscretions. Alicia had talked a lot about how even though she'd messed up her marriage, the important thing now was that she'd learned her lesson and that she was a changed woman. She'd claimed she would never hurt Phillip again, no matter what. That sort of sentiment was all fine and well, but from where Dillon was sitting all he could think about was one thing: once a slutty whore, always one. This was especially true of ridiculously spoiled women like Alicia who'd been given the best of everything since the day they were born. It was also women like Alicia who never learned from their mistakes and who always ended up doing whatever they wanted, regardless of whom they hurt in the process. Phillip would be a fool to marry that woman again.

But instead of airing such sinister thoughts verbally, Dillon finally said, "I don't know. Maybe sometime soon."

"I hope that's true," Alicia said. "She's a really good woman, Dillon."

Melissa smiled but didn't say anything.

Of course, Charlotte just couldn't help dipping in her two cents either. "She really is a wonderful person, and any man would be lucky to have her. Any man at all."

It was at moments like these when Dillon wished his father would divorce this tramp. Charlotte had made it known very early on that she didn't care for Dillon and that she would never accept him, so Dillon knew she'd only made that comment as a way to annoy him. She was indirectly taunting at him, making it known that

Melissa would be much better off with someone else, and it took everything in Dillon not to physically hurt her. Sometimes he even dreamed about hurting her, and he'd be lying if he'd said those dreams didn't give him great satisfaction. Charlotte was such a hypocrite and from what Dillon had heard, she'd done a lot of whoring around herself, the same as Alicia. So, no matter how much his father loved his wife and had forgiven her, Dillon knew who Charlotte was. He knew how deceptive she could be and that he had to watch out for her. He needed to be ready for any tricks she might toss his way, and he would be. That was a guarantee.

Chapter 3

It was Mother's Day, and surprisingly, Matthew's eyes welled up with tears. He'd just awakened only a few seconds ago, but for some reason, his mom rested heavily on his mind. These very sad feelings of his had caught him off guard because, although this was the second Mother's Day he'd spent without her, he hadn't felt this way a year ago. He hadn't shed even one tear or thought much about her, but now he knew that maybe it was because he'd still been too angry with her. Actually, he still was pretty upset and disappointed, but for some reason, today, he couldn't deny how much he missed both of his parents. He hadn't seen them in fourteen months, but it was starting to feel like more than a decade. If only his parents hadn't caused so many problems for him and had tried to be better people. Matthew knew all too well that everyone fell short at some point in their lives and that no one was perfect, but these last two scandals had been too much. First, his mom had paid two strangers to lie about Racquel and her mom, claiming they were child abusers, and then there was this whole Dillon Whitfield saga. Dillon, his new half brother. Dillon, who was now the oldest of their father's children and who clearly seemed to be his father's priority. Matthew had never met Dillon in person, but Alicia kept Matthew up to date on what was happening. Alicia had admitted that she didn't care for Dillon all that much and that she definitely didn't trust him, but for now, she tolerated him because she knew their dad wanted her to get along with him and make him feel welcome as her new brother. Matthew didn't have anything against Dillon, especially since it hadn't been his fault that their dad had disowned him, but Matthew still kept his distance. Dillon hadn't tried to contact him either, though, so Matthew knew the feeling was mutual. As a matter of fact, a couple of months ago, Alicia had tried to get the three of them together for dinner, but at the last minute, Dillon had offered some excuse as to why he couldn't make it. To be honest, Matthew had been relieved and so had Alicia.

Matthew wiped tears from both his eyes and looked over to the other side of the bed. Racquel was already up. They'd gotten into yet another argument last night, and they had soon turned their backs to each other in silence. Matthew had lain awake for hours, wondering, worrying, and thinking, but interestingly enough, he could tell Racquel had gone to sleep with ease. It was almost as if she didn't care what happened to their marriage, one way or the other.

Matthew swung his legs over the side of the bed,

got to his feet, and stretched his body. He slipped on his terry robe and then his slippers and went into the bathroom. After washing his face, he strolled into the kitchen. Racquel sat at the table, feeding little MJ a jar of baby food, but she never looked up. Apparently, she was still as angry as ever and was planning to keep this silent drill of hers going. But Matthew decided he would be a bigger person than that. He couldn't stand all this tension, so after pulling a carton of orange juice from the refrigerator, he poured himself a full glass and walked toward her and the baby. "Hey little man," he said, smiling. "So how's Daddy's favorite person in the whole wide world?"

Little MJ giggled and kicked his feet with much delight. But then Matthew looked at Racquel.

"Happy Mother's Day, baby."

"Thanks," she said, but never as much as glanced up at him.

Matthew played with MJ for a bit longer but since he didn't know what else to say to Racquel without setting her off, he walked into the living room. The TV was already on, so he scanned through the onscreen guide to see what looked interesting. Still, he couldn't help looking over at Racquel again. He was sorry that things had turned out so badly for them. Just last year, before little MJ had been born, they'd been hopelessly in love, yet now they could barely look at each other. There were even times when Matthew wanted to pack his bags, leave, and never come back there. It was his son that stopped him, though. Little MJ hadn't asked to be born into this world, and none of what was happening between Matthew and Racquel was his fault. Matthew also didn't want him and his son to live in separate households. He wanted to be a full-time father. He wanted to spend every moment he could with him. He didn't want to be like his own father, because for years his dad had spent many days on the road, traveling to one speaking engagement or book signing event after another. Matthew wanted to be there for his son, now and in the future. So his hands were tied so to speak. If he left Racquel, he'd be leaving his son, and if he stayed he feared he'd be stuck in misery for all eternity.

Matthew turned the channel to CNN, something he'd become accustomed to very early on in life because his dad had watched news shows daily. Seconds later, though, Racquel's cell phone rang.

She looked over at it, slightly frowning, but this wasn't unusual since she rarely wanted to talk to anyone. Still, she pressed the Send button and then placed the call on speaker so she could continue feeding MJ.

"Hello?" she answered.

"Hi, sweetie," her mother said. "Happy Mother's Day."

"Thanks. Same to you."

"So how's my little grandson doing on this beautiful morning?"

"He's fine. Almost finished eating his breakfast."

"And Matt?"

"Fine," she said dryly.

"Is everything okay, honey?"

"I'm good, Mom. How's Daddy?"

"He's doing well."

Matthew was a little shocked that Racquel had even bothered to ask about her father, because he'd sort of played at least some part in that whole DCFS fiasco. She did speak to him, but she wasn't nearly as close to him as she'd been before the incident.

"The other reason I was calling," her mother said, "is because I wanted to invite you guys over for dinner."

"I thought you said you weren't cooking this year and that Daddy was taking you out."

"I know, but this morning I decided it would be much nicer if we could spend some time at home. You know, with just the five of us."

"I really don't feel like doing anything, Mom."

"Honey, when was the last time you even went out somewhere?"

"I don't know."

"Well, we'd really like you guys to spend the day with us. We haven't seen you in over two weeks."

"Maybe tomorrow."

"Look, young lady. I'm not taking no for an answer. You need to get out, and that's that. We'll see you at one, okay?"

Racquel sighed so loudly that even MJ looked at her strangely.

"Honey, did you hear me?" her mother asked.

"Fine, Mom. We'll be there."

"See you then."

Racquel pressed the End button on her phone and looked over at Matthew. "I'm sure you heard, so if you wanna go you can. If not, you don't have to."

Matthew wanted to ask her why she was speaking to him that way, but all he said was, "What time do you wanna head over there?"

Racquel frowned and cast her eye at him like he was crazy. "Didn't you hear her say she wanted us there by one o'clock? I know you did because my phone was on speaker."

"Baby, please. All I meant was what time you wanted to leave. I thought you might wanna go early or somethin'."

"Twelve-thirty should give us plenty of time."

Matthew shook his head and flipped through the channels again. This time he turned the television to ESPN. It was NBA playoff time, but as he watched some of the highlights from the evening before, he was saddened all over again. For years, ever since he'd been a small boy, he and his dad had always watched regular-season football and basketball games together. They'd also watched playoff games for both sports, along with the Super Bowl and basketball championship finals. All of these memories were starting to be too much for him, and then if watching ESPN hadn't been enough, now he thought about his dad's church, Deliverance Outreach. He hadn't been to any church in months, and that bothered him. He hadn't been raised that way, and he missed Sunday morning worship. When he'd first moved in with his in-laws, he, Racquel, the baby, and her parents had gone weekly to the church her parents had attended for years, but once he and Racquel had settled into their own place and Racquel had basically turned against him, they'd stopped going altogether. Maybe he was thinking about his dad's church because Mother's Day was so hugely recognized at Deliverance Outreach, and his mom always looked forward to it. It was also tradition for his maternal grandparents to drive over from Chicago on Saturday for Mother's Day weekend and then attend service and have dinner with them on Sunday.

Now, as Matthew sat thinking and reminiscing, he thought about something else: he wondered if his mom missed him as much as he was starting to miss her. He was still having a very hard time trying to forgive her for all the problems she'd caused him, but he couldn't help thinking about some of the happy times they'd shared. She'd created enough drama and trouble to last a lifetime, but one fact remained: she was still his mother. She always would be, and nothing would ever change that. It was the reason tears streamed down his face, and he couldn't stop them.

Chapter 4

Dillon and Melissa sat listening as the choir neared the end of their second song of the morning. Dillon wasn't the most spiritual person you ever wanted to meet, but now that he went to church weekly without fail, it was starting to grow on him... well, at least it no longer bothered him to be there, anyway. He could think of lots of other things he'd rather be doing on such a glorious Sunday morning, such as watching NBA pregame highlight shows or one of his favorite old-time Westerns. But he came to church faithfully because this was yet another thing he knew his father wanted him to do, and he could tell his father respected him for it.

Sometimes it felt strange, though, because Dillon certainly hadn't come from a religious household. His mother had been a well-known stripper in the Atlanta, Georgia, area for years. Dillon hadn't learned this news firsthand, what with his mother dying in a car accident when he was just a tiny baby, but his aunt had told him as much as she could about her. His aunt had also insisted that although his mother hadn't lived the most honorable lifestyle, she had definitely believed in God. For some reason, this gave Dillon peace—maybe because a part of him couldn't help hoping that his mom had believed in God enough to make it into heaven. If she had, then Dillon hoped his father had been right when he'd told him he had a chance of seeing her again one day—that is, if he believed in God, too, and he accepted Jesus Christ into his heart as his personal Savior. Dillon was still pretty shaky in his faith, but again, he was willing to do anything if it meant seeing his mother again, so he was trying his best to do what his father had suggested.

When the choir members took their seats, a tall, late-thirty-something woman dressed in a black and white suit walked up to the glass podium, carrying what looked to be two or three envelopes. "Happy Mother's Day, everyone," she said, smiling.

"Happy Mother's Day," the congregation responded.

"Don't you all look absolutely beautiful this morning? Nothing like walking into the sanctuary and seeing the beautiful women of Deliverance Outreach. Amen?"

*Amen*s could be heard throughout the building.

"Well, as many of you know, I'm Cathy Reynolds and the reason I'm standing before you is so I can present our annual Mother's Day gifts! As always, I have an envelope with a check for five hundred dollars for both the oldest mother in our congregation and the youngest. So, without further ado, our first gift goes to Mother Bessie Mae Jefferson."

Everyone stood and applauded, and while at first Dillon didn't see anyone making their way to the front of the church, he now saw a tiny woman being escorted by two of the ushers. Dillon didn't pay a whole lot of attention to the kind of clothing older women wore, but even he couldn't deny how classy and beautiful the woman looked in her white suit, white hat, and matching shoes.

The members took their seats as Cathy walked down the pulpit steps to meet Mother Jefferson, hugged her, and then passed her the microphone. One of the ushers held her steady by her other arm.

"Nothin' but God," she said, though her voice was weak. "I tell you, I've come a long way from workin' in the cotton fields of Mississippi to now gettin' ready to celebrate my hundred and third birthday."

There was more applause and people smiling everywhere.

"There were times when I didn't know whether I would make it, but God had a different plan for me. This old body of mine has stood the test of time, I tell you. Heart surgery, a gallbladder operation, high blood pressure...but through it all, I'm still standin'. Thank God, I'm still here, and I'm doin' pretty good for an old lady...and I look pretty good, too, don't I?"

Laughter resonated from one end of the sanctuary to the other. Dillon laughed, too, and for a moment he wished he had a grandmother like Mother Jefferson. He could tell how loving and kind she was, and that she didn't have any ill will toward one human being. His own grandmother had passed away before he was born, and then when he'd met his father last year, he'd learned that his paternal grandmother had died some years ago also.

Melissa leaned closer to Dillon. "She's such a sweetheart, isn't she?"

Dillon nodded.

"Thank you all so much," Mother Jefferson said. "I love you, and God bless you."

As the ushers walked her back to her seat, most people stood up again and Cathy stepped back in front of the podium.

"Isn't Mother Jefferson the most precious woman you've ever seen? Such an amazing woman of God. Well, our next presentation goes to our youngest mother, Mrs. Mikayla Blake. Mikayla just gave birth to a beautiful baby girl two days ago, so she wasn't able to be here this morning, but our committee decided that she still deserved to receive this year's gift. She's only twenty-one, but she and her husband and the baby are doing fine. Because of Mikayla's type 1 diabetes, her pregnancy was a bit of a struggle, but they're hanging in there and they're doing as well as can be expected. We ask, too, that you would please keep their entire family in your prayers."

Dillon looked a couple of seats down at his father, who smiled at him. Curtis, Charlotte, and their children always sat together in the first row, and Dillon was proud to be a member of the Black family.

"And now for our fabulous first lady!" Cathy continued. "Lady Charlotte, will you please come up here?"

Charlotte waved at their parishioners as they stood in applause and when she strolled closer to Cathy, she walked up the red carpeted steps and embraced her.

When the excitement toned down, Cathy said, "Sister Black, we just wanted you to know how much we love you and appreciate you on Mother's Day and every day. So, on behalf of our Mother's Day committee and this entire congregation, we present you, our esteemed first lady, with this check in the amount of two thousand dollars."

There was more clapping, and Charlotte smiled.

Dillon looked on in amazement and wondered what was wrong with these people. Because to him, Charlotte seemed more like the devil's wife than she did a first lady. He wasn't by any means referring to his father as the devil. No, Dillon was referring to the *real* devil, the one living in hell. Dillon often thought, too, how appropriately Charlotte's parents had named her. Her name was in fact Charlotte, but the word *harlot* was mixed in very nicely and it described her to a tee. "Charlotte the Harlot," Dillon thought and wanted to laugh out loud like a child. Boy did this woman make him sick.

"Oh my," Charlotte began. "Well, first of all, I just wanna say Happy Mother's Day to all the wonderful mothers of this church. And to my own mom, who's also here with us," she said, smiling at both her parents. Then, of course, to this entire congregation...you all continue to be the most caring and loving people in the world, and Pastor Black and I will never be able to thank you enough for all you've done. I so appreciate this very special gift, and I have to say... it will certainly be put to good use!"

Many of the members chuckled, but Dillon didn't find his stepmother's words very humorous. Nothing was funny to him, because Charlotte the Harlot didn't deserve two nickels from these folks, let alone a whole two thousand dollars.

"As your first lady, I won't stand here pretending that I haven't made a lot of mistakes, because Lord knows I have. But for the first time in my life, I'm finally following God's direction and doing things the way I know He wants me to."

Dillon wondered when lightning was going to strike. This woman was faking and lying through her teeth. Who in the world did she think she was kidding? And the sad part was that while not all seemed to approve—specifically those who stared at Charlotte with stoic faces—he could tell many of these people supported her completely. They were blinded by her smile, good looks, and charisma, and Dillon was stunned. He couldn't believe it was this easy to con and deceive hundreds and hundreds of people. There must have been at least two thousand people present today, and that didn't count the two thousand who had likely attended the early service. He hadn't been there for that one, but he'd attended the early service a few times in the past, and the church had been pretty full.

"Thank you all so much for everything. I love you, I love you, I love you. Also, before I take my seat, I have a very important announcement to make, and actually, it's a truly wonderful surprise for all of you."

Dillon lowered his eyebrows, wondering what she was about to say.

"I guess I should begin by saying that this has by far been one of the toughest years in our family's life, but today, praise God..." Charlotte's voice trailed off with tears. "Today marks the return of my husband as senior pastor of Deliverance Outreach. So ladies and gentlemen, I am honored to introduce the man you've known and loved for years, your pastor, Reverend Curtis Black."

Dillon was flabbergasted. He could sort of hear all the chattering and clapping taking place, but at the same time he was sitting in his own world, trying his best to figure out how his father could have made such an important decision and not mentioned it to him. More important, he couldn't help wondering if Alicia had been told and possibly other family members. Dillon was so beside himself, he wanted to storm out of there, but he mentally calmed his nerves as best as he could and appeared unaffected by what was happening. Melissa grabbed hold of his hand, and he knew it was because she'd figured out how hurt he was over this.

The congregation was still in standing ovation mode, and now Curtis stood at the microphone. "Thank you," he said, holding either side of the podium. "Thank you all so much...God bless you...Thank you...Thank you so much...I love you all...God bless you."

When everyone had quieted down and finally taken their seats again, Curtis took a long, deep breath. "My, my, my. Well, today is the day the Lord hath made, so let us rejoice and be glad in it. And I guess it goes without saying that today I am a very happy man and I am also a very humbled and grateful man of God. As my wife mentioned earlier, this has been one of the toughest years of our lives, but thank God it has also been a wonderful learning period for all of us. It has been a process that we truly needed to experience. A little over a year ago, I stood here, letting you know that because I'd made a ton of mistakes it was time for me to step down as your pastor. And that's exactly what I did. I attended service each week the same as you, I participated in Bible study on Wednesday evenings as a member, and I read and studied my Word daily. Sometimes I studied from my home office for hours on end, and I'm here to tell you, it was very well worth it. Then there were days when I turned out all the lights and closed the shutters in my office and got down on my knees so I could meditate. I did this so I could listen and hear from God without any distractions. I spoke to Him regularly because I still had a lot of repenting to do. And it is because of all of this that I am totally recommitted to God's work and this entire ministry. I now see things completely different than I did before. I've learned so much and improved so many things in my life, I really wish more pastors would step down and take a backseat when they know they're not walking in God's purpose. When they know they're not doing all that God wants them to do and what He expects from them."

Dillon looked down the row at Alicia, who was all smiles, so again, he wondered if she was just as surprised or if she'd known about this newsflash all along.

"I finally feel as though I'm not just on the right path this time around," Curtis continued, "but instead I'm now on an eternal path when it comes to my relationship with God. And believe me when I tell you that there's definitely a difference."

"Amen," many of the members said.

"I'm also feeling very good about my relationship with my wife and children. Something that has taken a lot of soul searching and praying. My oldest son, Dillon, has been with us for a while now, and he and I have certainly come a very long way."

Obviously, we haven't come too far if you felt the need to hide this great news of yours from me. Dillon forced a smile, but he wasn't happy with his father at all.

"Son, I love you, and thank you for being patient with me. You're one of the most patient people I know, and thank you for allowing me to not only get to know you better but to do what I can to make things up to you. Had you not forced me to deal with my past and own up to my sins, I never would have stepped down and checked myself. I never would have spent this last year completely focused on God," Curtis said, smiling. Then he looked at Alicia and Curtina.

Actually, now that Dillon thought about it, Curtina normally attended the children's service over in one of the large seminar rooms, so he should have known something was up when he saw her sitting next to Charlotte. He could just about guess, too, that Alicia had been told very early on and that this was the reason she and Phillip were there as well, as were Charlotte's parents. They all drove over from time to time, anyway, but Dillon couldn't imagine Alicia preferring to spend Mother's Day with Charlotte versus spending it with her own mother in Chicago. No, Alicia was here for one reason: she'd been told that their father was returning to the pulpit.

"My two baby girls," Curtis beamed. "What would I do without you? It is true that one of you is well in her twenties, but Alicia, sweetheart, you will always be my baby girl, the same as my little Curtina."

Curtina and Alicia hugged and held hands, smiling.

"I will say, though," Curtis went on, "there's still someone missing. Someone I love with all my heart. My precious son, Matthew. I have never missed anyone as much as I miss him, and our family won't be complete until we have him back in our lives for good. Don't get me wrong, I know my wife and I are the reason he turned away from us, but ever since then, nothing has been the same. So I'm asking all of you to pray for our reunion with him and our little grandson."

Dillon's heart thumped wildly, and his breathing got heavier. Why couldn't his dad stop stressing over a son who didn't want anything to do with him? Why couldn't he just be happy with Dillon? Why wasn't one son enough for his father? Matthew had certainly been enough for many years, well before Dillon had come into the picture. So to Dillon, his father had simply lost one son and then gained a new one—end of story. But for some reason, his father wouldn't let it go—wouldn't forget about Matthew and move on the way he needed to. Maybe once he realized that Matthew would never forgive neither him nor that that witch, Charlotte, he would eventually give up. Maybe he'd finally forget he even had a son named Matthew.

Yes, that's what Dillon would hope for. He'd hope and wait for things to work in his favor. He just *hoped* it didn't take too long, though, because whether his father realized it or not, he wasn't as patient as Curtis believed him to be. Truth be told, he didn't have much patience at all...not when it came to getting what he wanted.

Chapter 5

Matthew drove his fire-red BMW—the one his parents had given him during his high school years—into the bank's parking lot. Then he coasted down the second aisle and pulled in next to a white SUV. Matthew was thirty minutes early, yet his boss had still made it there before him. She was a workaholic to say the least, and Matthew wouldn't have been surprised if she'd gotten to work before daylight. She'd done it before, and with the low interest rates they were offering on car loans, they had definitely been very busy.

Actually, Matthew was the opposite, though. He was the kind of employee who never walked in late, but he also never sat at his desk until about five minutes before start time. Today, however, he'd left the apartment a whole lot earlier because he hadn't been able to stand another minute with Racquel. A whole other day had passed, yet she still wasn't speaking to him. She was wallowing in anger and dwelling on the arguments they'd had over the weekend, and Matthew was tired of her attitude. Even as they'd driven over to her parents' yesterday afternoon for dinner, she hadn't said one word to him, unless you counted the curt answers she'd given him when he asked her certain questions. It was as if the only words she knew were *yes*, *no*, *maybe*, and *whatever*.

So, this morning he'd left as soon as he could and now here he sat, trying to gather his thoughts and waiting for the nervousness in his stomach to settle. He was starting to feel as though he couldn't cope, and that nothing in his life was right except the love he had for his son. He was actually beginning to feel depressed, and suddenly he wished he could talk to his father. Hear his voice and maybe ask him to pray for him and Racquel—ask his father, the wisest man he knew, for some good solid advice about his marriage. His father hadn't been the best husband to any of his three wives, including Matthew's mother, but nonetheless, his father had still been able to advise other couples with sheer excellence.

If only Matthew had the courage to pull his phone out and call him. If only he could find the words to say to his dad after all this time. But he couldn't, because his pride wouldn't let him. He couldn't just give in to his parents so easily, because they'd done too much. They had caused a massive amount of pain and humiliation in his life, and they didn't deserve to hear from him or ever see him again. Matthew wrestled with his decision, but then it dawned on him: he had to stay away from his mom and dad because if he didn't, they would soon start causing problems for MJ. That was the one thing he flat-out wouldn't tolerate.

Matthew relaxed against the headrest, weighing his troubles back and forth, until there was a knock at his window. It was Nicole Jordan, a gorgeous woman who was seven years older than he was and the same age as his big sister. She must be five foot ten and didn't wear more than a size eight. Her clothes always fit her perfectly, and married or not, a man would have to be blind not to notice her.

Matthew rolled down his window. "Hey, good morning."

"Good morning," she said, smiling. "Is everything okay?"

"Why do you ask?"

"Because you're sitting here with your eyes closed, and you're never here this early."

"Got a lot on my mind."

Nicole glanced at her watch. "You want some company?"

Matthew unlocked the passenger door. "Sure."

Nicole went around to the other side of the car and got in. "So what's wrong?"

"Everything."

"Wow, that's a lot."

"You're tellin' me."

"You wanna talk about it?"

Matthew rarely shared his personal business with anyone, let alone one of his coworkers, but if he didn't open up to someone he wasn't sure how he'd make it through his work day.

"My marriage is a mess, and I've never been more unhappy in my life."

"Gosh, I'm really sorry to hear that. Have you told your wife how you feel?"

"Yeah, but she basically couldn't care less. All she does is sit around the house, day in and day out."

"What about your son? I mean, is she a good mother to him?"

"Yeah, actually, she's too good."

"I guess I don't understand."

"He's all she cares about, and she doesn't think anyone else can take care of him. She doesn't even like it when I take him places. She's a nervous wreck from the time we leave until the time we get back. She calls my phone every fifteen minutes."

"That's not normal."

"You're telling me."

"Have you tried to get her some help? At the very least, the two of you should see a marriage counselor."

"I agree, but I've already suggested that to her, and she's totally against it. Says she's fine and nothing's wrong with her."

"Being married and unhappy is tough. I was married once, so I know how it feels."

"Really? How long were you together?"

"Hmmph. The quick answer is: too long. But we were actually married for five years. Our situation was a lot different from yours, though. I married a man who thought beating me and my son was some kinda sport."

"Wow," Matthew said. He couldn't imagine ever laying a hand on Racquel, and he had absolutely no respect for any man who did that kind of thing. And to beat a child? Matthew was mortified. "I'm really sorry that happened to you. I'm sorry for you and your son."

"Don't be," she said, stroking her long, coarse black hair to the side. "The important thing is that I finally took care of things. I found the courage to leave, and I haven't looked back."

"Does he ever try to contact you? Does he help take care of your son?"

"No, but I prefer it that way. I'm glad I don't have to see him or talk to him."

"How old is your son?"

"Six."

"When did you leave your husband?"

"Two years ago, but enough about me. That train is long gone, and I'm over it."

"I guess."

"So tell me about *you*. Of course, you can't work here and not know that Pastor Black is your father. Even though you've never volunteered that information."

"That's because it's complicated."

"You don't have a relationship with him?"

"I'd rather not talk about it."

"Sorry."

"No need to apologize. I just don't wanna talk about my family is all."

"Well, what about work? Is that off limits, too?" she asked, laughing.

Matthew couldn't help chuckling himself. "No, but what is there to talk about?"

"I don't know. Do you like it? Do you plan to stay here for a while?"

"I'd definitely rather be doing something else," he said. "And to be honest, I'd like to go back to school."

"Why didn't you go when you graduated?"

"I did, but then Racquel had the baby, things happened, and I dropped out so we could get married."

"Oh really? Where did you go?"

"Harvard."

"University?" she said, sounding shocked.

"Yep."

"And you left there?"

"Yep. Four-year scholarship and all, and now this is the result."

"You must really love your wife. Have to if you gave up four years at one of the most prestigious schools in the country."

"I did love her, and I thought she loved me, too. I also couldn't stand being away from my son for so many weeks at a time. Boston is a long way from here."

"I had no idea."

"My life is crazy. It's all messed up, and I don't know what to do about it."

Nicole placed her hand on his leg, and the flirtatious look in her eye made Matthew nervous. "Things'll work out," she said. "I know it may not seem like it now, but they will."

Matthew pretended her hand wasn't touching him and said, "It's almost eight, so we'd better get inside."

Nicole opened the passenger door but then looked back at him. "Just know that I'm here for you if you need me."

"Thanks" was all Matthew said. Not because he wasn't grateful, but because he wasn't sure how to take Nicole's generosity. He pushed the whole thing out of his mind, though, got out of his car, and locked it. They walked through the parking lot and over toward the building. As they headed closer to the entrance, however, his phone rang. He pulled it from the inside of his blazer and saw that it was Racquel. She rarely called him, so maybe she'd thought about things and had finally decided to call a truce. Maybe she was just as tired of all the bickering and drama as he was.

"Hey," he said, watching Nicole walk inside the bank.

"MJ is out of everything," Racquel said matter-of-factly, "so you need to stop at the store on your way home."

"It's not a problem," he said, trying to be as nice as possible. "Can I call you back later so I can make a list?"

"I already sent you an e-mail. See ya later," she said and hung up.

Matthew pulled his phone away from his ear and looked at the blank screen. He wasn't sure whether to curse or crack up laughing. The thing was, though, he never cursed and laughing just didn't seem appropriate. So he did or said nothing. He just stood there, looking like a fool, until he finally found the energy to walk inside the building.

He strolled through the lobby, over to his office, and sat at his desk. He immediately prepared for whoever his first customer of the day would be. Whether they'd be opening a new checking account, applying for a car loan, or purchasing a certificate of deposit, he would be ready. He would pretend he loved being a customer service representative, and that he simply couldn't be happier with his home life. He would display a huge smile and would go on with business as usual. He would do this because there was no way out. He was trapped, and there wasn't a thing he could do about it.

Chapter 6

Dillon was still furious. A whole day had passed, it was Monday morning, yet he still couldn't understand why his father hadn't told him about his decision to return to the pulpit. It just didn't make sense, a father not sharing such an important matter with his son, his oldest child. It wasn't fair, and ever since yesterday, Dillon hadn't been able to think about much else. He'd barely gotten two hours of sleep last night, a result of his tossing and turning and trying to rid himself of the pain and anger he'd felt. He just didn't know what it was going to take for his father to treat him with love unconditionally. It was bad enough that he'd gone fishing with a man who was no longer his son-in-law and hadn't as much as invited Dillon to come along, but now this thing yesterday was much worse. It was as if Dillon wasn't even a part of the Black family. A year ago, his father had seemed to go out of his way trying to make things right with Dillon, but now his father treated him like he was no big deal. He was just another person and nothing special at all.

Dillon leaned back in the chair in the kitchen, waiting for Melissa to finish preparing breakfast. Before moving to Mitchell, he'd had to work at a job he didn't love and report to some unappreciative supervisor, but thanks to his father's generosity he no longer had to answer to anyone. Although it was true that whenever the subject of coming to work for the church or going back to school came up, Dillon talked his dad in a different direction. He just couldn't see himself taking any old job, not when he was a son of the Reverend Curtis Black, and he wouldn't. His dad had gone on and on about having a plan and preparing for one's future, and while at first he'd been open to getting a job or even going back to earn his degree, once he'd realized Alicia didn't have a full-time job, he'd changed his mind. Alicia was an author of two or three novels and likely earned an income from those he was sure, but why should he have to work some thankless nine-to-five if his sister didn't? When the right position came along, he would take it, but until then, he would focus on bigger and better things, such as some of his entrepreneurial ideas. He had goals and dreams just like the next person, and he wouldn't ruin his chances of seeing those goals and dreams come to pass because of some petty level of employment.

Dillon watched Melissa place a veggie and cheese omelet on each of their plates, then add a couple of slices of whole wheat toast next to them and also a couple of patties of turkey sausage. He stared at her but the more he did, he became irritated. Sometimes he didn't mind being in her company, but there were other times like now when all he saw was a weak, pathetic female. Not to mention, as he looked back at things, he was surprised she'd been able to portray such a strong, independent woman last year when they'd pretended to be a happy couple who were about to be married. During each of the counseling sessions they'd had with his father, she'd been as vocal and as opinionated as Dillon had told her to be and she'd been so believable, his father hadn't realized they were running a scheme on him. Apparently, she was a great actor because she was nothing like that. She was spineless and naïve, and Dillon had very little respect for her.

Melissa set his plate in front of him, along with a glass of freshly squeezed orange juice, but Dillon looked at it and pushed it toward the middle of the table.

Melissa's eyes widened. "Baby, what's wrong?"

"What do you think is wrong?" he yelled.

"I'm really sorry about yesterday," she said. "I'm sorry about what happened with your dad."

"The whole thing is a big joke."

"Honey, maybe your dad wanted his news to be a surprise. Not just for the congregation but for you and the rest of his family."

"Please! You can bet Alicia knew days ahead of time and so did Charlotte's parents. I could tell just by looking at them."

"Maybe you should talk to him. Tell him how you feel, because maybe he doesn't realize he did anything wrong."

"No son should have to do that. A father should include his son in everything he does. Period."

Melissa drank some of her juice but didn't say anything.

Dillon felt his heart thumping faster. "He'll never treat me as well as he treats my two sisters. And when he spoke at church yesterday, he made it pretty clear that Matthew is still his pride and joy. He's still hoping and praying for their reunion. It's as if I don't even matter. And when I told him that you and I couldn't make it over for dinner yesterday, all he said was, 'Okay, son. We'll see you later then.' "

"I don't know," Melissa finally said. "Maybe it's just gonna take a little more time for the two of you to become closer."

"Yeah, right!" he said, frowning. "It's already been a whole year, so how much longer do you think I need to wait? How much longer should I sit on the sidelines waiting to be accepted? Waiting to become an equal with my sisters and my brother? And anyway, why are you defending my father? How dare you!"

Melissa got up and rushed around to where he was sitting. "Oh my God, Dillon, no baby," she said, caressing the side of his face. "I didn't mean it like that at all. I just hate seeing you so upset."

Dillon slid back from the table, got up, and slammed his chair over. "I hate this! I hate I ever came here."

Melissa went over to him and wrapped her arms around his neck. "Baby, don't. I know you're angry and hurt, but try to calm yourself down," she said, kissing him.

At first, he resisted, turning his head away from her, but soon he gave in and kissed her back, wildly and passionately. Their connection seemed genuine . . . until things turned ugly.

Dillon tore her robe open and slipped it down her arms and then ripped the neckline of her pajama top.

Melissa slightly pulled away. "Baby, wait. Let's go upstairs. Let's go where we can get comfortable."

Dillon breathed heavily and turned angrier. "I don't wanna go upstairs. I want it right here," he said, leaning against the counter and opening his own terry robe. "Now, what are you waitin' for?"

Melissa hesitated, and he could already see tears filling her eyes. He wasn't sure why giving him oral sex was the one thing she never wanted to do for him. She did everything else he demanded, but he always had to become forceful when it came to this.

"Did you hear me?"

Still, she stood solid in her tracks, acting as though she couldn't move.

Dillon didn't know why she pushed him to such outrage. "Why can't you just do what I tell you? You know what I want, now do it!"

"Baby, no . . . let's just go upstairs and make love the right way."

Dillon laughed at her. "First of all, we don't make love, we have sex. And secondly," he said, grabbing her by her hair and yanking her down to the floor on her knees, "you'll do what I tell you or else."

Jumbo tears streamed down her face, but all Dillon said was, "Don't make me tell you again, Melissa."

She cried more, but all Dillon cared about was that she took care of business. He'd given her many opportunities to leave Mitchell, many, many times, but she hadn't taken them. Said she wanted to stay with him forever. So now she belonged to him. He still hadn't changed his mind about marrying her, but until he found someone better and much more worth his while, she would do what was expected of her without question. Either that or there would be consequences.

Chapter 7

Matthew walked inside one of the largest superstores in the area and pulled a shopping cart away from a long row of them. He'd just gotten off work about a half hour ago and figured he'd better get this shopping business out of the way as soon as possible. He rolled the cart farther into the store and down one of the aisles. As it had turned out, the list Racquel had sent him was long and it didn't contain items only for MJ. She wanted him to pick up food for them as well. Then she'd listed other necessities, such as toilet paper, paper towels, and, of all things, her sanitary napkins. This was a first, and he couldn't believe she now resorted to having him purchase her feminine products. It wouldn't have been a big deal since he had always been willing to do anything for his wife, but what bothered him was that she now expected him to do everything. She burdened him with all outside responsibilities, so she never had to the leave the apartment. He was still shocked that she'd actually kept her word about having dinner at her parents'. They hadn't stayed very long, though—they'd returned home about an hour after they'd finished eating—and Matthew could tell her parents had been disappointed. They'd wanted to spend more time with MJ and Racquel, but she'd made up some lie about not feeling well and then announced that she wanted to go home and lie down. It was all a shame because spending time with her parents was the very least she could do, given all the help they gave her and Matthew. They faithfully paid her car note every month, and there were times when they covered her and Matthew's rent payment without being asked. They did it from the kindness of their hearts, and they also bought most of MJ's clothing and did whatever else they could to help out. But none of that seemed to matter to Racquel. All she thought about was getting back to her safe haven away from all the people who cared about her. It was interesting, too, how as soon as they'd arrived home yesterday afternoon, she'd quickly laid MJ in his crib and had rushed to turn on the television. One of the channels had aired back-to-back reruns of *Hoarders*, and she hadn't been able to plop down on the sofa fast enough. For the life of him, though, Matthew couldn't understand why she would want to watch this particular program for as much as two minutes. She was an awful housekeeper, and she wasn't far from being a hoarder herself. There was a time when he would come home from work every single day, spending at least an hour cleaning and picking up in every room. But when he'd realized that the more he cleaned up the more she messed up, he'd stopped. She didn't care one way or the other, and he'd given up on trying to keep their apartment presentable.

Matthew pulled various items from different shelves, then went down another aisle and spotted the maxi pads Racquel needed. He knew it was childish, but he hoped no one saw him standing there trying to locate the right brand and quantity she'd asked for. But so much for trying to be discreet.

"Hey you," a female voice said, and he turned around.

It was Racquel's best friend, Jasmine Green, and he smiled. He wasn't sure why, but just being in her presence was a breath of fresh air, and he was glad they'd run into each other. She'd been away at college for two years now, but she was still the same friendly girl she'd always been. She was exceptionally smart, and not one person in the entire school had questioned why she'd been named homecoming queen. As a matter of fact, he couldn't imagine anyone not voting for her, because Jasmine had a noticeably kind spirit and everyone liked that about her. He'd been named homecoming king that year as well, and though he could tell Racquel had been a little jealous of Jasmine for winning, Jasmine had deserved that win more than any girl who was graduating.

"So when did you get home?" Matthew said, hugging her.

"Friday. I left right after my last final, and I've been trying to call Quel ever since. I've left her a number of messages, but she won't call me back. Tomorrow, I was planning to call her mom."

"She rarely talks to anyone, so I'm not surprised."

"Is everything okay? I spoke to her a few times while I was gone but not nearly like I did the first year I was away. I just figured she was busy with the baby and married life. Plus, I had a really heavy course load this semester and a part-time job."

"I think she's depressed," he admitted. "Actually, I know she is."

"Oh no. Why? Because of what happened with little MJ when he was born?"

"Yeah. She's never gotten over what my mother did. When they took our son from her, well that changed everything. She hasn't been the same since."

"I'm so sorry to hear that, Matt. Wow."

"Maybe you should just stop by to check on her because she really needs to talk to someone. She won't really talk to me, and she doesn't have much to say to her parents either."

"I did think about that, but I hate showing up at anyone's house without calling. My mother always said people were being rude when they did that."

"You guys have been friends since what? Kindergarten? It'll be fine," Matthew said, but he knew in all likelihood that Racquel would be livid. Still, he was hoping that when she saw her best friend in the world that she would be happy, and that she might open up to her. There was a chance that maybe Jasmine could get her out of the house.

"I don't know," she said, pushing her oversized handbag farther up on her shoulder.

"Well, if you want, you can just follow me home and that way if Racquel gets upset, I'll take all the blame. I'll tell her you didn't wanna come without calling, but that I told you it was fine."

"I really do miss her, and I'm worried about her. Okay, I'll come."

"I really appreciate this."

"I still have to pick up a few things, so why don't I call you when I'm finished."

"Sounds good. Do you have my number?" he asked.

"No. Just call me so I'll have it."

As Jasmine recited her cell number, Matthew typed it into his phone and pressed Send.

When she saw his number display, she said, "Okay, got it."

"See you shortly," he said.

Jasmine went on her way to finish up her shopping, and for a second Matthew wondered if he was doing the right thing. He knew Racquel might be upset, but he'd already tried everything else. She wasn't listening to anyone, so all he could hope was that Jasmine's visit ended up being a positive thing. Even if it wasn't, though, it wasn't like he had anything to lose. The worst that could happen was that Racquel might yell at him the way she always did and then stop speaking to him. So what else was new? This sort of treatment had become her normal MO, and now he almost expected it from her. It was just the way things were. But today, he was taking matters into his own hands to try to help her. She might not think so, but he was doing this for her own good. He was doing the only thing he could think to do because, with the exception of trying to get Jasmine to talk to her, he was out of ideas. He was at his wit's end. He had been for a while.

Chapter 8

Matthew drove up to the front of the apartment complex, and so did Jasmine. He was still a little nervous about his decision to bring her home with him, but it was too late to change his mind about it. Plus, it was like he'd been thinking before, what did he have to lose? Not much at all, because things were already so bad between him and Racquel that he couldn't fathom them getting any worse.

He stepped out of his vehicle, opened the back door, and pulled out as many plastic bags as he could.

Jasmine got out of her car, too, and strolled around to where he was standing. "Need some help?"

"You don't mind?"

"Not at all."

Matthew passed her three of the bags he'd already taken out, shut the door, and they headed toward the building. They lived in a secure location, so he set two of the bags down and opened the door with his key. Once inside, he and Jasmine made their way up the first flight of stairs. Thankfully, he and Racquel had been able to rent a unit on the second floor because normally the elevator took forever, and they rarely used it.

When they arrived in front of the door, Matthew unlocked it, and they both walked in. They heard a TV playing from the bedroom and little MJ crying.

"Baby?" he said, calling out to Racquel and walking through to the kitchen. When she didn't respond, he set down the bags he was carrying and went to look for her.

Jasmine placed the other bags on the table and stood where she was.

"What are you doing?" Matthew yelled, walking into the bedroom. Racquel sat comfortably against two pillows, eating from a large bag of potato chips. Strangely enough, her hair was actually combed pretty decently. "Don't you hear MJ crying?"

Racquel looked at him and then back at the TV.

Matthew rushed out of the room and into MJ's and pulled him from his crib. "Awww, it's okay, little man. I'm so sorry. Are you hungry?" he said, holding the back of MJ's little head and rocking him. MJ screamed louder, and Matthew tried his best to calm him. Finally, he took him into the kitchen and passed him to Jasmine so he could fix him a bottle. When MJ saw that Matthew was getting ready to feed him, he cried a little less and he also laid his head on Jasmine's shoulder. He barely knew her, but maybe he'd cried so much, he was just happy to be held. There was no telling how long Racquel had been ignoring him, and she still hadn't come out of that bedroom to see about him.

Jasmine moved her body from side to side, continuing to comfort MJ, until Matthew took him from her. MJ drank his bottle so quickly and intensely, he acted as though he hadn't eaten in days. Something was very wrong. Racquel had a lot of issues, but one thing she never slacked on was taking care of their son.

"Do you think I should go talk to her?" Jasmine whispered.

"Of course, you should," Racquel said, strolling into the room, hugging her. "I thought that was you I heard."

"I saw Matt at the store and since I hadn't heard back from you, I decided to stop over."

Racquel never acknowledged any of Jasmine's phone calls and acted as though everything was fine. It was as if Matthew hadn't just come home and found MJ in his room all alone, crying for someone to come get him. She was also in a better mood than Matthew had seen in months.

"Girl, let's go sit in the living room," Racquel said, never once looking at Matthew or MJ. "You'll have to excuse all the mess."

Jasmine sat on the loveseat. "Now, Quel, you know you don't need to explain anything to me. I'm just glad to see you. It's been a long time."

"So how's school? Are you still loving it?"

"I am. Can you believe two years have already passed?"

"I know. Time is really flying, and before you know it you'll be graduating. You still majoring in fashion design?"

"Actually, that's my minor. My major is marketing."

"That's wonderful. I've been thinking a lot about going back to school myself."

Matthew glared at her in shock. He wasn't sure if this was some sort of façade she was putting on just for Jasmine or if maybe she'd truly had a nervous breakdown this time. He tended to think it was the latter because the one thing he simply couldn't shake from his mind was the fact that she was totally ignoring MJ. Normally, she never put him down unless he was asleep, which was part of the reason MJ had barely learned to walk. Even now, he was still a little wobbly because Racquel rarely gave him a chance to practice the way he needed to.

Jasmine smiled. "That would be wonderful, Quel. I hope you do."

"I'm really gonna look into it."

"Mitchell has one of the best universities in the Midwest."

"True, but my plan is to still go to MIT. My parents have always said they'd send me, and I'm really thinkin' about taking them up on their offer."

Matthew knew he must be dreaming. MIT? She was planning to go all the way to Cambridge, Massachusetts? Had she somehow forgotten she had a son and a husband? Jasmine must have been wondering the same thing because the look on her face screamed disbelief. She was just as confused as Matthew.

But he guessed Jasmine couldn't help asking her about their son. "So you're going to leave MJ?"

"Only until I graduate, and I'll be home during the summers, anyway. I'll be home for holidays, too. MJ'll be fine. He has his dad and his grandparents."

"Oh okay," was all Jasmine said.

Matthew's stomach swirled violently. The rest of his body fell numb. Her words sounded too real and like she meant what she was saying. She acted as though her mind was already made up, but what Matthew didn't understand was where this new attitude of hers was coming from. Just this weekend, they'd argued about her not doing anything around the house and not wanting to go out anywhere, yet now she was ready to pack her bags and take off to the East Coast? Not to mention, for four whole years? As it was, early this morning, she'd e-mailed him that list of things to pick up because she didn't want to have to leave the apartment. He'd only been at work for his normal eight hours and then gone to the store right after, so he couldn't imagine what had happened to her mind in such a short period of time. He was afraid for her, but he was more afraid for him and MJ.

"Hey, are you hungry?" Racquel asked Jasmine. She was changing the subject and still acting as though Matthew and MJ weren't there with them.

"No, I'm good. Maybe we can plan a day to go out

to lunch or dinner, though. That's if you're feeling up to it."

"Of course I am. We can go tomorrow if you want. How about Big Italy's at noon?"

Jasmine paused but then said, "Sounds good."

They chatted for another twenty minutes or so, and just as Matthew came back from laying MJ in his crib, Jasmine stood up.

"Oh well, I guess I should be going. But I'm so glad I stopped by."

"Me, too, girl," Racquel said, hugging her. "It really is good to see you."

"I'll call you in the morning," she said and then looked at Matthew. "See you later, Matt."

"Take care," he said, "and thanks."

Racquel walked her to the door and hugged her again. When Jasmine left, Racquel walked back through the living room, heading to their bedroom. She looked right past Matthew until he stopped her.

"So you're still not speakin' to me? You don't have anything to say?"

"About what, Matt? My decision to go back to school? Well, before you go all ballistic, I may as well tell you: my mind is made up, and I'm not changing it."

"What about MJ, Racquel? What about me?"

"I really don't wanna talk about this right now," she said, turning away from him.

"What's wrong with you? And when did you decide all this?"

"Didn't you hear what I just told Jasmine? I've been thinking about it for a while."

"So, you're just gonna leave us? Just like that?"

"Matt, why are you doing this?"

"Because this doesn't make any sense. And why were you ignoring MJ? Our son was in there crying his little eyes out, and all you were doin' was sittin' in our bedroom watching TV?"

"I'm tired! I'm tired of all the crying, all the diaper changing, the feedings, and everything else!" she screamed, walking toward him and stabbing him in his chest with her forefinger. "Do you hear what I'm saying? I'm tired of pretending like I love being a mother when there are days when I wish I'd never had MJ."

Matthew scrunched his eyebrows. "What are you talking about? Nobody loves being a mother more than you do."

"Yeah, I know you think that. Everybody does. But when your mother had DCFS take MJ away from me, I was so depressed I felt like I was losing my mind. But then, when I finally got him back, it was never the same. *He* was never the same. He cried all the time, he was sickly, and the only way I could keep him calm was to hold him all the time and stay at home with him."

"But you held him all the time before DCFS took him."

"It was different when I got him back. There was some sort of disconnect, and all this time I've never been able to shake it. I've tried to have the same bond with him, but I don't. I do love him, but taking care of him twenty-four hours a day, seven days a week is driving me insane. And I can't do it anymore."

"But what happened today? Why were you just letting him cry?"

Racquel stared at him. "Matt, I do that all the time. Just not when you're around to see it. Mostly, when I don't pick him up, he cries himself to sleep, and I cry right along with him. I leave him in his room, and I stay in mine."

"Dear God, no. Baby, please tell me you haven't been treating our son that way."

"I'm sorry, and I feel awful about it, but this afternoon I decided I couldn't pretend anymore. Now it's time I take care of me, and that's exactly what I'm gonna do."

"This is crazy," he shouted, storming past her. "As a matter of fact, *you're* crazy."

"Maybe I am, Matt, but I'm still leaving for school in September. I'll even give you a divorce if you want."

Matthew stared at her, speechless. She gazed at him, too, but then she finally walked away.

He had a mind to grab his son and leave there for good, but where would he go? His aunt Emma would gladly take him in if he asked her and so would Alicia, but he couldn't do that. He was too ashamed to let them see how terribly he'd failed as a husband, a father, and also as a person. More important, he truly loved Racquel and didn't want to lose her. For months, he'd been questioning whether he was still in love with her at all, but now he knew he was. He had realized it the moment she'd offered him a divorce for the second time. She'd done it with ease and with no real emotion, and now he could barely function. He could hardly keep a dry face, but he had to figure out what to do—about Racquel, his marriage, and, of course, his precious little MJ.

Chapter 9

The last thing Dillon ever wanted to do was take advice from the likes of Melissa, but as it had turned out he was preparing to do just that. She'd suggested yesterday that he sit down and talk to his father, so he was now only minutes away from the church. He still didn't feel as though he should have to tell his father to spend more time with him or that he should acknowledge him as his son a lot more than he had been. But the more he'd sat and wrestled with so many overwhelming thoughts, he hadn't seen where he had any other options. Maybe speaking with him face-to-face was the only way to get through to him, so Dillon had decided to give it a try.

Dillon drove into the church parking lot and rolled past his father's black SUV, which was parked in a spot specifically reserved for him, but when he saw Charlotte getting out of her Mercedes, he cringed. That witch now looked him dead in his face, smirking, but she refused to speak to him. It was as if he was a nonentity, and even with no verbal communication, the cunning and very disapproving look she tossed his way said everything.

Dillon got out of his black Cadillac Escalade, the same model his father owned, but as he walked past Charlotte's vehicle he couldn't help reading the sign in front of it: RESERVED FOR FIRST LADY BLACK. What a joke. That woman didn't deserve as much as a cool drink of water on a hot day in the desert, let alone a reserved parking spot. She so had everyone fooled, even her own husband, but not Dillon. He knew her better than she realized, and what he was mostly waiting on was for her to slip up again and hurt his father. Dillon had heard lots of awful stories about her past, and with tramps like Charlotte it was only a matter of time before they slept around again. When she did, Dillon would take full advantage of the situation. He wasn't sure how exactly, but he knew he'd enjoy her demise.

As Dillon went inside the church, his phone rang. He pulled it out and frowned when he saw that it was Melissa. He couldn't imagine what she could possibly want, especially since it had been only a half hour since he'd left home. She was so clingy and such a pest sometimes, so he quickly pressed Ignore and kept walking.

"How are you, Miss Lana," he said when he walked into the administrative offices.

"Hey, Dillon," she said, smiling brightly. "How are you?"

"I'm good. Just here to see my dad. You?"

"Doing well, so I can't complain."

Dillon smiled back at her. Lana had always treated

him with the utmost respect, and he'd liked her from the very beginning. Even when none of them had known who he was when he'd first begun attending the church, he could tell how kind Lana was. His father saw her as a mother figure, and Dillon understood why. She was genuine, and she cared about people. She was someone that trick, Charlotte, could learn from.

"Your dad is waiting for you, son, so please go right in."

"Thanks, Miss Lana."

Dillon knocked and opened the door almost at the same time.

"Hey son," Curtis said, smiling, walking toward him and hugging him.

"Hey Dad," he said, glad that Charlotte wasn't in there.

"So what's goin' on?" he asked, strutting back around his desk and sitting down. "You finally ready to take me up on my offer? Ready to come work for the church?"

Dillon hated when he brought this up. He did it all the time, but working here was the last thing Dillon wanted to do. He knew he needed to be diplomatic in his response, though.

Dillon took a seat in front of him. "No... at least not yet, anyway. But if I don't find something in a couple of months or so, I'll think more about it."

"I'm glad, son, because sitting around with no real responsibilities isn't good. An idle mind is the devil's workshop."

Good grief. Why was his dad doing this? Why was

he trying to force Dillon to take a job he didn't want or force him to go work for anyone? It wasn't like he was broke and unable to pay his bills—his father had seen to that when he'd given him that money—so why couldn't he let well enough alone and simply let Dillon find his own way? More important, why couldn't he spend more time focusing on them as father and son versus mentor and mentee? He didn't need his father's career advice, what he needed was his love and understanding.

Dillon leaned back in the chair. "I know, and I'll decide on something soon. What I'd like to do is start my own business."

"There's nothing wrong with that either. What kind of business are you considering? Maybe I can help you with that."

Why wouldn't he just leave this alone?

"I've been playing around with a few ideas, but I haven't decided on anything."

"Well, in the meantime, you could also go back to school. We've talked about that before, too."

No, you've talked about it. All I've done is listen. "Maybe," Dillon finally said. "We'll see."

"At least think about it, son. Nothing would make me happier than to see you enter a reputable university. I wanted the same thing for Matthew and wish he'd stayed at Harvard," he said in a slightly sad tone. "But enough of that. What did you wanna see me about?"

"Us."

"Meaning?"

"I don't feel included. After all this time, I still feel like an outsider and like I don't count."

Curtis squinted his eyes. "Really? Why?"

"I just do. I mean, Dad, you didn't even tell me you were gonna return to the pulpit. And to me that's the kind of thing a father would immediately share with his son."

"Is that what this is all about? I guess it never dawned on me that I hadn't."

"But Dad, I was just at your house on Friday. Then two days later you made the announcement."

"Yeah, but I'd made the decision to return a few weeks ago. So when you were visiting on Friday, it never crossed my mind. That's probably why no one else talked about it either."

"Oh, so Alicia and Phillip knew way back when also?"

Curtis sighed and leaned his elbows on his desk. "Actually, they did. But only because Alicia called me the day I'd made up my mind."

"But you still never thought to call and tell me, too?"

"Son, I just didn't think about it, but it wasn't on purpose. I know this might be hard for you to understand and it also doesn't justify my actions, but my role as a father to you is still evolving. I love you, and I would do anything for you, but when you meet a child for the first time at twenty-seven years old, it takes a lot of adjusting. So it's not like I didn't wanna call you or that I chose not to call you, I simply just didn't think about it. Even when we had conversations after

I made my decision, it just didn't enter my mind. I didn't think about it."

Dillon heard what he was saying but mostly he dwelled on "my role as a father to you is still evolving." So what did that mean exactly? When would it be *finished* evolving, and when would he finally be accepted as a legitimate son and not treated like some bastard child nobody wanted?

"But," Curtis continued, "I'm really sorry, son, because I had no idea. I'm sorry your feelings were hurt by this."

"It's not just that. It's everything. You never even invited me to go fishing with you and Phillip. And I'm starting to wonder if I'll ever fit in period and if you'll ever love me the way you love your other children."

"How could I not? I know I abandoned you when you were just a baby and that there's a lot of bad history, but if I didn't love you, son, I wouldn't have called you to my hospital bed the way I did. I certainly wouldn't have apologized to a son who lured me out to a strip club to be beaten half to death. I wouldn't have done that if I hadn't wanted to become a father to you. Love is something that has to grow, and over the last year I've definitely come to love you more and more."

"It's still not the same. When I see you with Alicia and Curtina, it's different. It's like they're everything to you. Even when you talk about Matthew, who you haven't seen in forever, the love you have for him is obvious. But with me, it's like you could take me or leave me and you'd be fine."

"That's just not true, and I'm sorry you feel this way."

"Then there's your wife," Dillon said, definitely not wanting to leave her out of the conversation.

"What about her?"

"She hates the sight of me. She hates everything about me, and she makes me uncomfortable."

"Your being my son has taken some getting used to for her. But it'll happen, and things will be better."

Dillon looked at his dad but knew a loving relationship with Charlotte was out of the question. Just as he was about to say something else, though, his dad's phone rang.

"Hey Lana . . . oh yeah that's right . . . I didn't realize it was so late . . . I'll be there shortly," he said and hung up. "I'm sorry to cut this short, son, but I have a staff meeting to get to. I guess my time sort of got away from me."

Wow. So, here Dillon was face-to-face with his dad, pouring his heart out, yet his dad was getting ready to rush off to some church meeting? Didn't he know family came before anything? Couldn't he see how upset Dillon was and that what he needed was for his father to pay some attention to him? Reassure him that he truly did love him and that he was proud to have him as a son?

Curtis grabbed his leather pad folio and a pen and got up. "Why don't we talk this evening, son?"

Dillon stood up. "I guess."

Curtis placed his arm around Dillon's shoulder. "I'm serious. It sounds like you have a lot of doubts about our relationship, and I want us to work on that."

Dillon didn't say anything, but when they walked out of Curtis's office, they hugged and Dillon went on his way. Instead of feeling better about things, though, he felt worse and he wanted out of there. But to his great disappointment, as he continued down the hallway, he just so happened to look inside Charlotte's office. Her door was wide open and as soon as she spied him, she laughed in a sarcastic sort of way and shook her head at him. She laughed like he was the most pathetic thing she'd ever seen, and before he'd realized it he'd stepped inside and slammed her door.

It was amazing how quickly that dirty smile of hers vanished.

"What are you doing?" she asked, clearly not knowing how to react. "Get out of here, Dillon."

"Just shut up, Charlotte. You've been taunting at me for more than a year now, and I'm sick of it."

She picked up her office phone, looking scared to death. "I'm calling security."

Dillon rushed over and snatched the receiver away from her. "You're not callin' anybody."

Charlotte stood up and backed away from her desk. "I'm not afraid of you."

Now Dillon was the one laughing. "Yeah, well, you should be. You should be terrified, because I'm not someone to be played with."

"You'd better get out of my office," she said. Her tone was stern and threatening. "And if I were you, I'd pack my little rags and head back to wherever it is you said you came from. Because nobody wants you here, Dillon. You're beneath the rest of us, and nothing will ever change that."

"Look, skank. You'd better check that nasty attitude of yours or else."

"Or else what? And who're you callin' a skank? It sounds to me like your *mother* was the skank of the century. The woman was a veteran stripper."

"Don't you ever mention my mother to me." Dillon spoke through clenched teeth, fighting with all his might, trying not to grab Charlotte.

"You wait until I tell Curtis about you being in my office."

"You're not gonna tell my dad anything."

"Just watch me."

"If you say one word, then I'll just have to tell him your little secret."

Charlotte laughed out loud again. "Please. I don't have any secrets."

Dillon didn't have a thing on her—at least not yet—but he sensed a certain nervousness about her, and that told him he was on to something. "Everybody has secrets, sweetheart, but the secret I'm talking about...well, let's just say if my dad ever finds out about it, you'll be signing divorce papers. He'll never even speak to you again. So just keep pushin' me, Charlotte. Keep messin' with me, and I'll sing like a Grammy winner."

"I want you out of here," she said, clearly frustrated, so now Dillon wondered what secret she was in fact keeping from his father.

"See ya later," Dillon said, laughing. "Charlotte the Harlot."

Dillon walked out of her office and for some reason, he felt relieved. He'd finally gotten something on Charlotte. He wasn't sure what it was exactly, but he was certainly going to figure it out. He would dig deep, searching for proof of whatever it was she was hiding, and he would use it against her. He would make her sorry she ever met him in the first place.

Chapter 10

Matthew dried off MJ and smoothed baby lotion over his little body. MJ smiled joyfully, the way he always did, but Matthew could barely keep his eyes open. He'd tried his best to fall asleep—because Racquel certainly hadn't had a problem doing so—but he hadn't been able to. He'd had too much on his mind, and he was troubled about his future. Everything was falling apart, and to make things worse, Racquel didn't care about any of their problems in the least. Matthew was shocked, of course, at how suddenly she'd turned into this upbeat twenty-year-old with brand-new college ambitions, but what he mostly couldn't fathom was her lack of concern for MJ. She'd gone from loving their son, protecting him and obsessing over him, to now not paying him any attention at all? Things just didn't add up, and for the life of him, Matthew couldn't understand it. He wanted answers—needed answers—but Racquel wasn't giving any explanations. At one point, she had mentioned how it was time she took care of herself, but it still didn't make sense. This strange turn of emotions wasn't normal, and Matthew knew she needed help.

"So you all ready, little man," he said to MJ and kissed him on the cheek. He finished putting on his son's pants and shirt, and now he just had to grab his bag and get his keys. After last night's drama, he'd called Aunt Emma and asked her if she could keep MJ for them. He hadn't told her why, but she'd said yes and hadn't asked any questions. He was glad about that, because he didn't want to hear any of her lectures about his parents. She was never rude or overbearing, but every now and then she tried to talk him into forgiving his parents and going over to see them. She talked a lot about letting bygones be bygones, and she frequently reminded him of how short life was. He never said anything out of the way to her, because he would never disrespect her, but he never commented when she brought up the subject, either. He also didn't want to tell her how bad things were between him and Racquel, because he didn't want his parents to know about that. Before he'd ended his relationship with them, they'd both advised him to stay in school and had thought he was too young to be getting married. But he hadn't listened.

When Matthew carried MJ out to the living room, he looked at Racquel but she pretended she didn't see them.

"I'm taking MJ over to Aunt Emma's."

"That's a good idea. He loves her."

Matthew stared at her for a few seconds but then

picked up his keys and walked out the door. There was so much to say, yet nothing to say at all. It felt like he was dreaming, but he knew this disaster was very real—it was more like a living nightmare.

After buckling MJ into his car seat, Matthew double-checked it, making sure he was secure, and went around to the driver's side. Before he got in, though, he just so happened to look toward the building and up at the second floor. Racquel was looking down at him from the window. He watched her, but soon she closed the mini-blinds as though she hadn't seen him.

As Matthew drove away, he positioned his Bluetooth and called his mother-in-law. Vanessa answered on the second ring.

"Hello?"

"Hi, Mom."

"Hey, Matt," she said with a smile in her voice. Sometimes she seemed more like a mother to him than a mother-in-law, and right now he needed that.

"How are you?"

"I'm good. Just trying to get a little work done, but how are you? And how're Racquel and my little grandson?"

Matthew felt tears filling his eyes and though he had his sunglasses on and no one could see them, he was ashamed. Here he was, some six-foot-two twenty-year-old, yet he was hurting and wanting to cry like a child. It was so embarrassing, but he couldn't help himself.

"Things are really bad."

"What's wrong?"

"It's Racquel. She's decided to go back to school. She says she's leaving in September."

"What? Well, she sure hasn't mentioned anything to me or her dad."

Matthew told Vanessa how he'd seen Jasmine at the store and how he'd invited her over to talk to Racquel. Then he told her about how she'd admitted to treating MJ.

"I just can't believe what I'm hearing," she said. "Oh my goodness, Matt. So she's been letting MJ cry himself to sleep?"

"Yeah. Then, this morning when I told her I was taking him to my aunt Emma's, she was fine with that, too. She doesn't care about either of us anymore."

"Oh Matt, something's very wrong with her."

"I know, and she also said she would give me a divorce."

"I am so, so sorry this is happening. The two of you have been through so much, and it really breaks my heart."

"I just don't know what to do."

"Well, I will tell you this. While I didn't think so before now, I think Racquel is dealing with postpartum depression. Her dad and I have always known she was depressed and that's why we've always tried to make her get some help, but we didn't think it was related to MJ. We just thought it was because of MJ being taken from her. We didn't think it was postpartum, because Racquel has always seemed so in love with MJ. She's never wanted to be without him."

"I thought MJ was her entire world, but now we know otherwise. She hasn't touched him or said anything to him since I got home yesterday."

"We have to talk to her. So, can you ask your aunt Emma if she can keep MJ a little longer this evening? That way her dad and I can come over. Maybe if the three of us sit down with her together, she'll listen."

"She's never listened to us in the past, but I'm willing to try."

"What time can you be home?"

"About six."

"Okay, then, we'll meet you at your apartment."

"Thanks, Mom. And I'm sorry to bother you with all this."

"Racquel is our daughter, MJ is our grandson, and we love all three of you, honey. Don't you ever forget that."

"I love you, too."

"Now, drive safe and try to have a good day at work."

"I will," he said, but he knew that was impossible. Until things were handled with Racquel, he didn't see how he could enjoy anything. Especially not a job where he had to see and talk to people, because right now, all he wanted was to go home, close up in his bedroom, and sleep his troubles away. This was certainly out of the question, though, since he couldn't afford to miss as much as a couple of hours, let alone a full day. Still, that's what he wanted to do...but so much for wishful thinking.

Chapter 11

As soon as Matthew turned the key and walked inside the apartment, Racquel shot him a look of fury. Her parents were sitting on the loveseat, Racquel on the sofa, and she acted as though she wanted to kill Matthew.

"Hey Mom and Dad," he said.

"Hey Matt," Vanessa said.

Neil smiled. "Hey son."

"Hi, baby," he said to Racquel, but she just stared at him, speechless.

It was interesting, though, because Racquel looked better than Matthew had seen her look in months. Her hair was freshly done, her makeup was flawless, and she wore a beautiful fuchsia blouse with a pair of off-white dress pants. At first, he wondered why she was all dressed up, but then he remembered that she'd scheduled a lunch date with Jasmine for earlier today. Still, this was another lifestyle change for her because normally she never took time to do her hair or makeup, and she'd stopped caring about clothes a long time ago.

If she wore anything, it was usually a T-shirt and a pair of jeans or a T-shirt and a pair of jogging pants.

Matt sat down on the opposite end of the sofa.

"Well," Neil said, "I guess there's no easy way to say this except to say it. Honey, you need help."

"What kind of help, Daddy?"

"Help with your feelings and whatever else is bothering you."

Racquel folded her arms. "Nothing's bothering me."

"Honey, please," Vanessa said. "You're not yourself. You haven't been for a while."

"And I've been telling all of you *for a while now*, that I'm fine. So why can't you just accept that?"

"Because, sweetheart," she said, "you're not fine, and we think you have postpartum depression."

Racquel jerked her head toward Matthew. "What did you tell them?" she yelled. "That I'm a bad mother?"

Matthew turned away from her.

"I know you told them bad things about me, Matt. How dare you."

Neil scooted to the edge of his seat. "Honey, it wasn't like that. We're all here because we love you, and because we want you to talk to someone."

"You spineless idiot!" she said, picking up a magazine and throwing it at Matthew.

"Racquel!" Neil shouted.

"I hate you," she told Matthew. "I hate I ever married you."

Matthew breathed deeply, trying to gain his composure.

"Honey, please don't do this," Vanessa told her. "You know Matt loves you, and that he only wants the best for you."

"Exactly," Neil agreed. "When the two of you decided to get married, you became one. You became husband and wife, and that means you have to stick together when times get hard."

Racquel crossed her arms tighter and also crossed her legs. "Hmmph, is that right, Daddy?"

"Yeah, it is."

"Well, if you haven't done the right thing in your own marriage, what gives you the right to tell me what to do with mine?"

Matthew knew where this was headed, and he wished there was something he could do to stop her. It was too late, though.

"Daddy, you've messed around on Mom for years, and everyone knows it. It's so humiliating. I mean, here you are a top neurosurgeon, yet you can't stop sleeping with all these women? I'm sorry, Daddy, but you're the last person who should be telling anybody about their marriage."

Vanessa looked mortified, and Matthew wanted to choke.

"Young lady, you're completely out of line," Vanessa said. "You're being disrespectful, and your father doesn't deserve that. *I* don't deserve that."

"Mom, please. Have you forgotten what happened last year? Have you forgotten how Daddy knew Charlotte was behind that whole DCFS madness, yet he didn't say anything? He'll never admit it, but the reason he didn't expose her is because he was trying to sleep with her. Daddy was actually trying to sleep with my mother-in-law, Mom!"

"That's enough!" Vanessa said.

Racquel raised her eyebrows. "Okay, then if I can't talk about Daddy, then let's talk about you. Let's talk about how you basically forced me to drop that lawsuit. I'd told you from the beginning that I wanted to take that witch to the cleaners for what she did to me. But, no, you wanted the whole thing to be over with. Then you convinced me to give up as well."

"Because it was the right thing to do, Racquel. That whole lawsuit craziness was taking a toll on all of us. It was tearing our families apart, and then it dawned on me that if we took Charlotte for everything she had, we'd be doing the same thing to Curtis. And honey, he hadn't done anything. It was all her."

"You let her get away with hurting me, Mom, and you never should've done that. You should've fought until the end, and I never should've listened to you. I should've kept my part of the lawsuit going regardless of what you decided to do."

"Honey, it just wasn't worth it," Vanessa tried to explain. "It wasn't worth having MJ growing up and finding out that one of his grandmothers sued the other for everything. Sometimes it's better to let go and let God."

Racquel ignored her mother's last comment and turned to Matthew. "It's your fault, too. You should have stood up for me, Matt. You should have helped me take that lunatic mother of yours to the poorhouse. We should have taken her for everything she had. But like I said, you're a spineless idiot."

Matthew still didn't say anything. He knew he was acting like a wimp, but what no one knew was that his pain was slowly turning to rage and he'd had just about enough of Racquel for one evening.

"But you know what?" she said. "That's all beside the point. I'm putting that drama behind me and moving on. So all I need to know is whether the two of you are still gonna pay for my education the way you promised."

Matthew stared at her in amazement. What nerve. Here she'd sat, calling her father the biggest whoremonger in the country and then spoke to her mother like she was her greatest enemy, yet now she wanted them to pay thousands of dollars for tuition? Not to mention room and board? Matthew didn't even know who Racquel was anymore.

Neil and Vanessa looked at their daughter but didn't speak.

So she asked them again. "Well, are you? Because I've already spoken to MIT admissions. I talked to the woman who'd worked it out for me to start last fall, and she's pretty sure she can get me back in for this September. I also told her that you'd be paying cash for everything."

Matthew scrunched his forehead. Did she really think they were going to just up and send her away when there was clearly something wrong with her?

From the look on her face, though, he could tell she did. She saw not a single thing wrong with what she was asking.

Neil still said nothing, and Matthew could tell he was livid about those infidelity accusations. Vanessa finally answered her, though.

"If you're really ready to go back to school then we will totally support you, but only after you see a doctor."

"What kind of doctor, Mom? And for what?"

"A psychologist."

"What you mean is a psychiatrist. A doctor who sees crazy people."

"We just want you to sit down with someone. Let them counsel you."

"Counseling is for crazy people, and I'm not crazy."

"We're not saying you're crazy. But the fact that you no longer want to have anything to do with MJ means something's wrong."

Racquel looked at her mother, then at her dad, then at Matthew. "Oh, I get it. The three of you think this is some kind of intervention, don't you? Well, you can intervene all you want, but not with me. So please leave," she said, standing up.

"Really?" Neil said, getting to his feet. "Our own daughter throwing us out. After all we've done for you."

"Honey, I'm begging you," Vanessa said. "Please let us help you."

"I said, get out, Mom!"

Vanessa stood up and broke into tears. Neil took her

by her arm and led her to the front door. Matt walked into the hallway with them.

"I'm sorry," he told his in-laws.

"It's okay, son," Neil said, rubbing his back. "This isn't your fault, and no matter what we all say or do we can't make Racquel get help. As long as she's not a danger to herself or anyone else, we can't force her to see anyone."

"I just don't understand what happened to her," Vanessa said, sniffling. "I always thought she was depressed and that's why for months now, I've tried to convince her to get help. But I've never heard of postpartum happening a whole year after a child is born."

"But it is possible," Neil said. "I spoke to our head of psychiatry this afternoon right after you called me, and he said he's seen this before. It's not as common, but he's had a couple of patients who seemed to love their babies more than anything in the beginning, but then they became so overwhelmed with the responsibilities of motherhood that they eventually distanced themselves from their child altogether. He said Racquel may have somehow decided that MJ is the reason she doesn't have the freedom most young people do. She might even be blaming him for not entering MIT when she was supposed to."

"But that's crazy," Matthew said. "MJ didn't ask to come here. Racquel and I decided that for him."

"I know, but women who suffer from postpartum depression can't see it that way. So all we can do is pray she'll agree to see a doctor and keep a close eye on her...and you definitely shouldn't leave MJ here with her during the day, so taking him to your aunt Emma's was the right thing to do. We'll be glad to pay her."

"I can keep him sometimes, too," Vanessa said.

"Thank you both," he said, hugging them.

"We're here for you, son, day or night," Neil assured him.

Matthew watched them walk down the stairway, and then went back into the apartment.

Racquel started in on him immediately. "I know you called them over here."

"I never asked them to come anywhere."

"Liar!"

"I'm not doing this with you, Racquel," he said, picking up his keys.

She jumped in front of the door. "You don't have a choice."

"Get out of my way, Racquel."

"Wimp."

"Please move, Racquel."

"Idiot."

"I'm asking you nicely, Racquel."

"Coward."

Matthew felt himself getting angrier by the second, and if she didn't move soon he was going to explode. He'd never hit a girl in his life, but this name-calling was pushing him too far. He was trying to ignore her, but this was the only way out to the parking lot and he needed to go pick up MJ.

"Please move out of my way, Racquel!"

"Or what?"

Matthew reached for the doorknob, but she shoved him into the sofa table, and the lamp crashed to the floor.

"What's wrong with you?" he screamed.

Racquel ran up to him. She slapped the side of his face so hard he had to shake it off. At five-nine, she was five inches shorter than him, but it felt like a man had struck him. The forceful impact of her hand had left his jaw stinging.

She swung her arm back again, but this time Matthew grabbed it. "Stop it, Racquel. Stop actin' crazy."

"Get your hands off me!" she said, turning and twisting and trying to get loose.

"Then stop it," he said, gripping her arm tighter than before.

"Fine, just let me go."

"Are you gonna settle down?"

"Yeah, now let me go!" she said.

Matthew wasn't sure if he could trust her, but thankfully when he released her, she stormed out of the living room and into the bedroom. Still, he stood there trying to catch his breath. Mostly, though, he wondered how long he'd be able to put up with this kind of insanity. He loved Racquel, but he wouldn't keep living like this. He knew she wasn't herself, but what if MJ had been there with them a few moments ago? What if he'd seen his mother acting psychotic? He was only one, but he was still noticeably impressionable and very much aware of his surroundings. Matthew was going to pray for things to get better, but if they didn't, he'd have to figure out something different. He'd have to pack up MJ and move elsewhere.

Chapter 12

After leaving the church, Dillon had driven around for hours. At one point, he'd found himself eighty miles away in a tiny town just south of Mitchell, but now that he was home he still didn't feel any better. If anything, he felt worse about his relationship with his father. He'd replayed their entire conversation over and over in his mind, but for the life of him, he couldn't see where any of his father's words had been genuine. He'd apologized to Dillon for not telling him about his announcement to the congregation and then explained that their relationship was still "evolving," but Dillon hadn't viewed his father's sentiments as anything more than theatrics. It was as if he'd said all the things he'd thought Dillon wanted to hear, yet he wasn't planning to do anything to make things right. He didn't seem to care about all the concerns Dillon had laid out for him.

Dillon sat in front of his laptop computer in the bedroom that Melissa had turned into office space. Actually, it was sort of a family room, too, and it was a little overcrowded, but this was where he spent a lot of his time when he needed to think and didn't want to deal with her. However, his locking himself away never seemed to stop her, and when he looked up, he saw the door opening.

"Can I get you anything, baby?" she asked.

Dillon turned back to his computer screen. "No."

"Are you sure? I made some shrimp fettuccine, and I know you like that."

Dillon ignored Melissa's last comment, pressed a few buttons, waited for the Google search engine page to appear, and typed in the words *Deliverance Outreach*.

"Baby, what's wrong?" she continued.

Dillon sighed and then frowned at her. "Melissa, why can't you just take a hint? Why do you have to keep harassing me when you know I don't wanna be bothered?"

"I'm sorry. I'm only trying to be here for you."

"Well, right now, I wanna be left alone."

Melissa eased the door closed. She was starting to irritate Dillon more and more, and he wasn't sure how much longer he could take it. He didn't want to kick her out on the street, because he knew she had no place to go, but eventually something would have to give. What she needed to do was find a job and find her own place to stay.

Although he understood all too well what it was like to not want to take just any job that came your way, because he was sick of his father trying to get him to do that very thing. He didn't want to work at the church, and although he'd never come straight out and told his father that, he wished his father would stop pestering him about it.

Dillon glanced over at a bronze-framed photo of him and his mom. It had been taken the day he was born. Oh how he wished she'd lived a lot longer and that he'd been old enough to remember her. His aunt had done the best she could for him, and he was grateful for that, but it still hadn't been the same as being loved and raised by your own mother. He knew this because he'd spent years trying to imagine what it would have been like to receive a mother's love.

Dillon pulled up the church's website and then clicked on his dad's bio page. The first thing he saw was an official family photo that included his dad, Charlotte, Alicia, Matthew, and Curtina. Of course, this was an older photo, so Dillon was nowhere to be found, and he wondered when his father would have a new one taken. When would he include Dillon so that the world would know there were four children in the Black family and not three? But then, Dillon was sure his dad would never want to take down a photo of his precious Matthew. It wasn't like he'd be able to get Matthew to take a new one with all of them, not when Matthew wouldn't have anything to do with them. Which to Dillon was plain ludicrous. He'd been thinking this for a while: why worry about a son that no longer cared anything about you when you had another son who loved you and thought the world of you?

Dillon stared at the Black family photo and suddenly

thought about his aunt Susan. She'd left him several messages over the last week or so, but tonight, he needed to hear her voice. He needed to be comforted and told that everything would be all right.

He leaned back in his chair and dialed her number.

"Hello?"

"Hey, Auntie, how are you?"

"Dillon? I'm fine. How are things with you, honey?"

"Okay, I guess. Could be better, though."

"Well, that doesn't sound too good."

"I just wish I'd met my dad way before a year ago. It would've made such a difference."

"I wish you had, too, but at least you were able to meet him when you did. And on top of that, everything turned out fine."

"But that's just it. Everything isn't fine, and I'm not sure what else to do."

There was dead silence, and Dillon wondered why she hadn't commented.

"Are you still there?" he asked.

"Yes, I'm here."

"Did I say something wrong?"

"No, I guess I'm a little shocked to hear this. I thought things were going great... although you know I never thought it was a good idea for you to move there. I just didn't want you to get hurt."

"Well, the only reason I'm hurt is because of my two sisters and the memory of a brother who never comes around. They're always in the way, and that interrupts the time I could be spending with my dad."

"I'm sure you won't understand this, but can I be honest?"

"Go ahead."

"I know you want things to be great between you and your father, but I don't think you can ever expect him to love you the same as he loves his other children. He's been with all of them since the day they were born."

"Not Matthew. My dad didn't meet him until he was seven."

"Still, he was just a little boy, and your dad has loved him and been around him ever since. Your dad is also married to your brother's mom."

Dillon cringed at the thought of Charlotte. "But none of that should matter. I'm just as much my dad's son as Matthew. Actually, I'm his firstborn, and that should mean everything."

"But you don't have a lot of history with him. You haven't known him long enough to have the kind of relationship fathers and sons usually have. Not the kind when they've been together for years. Relationships take time, honey, and simply having the same blood running through your veins isn't always enough."

"Well, it should be. Family is family, and I've loved my dad from the moment he accepted me. As soon as he acknowledged me as his son."

"I understand that, but you can't expect your dad to feel the same way. For your sake, I wish he did, but honey, he's human and he can't help it."

Now Dillon hated that he'd called her. She wasn't saying any of the things he needed her to, and he was becoming a little tired of all this negative chatter. He loved his aunt, but if she didn't change her thinking very soon he'd have to hang up.

"If you ask me," she continued, "I think you should leave there and come back to Atlanta. You need to come home."

"This *is* home, Aunt Susan. I don't have a mom, so home is where my father is."

"But look how you're feeling. Look how upset and sad you are."

"It won't always be this way. Eventually, my dad will come around. He has to."

"I know you want that, but I think you need to be more realistic about this. As it is, you've been there for a good while, and nothing's changed. And Dillon, honey, you haven't even been here to see me in over a year."

"I have to go, Aunt Susan," he said matter-of-factly. It was bad enough that she was insisting his dad would never love him, so he certainly didn't want to hear anything about his choice not to visit her in Atlanta. Didn't she know he had other priorities right now and that he would get back down there when it was convenient? Couldn't she see how important his father was to him?

"Honey, I know you're upset, but I wish you'd listen to me. I wish you'd think hard about this and then move on."

"It was really nice talking to you, Aunt Susan, and I'll try to call you next week, okay?"

"You take care of yourself, honey," she finally said.

"And know that I love you. I never had my own children, so to me you were more my son than you were my nephew. I couldn't love you more, even if I'd given birth to you, so please don't forget that."

"I love you, too," he forced himself to say, but he was glad the conversation was over.

When he laid his phone down, he felt like bursting into tears but he fought back the urge. No matter how hurt he was, he wouldn't punk out like some weak little kid. Still, he couldn't help thinking about the way everyone always seemed to abandon him. First his mom had committed suicide, something his dad had driven her to, and now his dad acted as though he didn't care about him—at least not as much as he'd seemed to care about him when they'd first met. But then Dillon thought about something. The only way for a person to ever get what he or she wanted was to take it. The only way to get his father to pay more attention to him and love him more was for Dillon to take drastic measures—maybe not drastic per se, but he had to do something that would get his dad to take notice and see him as his most important child. He needed to prove to his dad that he was the most loyal of his offspring, the one his dad could count on until death. Then, once his dad realized this, life would be good. Everything would be perfect, and Dillon would finally have the kind of fatherly love he'd always wanted—the kind of love he deserved.

Chapter 13

Matthew sat inside his office, gazing into thin air, trying to figure out how all this had happened. He'd made the mistake of having sex before marriage, made the mistake of getting Racquel pregnant, and made the mistake of dropping out of college and getting married to her. But he'd never imagined that things would spin so utterly out of control. It was a new day, but he still couldn't forget what had occurred less than twenty-four hours ago. Racquel had treated her parents like villains, she'd hauled off and slapped him like a heavyweight champion, and she was still blatantly ignoring her own son. She'd done so again last night when Matthew had brought MJ home, and this morning she hadn't as much as come out of the bedroom while Matthew was getting him dressed. At first, Matthew had considered saying something to her, asking her why she was treating MJ so badly, but he'd decided against it. On the one hand, he'd thought it might be good to engage her in conversation, thinking that maybe it would help her, but on the other, he realized it might be best just to leave her alone. He also had to admit that he'd worried all night about what she might do next—what she might do to him, or heaven forbid, to poor little MJ. Matthew didn't want to believe she'd go that far, but as it was, she'd already shown a side of herself he hadn't counted on, so he needed to be careful. He needed to be much more cautious when it came to Racquel than he had been.

Matthew looked up when he heard his coworker Nicole calling his name.

"Hey, you okay?" she said, smiling but also looking concerned.

Matthew smiled back at her. "I'm good."

"You sure? Because if so, we have a couple of customers waiting."

"Oh."

"One is looking to apply for a car loan, and the other wants to purchase a CD. Any preference?"

He would get a commission either way, but to be honest, he'd rather do the CD because it would likely be quicker. That way, he wouldn't have to spend much face-to-face time with anyone.

"I'll do the CD," he said.

Nicole nodded and walked away.

Matthew tidied up his desk a bit, moving a few folders to the side.

Nicole returned to his office. "Matt, this is Mrs. Downing."

Matthew stood up. "Please have a seat, Mrs. Downing."

"Why thank you young man," the motherly, sixtyish woman said.

She looked familiar to Matthew, but he couldn't place her. Still, he took a seat, too. "So, ma'am what can I do for you today?"

"Well, yesterday I closed a savings account at my other bank, and I've decided to get a one-year CD from you. But if you don't mind, can I say something?"

"Of course."

"I really miss you, Matthew," she said, smiling. "We all miss you."

Matthew stared at her, sort of clueless about what she meant. Although, if he had to guess...

"I've been a member of Deliverance Outreach for years now," she said, "and although I know it's not my business, I hate how things turned out between you and your parents."

Matthew swallowed hard and wasn't sure what had come over him, but suddenly he felt homesick. Maybe because he missed his parents more than ever before, and also because he could tell this woman had a kind heart and genuinely cared about people. If he could, he would get up, walk around his desk, and hug her, but he knew that would be unprofessional and immature, so he didn't.

"I can tell from the look in your eyes that you miss your mom and dad, too. Am I right?"

Matthew smiled at her, but he couldn't will himself to admit the truth to her. His pride and shameful thinking wouldn't let him. He was also glad he had an office with a door. He hadn't been assigned one because he held a management position but because the bank wanted to give new customers their privacy and to protect their confidentiality. This was good because he would never want Nicole and her customer to hear all that Mrs. Downing was saying. She wasn't a loud woman, but she also wasn't whispering, and Nicole's office was right next to his.

"Did you know your dad decided to return to the pulpit?"

Matthew could tell she honestly didn't know whether he'd been told or not, but actually he had. Alicia had called him during his drive to work this morning and casually mentioned it. Normally, she didn't talk about their father to him, because she knew Matthew never liked it, but he could tell she hadn't been able to keep this particular news to herself. He'd heard the excitement in his sister's voice, and deep down, he'd sort of felt happy for his father. He was angry with both his parents, but no matter how many sins his dad had committed, no matter how many times he'd disappointed Matthew, there was no denying that his father was a great pastor. Still, when Alicia had told him the news, he hadn't commented, because he'd been too upset about his situation with Racquel. Actually, he'd wanted to tell Alicia about everything he was dealing with, specifically about the scary change in Racquel's personality, but he hadn't been able to. He'd been too hurt to talk about it, and more important, the reason he hadn't told her the truth was for the same reason he hadn't told Aunt Emma. He didn't want his parents to know. There was no doubt that he could trust Alicia to keep a secret, but the reason he couldn't trust her with this was because he knew she might think he needed help from his mom and dad and that telling them was the right thing to do.

Matthew realized he'd been in deep thought and that he hadn't fully been listening to this nice woman because he heard her say, "Son, are you okay? Is everything all right?"

"I'm fine, Mrs. Downing."

"You know, son...I hope I'm not out of line, but nothing should ever come between a child and his parents. I don't care how bad things get. It's no secret that your mom did a terrible thing to you and your wife, and I know your father hasn't always done the right thing either, but in the end, they are still your parents and they still love you. I can tell you love them, too."

Matthew swallowed hard again. He wished Mrs. Downing would talk about something else. He wished she would focus on the CD she'd come there to purchase, but she wouldn't.

"You've always been a wonderful young man, Matthew, and though I know you're hurting, I really do wish you'd call your parents. Or better yet, just get in your car and go see them."

Tears flowed down Matthew's face, and although he felt like a gigantic fool, sitting in a place of business, crying, he also felt relieved. His problems hadn't been fixed, but somehow his tears gave him a much-needed sense of release. It was as if he could breathe easier and wasn't consumed with as much bottled-up pressure. He also now felt as though he could make it through his work day. His father used to say that God always sent the right people when you really needed them, even if you weren't expecting them. So, thank God for Mrs. Downing. Thank God for unexpected angels.

Chapter 14

It was shortly after five, and Matthew was glad to be off work. What a day it had been, as he'd experienced just about every emotion known to mankind. He still wasn't happy about breaking into tears in front of Mrs. Downing, but even though hours had passed, he felt better than he had before she'd walked into his office. She'd also given him a lot to think about when it came to his parents, and he couldn't ignore that either.

Now, though, he was in his car and preparing to call Jasmine. He'd sort of been wanting to do so ever since she and Racquel had gone to lunch yesterday, but he hadn't been sure if Jasmine would feel comfortable telling him any of what Racquel might have said. It was true that she and Jasmine had lost touch over the last few months, but they were still best friends, and Matthew knew who Jasmine's loyalty rested with.

Matthew dialed her number, repositioned his Bluetooth device, and drove out of the bank's parking lot. She answered right away.

"Hey Matt."

"Hey, how's it goin'?"

"I'm good. You?"

"I could be better, but you know how that is."

"I was really hoping to talk to you, and the only reason I didn't call was because I didn't wanna take a chance on Racquel overhearing our conversation. I also didn't want to bother you at work."

"So how did things go yesterday?" he asked.

"Well, to be honest, I've never seen Racquel any happier. She went on and on about how free and relieved she is, and how she can't wait to leave for school this fall."

"Did she say anything about me or MJ?"

"No, she didn't, and that's what I don't understand. That's why I know something's very wrong with her."

"It's as if she went to sleep one night and then woke up a totally different person. It's like she no longer cares about anyone but herself. Which would be fine if she didn't have a husband and a son. She's acting like MJ and I don't even exist."

"I know, Matt, and I'm really sorry."

"Actually, her parents and I sat down with her yesterday evening, but it turned into a total disaster. She went off on all three of us."

Matthew didn't bother telling her that Racquel had slapped him silly, because he was too ashamed. He just couldn't bring himself to admit that his twenty-year-old wife had turned abusive.

"What happened?" Jasmine asked. "What did you say to her?"

"We told her we wanted her to see someone, and that's when she really got mad. She went ballistic. Her parents believe she has postpartum depression, though."

"Can that happen this long after having a baby?"

"Yeah. My father-in-law confirmed it with one of his colleagues at the hospital."

"Wow. So I'm guessing she doesn't think she has a problem at all."

"She doesn't. And sadly, we can't force her to get help if she doesn't want it."

"This is crazy, Matt. I know Racquel has been through a lot, but I never would have thought things would turn out so badly."

"Yeah, well, try to imagine how I'm feeling. I'm basically numb, and I'm not sure how to deal with this. I don't even feel all that comfortable being in the house with her."

"You don't think she'll try to harm you or MJ?"

"I don't know. I hope not, but that's why I'm gonna keep taking him to Aunt Emma's every morning. I'm actually on my way to pick him up now."

"I just hate this. I hate what's happening, and I hate talking about her behind her back."

"But we're only doing it because she needs help."

"I'll keep talking to her every day," she said, "and I'll let you know if anything changes."

"I really appreciate that, Jasmine. A lot."

"No problem. I'll talk to ya later."

Matthew set his phone on the seat, but as soon as he did it rang. He smiled when he saw that it was one of his two best friends, Jonathan. He, Jonathan, and Elijah had been as close as brothers since childhood.

"Hey man, you here?" Matthew asked.

"Yep. Just got home this afternoon. So did Elijah. What's up with you?"

"Man, you don't even wanna know."

"So what's up?"

Matthew hadn't spoken to either of his boys in a couple of weeks, mostly because they'd both been studying for finals and partly because he didn't want to have to tell them that his marriage was falling apart. Jonathan and Elijah both liked Racquel, but they'd never thought he should marry her. He remembered how they'd both shaken their heads at him when he'd told them.

"Jon, man, things are bad," he said and then told him everything from A to Z—except the part about Racquel slapping him. Jonathan would never understand that or tolerate something like that from anyone.

"So she wants nothin' to do with little MJ? And she also wants a divorce?"

"That's pretty much it."

"Wow, man, we tried to tell you. You never shoulda married her. You coulda stayed at school and still been a father to your son."

"Yeah, but you know I wanted to do the right thing, and I really do love Racquel."

"Shoot, maybe. But sometimes love isn't enough, my friend. Sometimes, mistakes are made and we have to move on and get past them."

Matthew was quiet. He knew Jonathan was making some good points, but his words weren't making him feel any better.

"So where's MJ now?" Jonathan asked.

"At my aunt's. I've been taking him there all this week."

"You're still not talkin' to your mom and dad?"

"Nope."

"Man, I know you don't wanna hear this, but life is too short for all this drama. They messed up, we all know that, but I gotta tell you. I can't imagine not seein' my parents for more than a year. I can't even imagine goin' a whole week without talking to them on the phone."

"That's easy to say because you have normal parents who have always tried to do the right thing. They've never hurt you or humiliated you."

"Well, it's not like they've been perfect. Nobody is. But I'm just sayin', man. Those are your parents, and they really miss you."

Matthew knew Jonathan still spoke to his parents and that he also went to see them whenever he came home some weekends and holidays, but Jonathan had learned a long time ago not to tell Matthew about it. Elijah visited Curtis and Charlotte, too, whenever he was in town, but he never mentioned his visits to Matthew either.

"Anyway, so when are we gonna get together?" Jonathan said.

"Tomorrow?"

"That's what's up. I'll call you when you get off work."

"Talk to you then."

"Later, man, and you hang in there."

Matthew dropped his phone back on the seat, but when he looked to the right he saw the main street leading to the one his parents lived on. At first he debated, but the next thing he knew, he'd turned down it. He wasn't sure what had made him do so, although maybe it was the conversation he'd had with Mrs. Downing. Her words had truly gotten to him and touched him in a way he hadn't planned on, and ever since then, he hadn't been able to get his parents out of his mind—not to mention the words he'd just heard from Jonathan about them. Matthew also hadn't seen Curtina in a while because, lately, she hadn't been over to Aunt Emma's on any of the days he'd been visiting. He missed his baby sister a lot, though, and he knew she missed him, too.

Matthew drove past the house, peering through the wrought-iron gates and up the driveway. Though a part of him was glad he hadn't run into his mom or dad, a part of him wished he had. He wouldn't have stopped to talk to them or anything, but maybe if he'd at least been able to *see* them, he wouldn't feel as though he missed them so much. Maybe if he saw them, he'd be reminded of all the terrible things they'd done, and he could go back to living his life without them.

As Matthew continued farther down the street and away from the house, he stopped at a red light. He sat there waiting for it to change, but as he did, he spotted a black Escalade SUV that looked exactly like his dad's. His stomach churned nervously, and he took a deep breath. Strangely enough, though, when the light changed and he accelerated, he realized it wasn't his father at all... it was his brother, Dillon. They both stared at each other in passing, and Matthew couldn't help feeling a little jealous, because if Dillon was traveling this close to his parents' home, he was likely on his way to see them.

Matthew sighed and kept driving. His life was a mess, and he was starting to feel as though the stress was too great to deal with. He had so many unresolved feelings and issues, and he was starting to feel sad again. What he wanted was to be happy and problem-free—what he needed was a miracle.

Chapter 15

Dillon's heart raced, and he felt as though he were hyperventilating. His body was hot, and he had to catch his breath a few times. But what were the chances? Here he'd been driving toward his dad's house, just for the sake of doing so, and out of nowhere he'd seen Matthew. Had Matthew actually been over to see his dad and Charlotte? Had he finally forgiven them and called a truce? Had his father welcomed his precious little Matthew back with open arms and would no longer have any use for Dillon?

Dillon's heart beat faster than before, and he punched his steering wheel with his fist. He just couldn't win. He'd already been devising a plan to get Charlotte out of his way—he'd spent the better part of last night and this morning plotting it—but now there was a chance his brother might be back in the picture?

Dillon drove past his dad's house, but he didn't see anyone. Of course, there was no way to tell if Matthew had been there or not, but just the thought of it gave

Dillon pause. It infuriated him and worried him, and he had to find out.

So he called his dad.

"Hello?" Curtis answered.

"Hey Dad, it's me."

"Hey son. How are you?"

"Good. So what's goin' on?"

"Just sitting here in my office preparing for Bible study. I need to leave for the church in about a half hour, though. Can I call you back when I'm driving?"

He sure was rushing Dillon off the phone, and Dillon knew it was likely because he was now focused on Matthew and didn't want to talk to him.

"I'll let you go," Dillon finally said, wanting to slam his fist into his steering wheel again.

"Are you coming tonight?"

"To Bible study?"

"Yes, it would be good to have you there."

"No, not this time. Maybe next week."

"Okay...well, why don't I just call you afterward? That way we'll have more time to talk."

"Whatever works best," Dillon said.

"Talk to you later, son."

It took every ounce of constraint Dillon could muster not to fling his phone against the windshield. He couldn't believe his father was ignoring him once again. Maybe what he should do, though, was call Charlotte. He'd never done so in the past, but his dad had given him her number months ago, in case he ever needed it. The reason he wanted to call her now was because if Matthew had in fact been to visit, Charlotte would be glad to rub Dillon's face in it. She would boast about Matthew being back in their lives and how Matthew would now be his father's only priority. She'd brag about it for her own enjoyment and also to make Dillon feel bad. Only thing was, he didn't want to call her when his father was around because for all he knew, that witch might be in the room with his dad.

So instead, Dillon set his phone down on the passenger seat and kept driving. He had a plan, but now with this latest Matthew development he had to work faster. He had to break up that little union between his father and that deceitful tramp he was married to. If he could manage that, Matthew would be a nonissue. If Dillon showed his father who his wife truly was, his father would be indebted to him. He would finally see which of his children had his back, and this was all Dillon wanted.

When Dillon arrived home, he walked inside and rushed straight into the bedroom where Melissa was.

"Take off your clothes," he said.

Melissa gazed at him strangely and at first she hesitated—until she saw the angry look in his eyes. It was then that she began unbuttoning her shirt, but when she seemed to be taking far too long doing it, Dillon yanked her blouse apart with both hands and buttons flew in every direction. Dillon hated having to do this kind of thing, but he was frustrated and feeling rejected, and though he wished he could be with another woman besides Melissa, he needed her to take care of him. He wasn't sure why, but he'd noticed as of late that sex always made him feel better about everything. It calmed his nerves and settled his thoughts very quickly. It allowed him to be in total control of his life, and he needed that.

When he'd finished with Melissa, he lay there, practically out of breath and feeling satisfied. She lay in silence. Dillon thought about a lot of things, but it wasn't long before he thought about Charlotte again and his plan to destroy her. He also thought about the fact that he was going to need Melissa's help.

"I need you to start researching everything you can about Charlotte. All the way back to her childhood. I'll even pay for a hired professional if you need one."

"Why?" she asked.

"Because getting rid of her is the only chance I have of becoming close with my dad. It's the only way."

Melissa turned away from him.

Dillon frowned. "You don't have a problem with that do you?"

Melissa sighed. "I just wish there was another way."

"Like what? Waiting? Because I've been waiting for months for things to get better, and they haven't. And I know it's because Charlotte is constantly badmouthing me to my dad. She hates me, I hate her, and she's got to be eliminated."

"I'm not sure I'll be able to find anything, because so many of Charlotte's secrets have already been exposed. Things have been publicized about her for years."

Dillon propped himself up on his elbow, reached his hand under Melissa's chin, and whisked her face toward him. "You'll do what I tell you. You'll find the kind of dirt I need on Charlotte, or you can pack your things and get outta of here."

Melissa stared at him in horror, but fear was a good thing. When people feared you, they did what was expected, so that there would be no consequences. Back when he'd needed her help with concealing their identities from his father, Dillon had been forced to get rough with her a couple of times then, too—she hadn't felt comfortable lying to anyone or deceiving them, but Dillon's aggressiveness had been the reason she'd done such a great job. It was the reason she'd worked hard and had done what was required. She would do an excellent job again . . . or else.

Chapter 16

Matthew walked inside Aunt Emma's house and hugged her.

"So how was work today?" she asked, heading back toward the kitchen.

"It was okay."

"Just okay?"

"It was fine," he said but only because he knew that's what she wanted to hear. She didn't respond, though, which meant she knew his first answer had been an honest one.

"That son of yours is sleeping away, and dinner should be finished in a few minutes."

"I'm gonna go look in on him."

Matthew went into Aunt Emma's bedroom and smiled at his beautiful little son. He was surrounded by a pillow on either side of his body so he wouldn't roll over and fall out of the bed, and he slept peacefully. MJ was so innocent and helpless. All babies were, and they never got to choose their parents. Their protectors. The two adults who were supposed to love and cherish them, no matter what. Matthew stood admiring his son, but the thought of Racquel erased his smile. What was he going to do? How was he going to fix things? How would he ever be able to convince Racquel she needed help? He was carrying a very heavy burden to be so young, and for some reason, he thought about that famous saying his grandmother recited a lot: when you make your bed, you have to lie in it. If only Matthew could turn back time and do things differently, he would. He wouldn't have sex before marriage, or even if he made that mistake, he wouldn't do it without wearing protection; he wouldn't leave Harvard until he graduated, and he wouldn't marry any woman until he'd gotten at least a master's degree.

Matthew gazed at his son and couldn't remember ever feeling so downtrodden. He was beyond miserable, and he wasn't sure how much longer he could handle the awful heartache of being an unhappily married husband and father. He loved his son, but what was he supposed to do about a wife who had made it clear that she was ready to move on—a wife who wanted to start a brand-new life without him and MJ?

When Matthew left Aunt Emma's room and went into the dining room, he saw Aunt Emma setting a couple of dishes on the table. It was only Wednesday but she'd cooked so much food, it seemed more like Sunday. Baked chicken, macaroni and cheese, mustard greens, and sweet potatoes. She'd asked him this morning if he could stay for dinner this evening, and though he'd sort of wanted to decline her invitation—

because of how depressed he felt—he was glad he'd accepted. His grandmother's sister was the best cook he knew and even as a small boy, he'd loved spending time with her. She and his grandmother weren't all that close—thanks to his grandmother sleeping with Aunt Emma's ex-husband, a story he'd overheard his parents discussing years ago—but his mom was very close to Aunt Emma, and Matthew had pretty much seen her every week of his life from the time he was seven. She'd also babysat him whenever his parents had needed her to, and now here she was doing the same for him with MJ.

After a few more minutes passed, his cousin Anise walked in. She was Aunt Emma's only child and his mother's first cousin, but sadly, Cousin Anise didn't care for his mom for the same reason Aunt Emma didn't have much to do with his grandmother: his mom had slept with Cousin Anise's ex-husband, David, behind her back and she'd found out about it. This had all occurred before Matthew's parents had married, but at one point, David had wondered if Matthew was his son. It hadn't been true, but even now, Matthew shook his head at the thought of it because it reminded him of just how many people his mother had hurt.

"Hey Matt," Anise said, setting her handbag down and hugging him. He could tell from the suit she wore that she'd come straight to her mom's from work.

"Hey Cousin Anise."

"It's so good to see you, and where's my handsome little baby cousin?"

"Asleep."

"Awww. Well, I hope he wakes up soon. I just love him."

Matthew smiled and sat down at the table.

"Hey Mom," Anise said, hugging Aunt Emma. "Can I help you with anything?"

Aunt Emma set down a glass pitcher of homemade sweet tea. "No, I think this is just about it."

"So, Matt," she said, "how's work going?"

"It'll do."

"Well, you know I think you should go back to school. Even if only part-time or online."

"I've thought about it, but all the programs I looked at are way too expensive."

"Doesn't your job offer tuition reimbursement?"

"Yeah, but I haven't really checked into it."

"Well, you should. And there are always student loans to consider, too. I know you don't want to end up with tons of debt, but I think getting an education will make a huge difference for you. I mean, Matt, you did so well all the way through high school, and you're such a smart young man."

Matthew heard what she was saying and though he would like nothing more than to go back to school, right now taking any classes, part-time or otherwise, was out of the question.

He and Anise chatted for a while longer until Aunt Emma finally sat down and said grace.

"Dear Heavenly Father, thank you so much for the food we're about to receive, and thank you for allowing my daughter, great-nephew, and great-great-nephew to come together this evening as a family. Lord we ask that You would use this food for the nourishment of our bodies and that You would continue to bless each of us in our daily lives. In Jesus' name, Amen, Amen, Amen."

The three of them passed the various dishes around, serving themselves, but when Matthew bit into one of two chicken thighs he'd laid on his plate, he wanted to close his eyes. It tasted that good; almost like it was fried.

"So, Matt," Aunt Emma said, "how's Racquel doing?"

He'd been so hoping that neither his aunt nor cousin would bring her up, and now he had to figure out how to answer. But the more seconds he sat in silence, he found himself wanting to tell them everything. He wanted to tell the truth and release the anguish he was starting to feel again. Mrs. Downing had helped him with that a little when she'd given him advice about his parents, but what he needed was to tell someone else about Racquel. Jasmine knew about her and so did Jonathan, but he needed to tell his great-aunt, which was the next best thing to telling his mother. His cousin Anise only wanted the best for him, too, so he didn't mind her hearing also.

"Things are awful between us. She hasn't touched MJ in a couple of days, and she says she's leaving for school in the fall."

"Oh my goodness, Matt," Anise said. "I had no idea."

Aunt Emma reached her hand over and laid it on

Matthew's. "Lord have mercy, honey, I'm so sorry to hear that. I knew something was wrong when you asked me if I could keep MJ for you, but I just thought maybe you and Racquel had had an argument."

"Well, it's much more than that. She says she wants to be free, and she even offered me a divorce."

"Gosh, Matt," Anise said. "This just doesn't sound right. Not coming from a woman who rarely put MJ down even when he was sleeping."

"I know, but my in-laws think she's dealing with postpartum depression."

They looked at Matt in shock, and he knew it was because they likely didn't believe this was possible, because MJ had turned one already. But once he explained it to them, they understood.

"I'm going to pray for that young lady like I've never prayed before," Aunt Emma promised him. "And you and MJ, too."

"I really appreciate that," he said.

"We'll both be praying," Anise added.

Matthew believed wholeheartedly in prayer, and for a while he'd been praying, too, but to him things had only gotten worse. He wasn't saying that he wasn't grateful for his aunt's and cousin's nice gestures, but he wasn't very optimistic about the results. If ever there had been a time when his faith had waned, it was now, and he couldn't help it.

The three of them chatted about one thing or another and ate some of the apple pie Aunt Emma had made from scratch, but then Matthew's phone rang. It was Jasmine, and he wondered why she was calling.

"Hey Matt, Quel just stopped by my house," she whispered.

"Really? Why?"

"She's trying to get me to go out to a club with her, and Matt, she had on the shortest, tightest dress I've ever seen."

Matthew's heart skipped a beat. He wasn't sure why, what with Racquel being capable of just about anything these days, but he'd never known her to dress that way or want to hang out at bars. She was too young, anyway.

"How does she expect you guys to get in?"

"I asked her that. She said she met some guy at the store who works the front door."

"What guy?"

"I don't know."

"Are you going with her?"

"I don't want to, but I sort of think I should."

"If you don't mind, I wish you would so you can keep an eye on her."

"That's what I was thinking. I'll call you when I'm back at home."

Matthew set his phone down, wondering what would happen next. There was just no telling.

Chapter 17

It has half past midnight, and as soon as Matthew hung up from Jasmine's call, he got out of bed, shut MJ's bedroom door, and went into the living room and waited. In the meantime, he turned on the television, found a repeat airing of an earlier basketball game, and muted the volume. When Racquel staggered in, he wanted there to be complete silence so she would hear everything he had to say to her. He was tired of this drama, and he was going to let her have it. Jasmine had told him that Racquel was on her way home and that while she'd had way too much to drink, she'd gotten angry when Jasmine told her she shouldn't be driving. Thankfully, Jasmine had driven them to the club, but what she hadn't been able to do was stop Racquel from getting behind the wheel of her own car when they'd returned to Jasmine's house. Still, Jasmine was now following her to the apartment just to make sure she got there safely, and they were only five minutes away. Matthew wasn't sure what to expect, but what he did know was that he'd been worried sick all evening and hadn't slept a wink. He hadn't been sure why, but the whole time he'd thought about his mom and the drinking problem she'd had a couple of years ago. Of course, he'd hoped Racquel wouldn't do any drinking, but now he knew she had and he was furious. She was going too far with this hanging-out-at-clubs-getting-drunk thing, not to mention the way she was endangering innocent people. She was actually driving under the influence, and this was yet one more shenanigan of hers he didn't understand.

Matthew tried to figure things out but when he couldn't, he sat waiting for a few more minutes. Finally, Racquel slipped her key into the lock. When she walked inside, she stumbled toward the sofa where he was sitting, gawked at him, and cracked up laughing.

"Where have you been Racquel?"

She kicked her high-heeled sandals off, almost tripping and falling to the floor, dropped her shoulder bag, and strolled closer to Matthew. "Out."

"Out where?"

"Just out."

"Doing what?" he said, looking at her and frowning. "And why are you wearin' that slutty outfit?"

"Because... it looks... good... on me," she said, slurring her words.

"This is ridiculous."

Racquel straddled his lap and grabbed the sides of his face.

"Move, Racquel. Get off me."

"Awww, baby, don't be like that. You know I love you."

Her breath reeked of alcohol, and Matt turned his head away from her.

She quickly turned it back and kissed him ferociously...and Matthew hated himself for liking it. He hated himself for wanting her so badly. How could he when she'd turned against him, slapped him, and she never as much as looked at their son anymore? They were living in total dysfunction, worse than the way those people lived on those reality shows Racquel watched all the time; yet, he couldn't help the way he felt. No matter what problems they were having, he was still a man with needs, and Racquel was still his wife. He didn't want to give in to her, not unless she was truly sorry and she was ready to love him again and work on their marriage, but her sexual advances—all the kissing and caressing she was doing—were making him weak. It was as if he didn't care about her obnoxious and uncaring attitude and that all he could think about was getting what he wanted from her. What he hadn't had in months. What a husband deserved to get from his wife. She'd been holding out on him just to make him suffer, but now she was offering herself to him, and he would take it.

She kissed him roughly, and Matthew let her have her way with him. He silently gave her permission to do whatever she wanted, which was exactly what she did. She was drunk, out of control, and acting like a street woman, but Matthew was fine with it—he actually encouraged it.

Chapter 18

Dillon closed his eyes, enjoying the soothing hot water running across his chest. There was nothing like taking a relaxing shower, not to mention this was usually where he mapped out his thoughts and plans and decided on his next move. As a matter of fact, he'd thought of the perfect plan just now and wished he'd acted on it a long time ago—he was going to legally change his last name to Black. Of course, the idea had occurred to him right when his father had learned who he was, but it hadn't been until last night before going to sleep that he'd realized how changing his name might help him. It would make church members and other acquaintances see him as a legitimate Black family member, and he wouldn't have to work so hard trying to prove that he belonged. He wouldn't get rid of his mom's surname, but the more he spoke it out loud, the more prestigious Dillon Whitfield Black sounded to him, anyway. It had a certain ring to it, and Dillon couldn't wait to head over to the courthouse to get the ball rolling. It was the reason he was up so early.

He'd checked their county's website and learned that once he filled out the application and paid the filing fee, all he would need to do is schedule a hearing date with the county clerk so he could go before a judge. So it didn't sound as though this process would take more than a few weeks, and if all went well, he'd have his new name pretty quickly. Now, his thought, too, was that he should call and tell his dad about it, but then he decided that Father's Day would be a much better time. It was only a month away, and this would be his gift to him. If, for some reason, things weren't finalized in time, he would at least show him the paperwork, which would still make his dad just as happy.

Dillon turned the pewter knob, making the water hotter, and turned his back to it. Then he got out, barely dried his body, and wrapped a thick terry towel around his waist. He took another towel and dried his hair and then went into the bedroom. He was about to get dressed, but then he decided to go check on Melissa's progress in the den.

"So have you found anything?" he asked.

"Not really."

"Well, if you don't find something soon, you need to hire a private investigator. I told you that last night. Pay them whatever they ask for."

"I will."

"I'm going out for a while, but my clothes need to be washed. I have some stuff for the cleaners, too."

"Oh . . . I was thinking I'd wait a couple of days . . . until we have a few more pieces to add to the load."

"I hate seeing dirty clothes and you know that. I want them washed today."

"Okay, baby, I'll do it."

Dillon rolled his eyes in disgust. She always had to try him. It was as if she liked making him go off.

"I'm outta here," he said.

"Baby, wait."

Dillon pursed his lips. "What, Melissa?"

"Can I ask you something?"

"Depends on what it is."

"Why do you hate me so much?"

Dillon threw his hands in the air. "Oh, here we go."

"I'm sorry, but I just wanna know because I do everything I can to please you. Everything...but it's never enough."

"Yeah, but didn't I give you an opportunity to leave? Haven't I always told you I would never marry you? I've always been honest about that, so why are you complaining?"

"Do you hate me because you're seeing someone else?"

Dillon laughed and shook his head. "You know what? You just get back to doin' what I told you. Good grief," he said, leaving the room.

After all the times he'd declared to her, "I don't love you, Melissa," she still had the audacity to question him about their relationship. Wasn't it humiliating for her? Especially since he'd always made it clear that he didn't love her. He actually wondered where these sudden inquiries were coming from. He wasn't going to worry about them, though, not when she was nobody important and she didn't have a dime to her name. He was doing her a favor just by letting her live with him for free, so he didn't know what her problem was. He didn't know why she couldn't be happy with the way things were, when she knew nothing was going to change between them.

Dillon went back to their room, slipped on his jeans and white V-neck pullover and headed out to the garage. He never bothered telling Melissa he was leaving, but as he backed halfway out of the driveway, he rolled down his window and spoke to his lawn guy, Roger. Roger was maybe in his late thirties, and he did a great job with cutting the grass, but he wasn't the brightest person Dillon had ever met. As a matter of fact, Dillon sometimes wondered how he'd been able to start his own business. He was a little on the country side, too.

"Hey Mr. Whitfield, how you?"

"Can't complain. Nice day today, isn't it?"

"Yep," he said, eyeing Dillon's SUV. "Man, I sho do like that ride of yours."

Dillon smiled. "Thanks. To tell the truth, I like it myself."

"I'd give anythang to drive somethin' like that."

"If you keep working the way you do, you'll have one in no time."

Roger laughed, with two teeth missing—one on the top right and one on the lower left. "Nah, I don't think so, Mr. Whitfield. Cost too much money for me."

"You never know," Dillon said, but Dillon knew Roger was right. He would probably never own anything slightly close to what Dillon was driving. "Well, I'd better get going. See you later."

"Take care, Mr. Whitfield."

Dillon wasn't sure why Roger never called him by his first name, especially since Roger was easily ten years older than him. Maybe it was just his way of offering respect to a client.

Dillon drove out into the street, but before he could drive away from the house, his phone rang, and he got irritated. What did she want now?

However, when he looked at the display, he saw an unknown number from the Atlanta area. It was likely his aunt calling him from work.

"Hello?" he said, turning onto the next street and heading out of the subdivision.

"Dillon?" a woman responded.

"Yes."

"My name is Tina. I'm a very close friend of your aunt Susan's."

"Is she okay?"

"No, sweetie, she isn't. She passed away a couple of hours ago."

Dillon pulled his SUV to the side of the road and stopped. He sat listening to the woman, but he no longer heard a word she was saying because all he could think about was the way he'd rushed his aunt off the phone last night. She'd told him how much she loved him, but he hadn't wanted to hear it—he hadn't wanted to discuss anything accept the love he needed from his father, and now the one person who truly did love him was gone. The woman who had raised him and who had done everything she could for him was no more—and all she'd wanted was for him to come see her. Now, as he thought back to their conversation, he couldn't help realizing that her plea had sounded a little desperate. So maybe she'd been sick and hadn't told him. He couldn't imagine her keeping that kind of a secret, but now he wondered. Then he cried like an infant.

Chapter 19

What a night. Matthew couldn't remember the last time he'd needed Racquel so badly, and to his surprise, she'd given him all he could want and then some. It had almost been like being with another woman because even during some of their happier times, she'd never been so forward and aggressive. He wasn't sure if her intense desire to make love to him stemmed from her being intoxicated or if maybe she simply missed him as much as he missed her—and maybe she'd had a huge change of heart. He chose to believe the latter because it made him feel better and also because he didn't want his wife to have to drink just to be with him. He couldn't deny, though, that she was definitely a happy drunk. She hadn't said a harsh word to him, and she'd told him multiple times how much she loved him. She'd laughed a lot, too, mostly at her own jokes, but she'd laughed nonetheless, and Matthew liked that Racquel better—as opposed to the bitter, angry, and cruel Racquel he'd been dealing with for far too long.

Matthew inhaled and exhaled, stretched his body, and then glanced over at the clock on his nightstand. He'd thought it was much earlier, but it was already seven o'clock. He normally got up at six, which gave him plenty of time to get dressed, feed MJ, and then get him ready for Aunt Emma's. But today, he was going to call into work to let his boss know he wouldn't be in until around noon.

Matthew looked over at his wife, who was still sleeping, wondering how she was going to react when she woke up. Maybe he was being naïve, but what he hoped was that she would tell him she no longer wanted to leave them and that she would then rush into MJ's room, scoop him out of his crib, hug him as tightly as possible, and tell him she loved him more than life itself. That's what Matthew hoped for, anyway.

He lay there thinking back over his life, thinking about his job at the bank and thinking about his future. Mostly, though, he waited for Racquel to open her eyes so he could talk to her. Maybe they would even make love again, or better yet, he'd take the day off so they could spend it together.

Sadly, though, when he looked over at her again, he saw her staring straight at him, and she seemed repulsed by his presence.

"What are you lookin' at?" she spat.

Matthew faced the ceiling again and closed his eyes. His worst nightmare had been realized. She'd sobered up and had turned vicious again.

"I hate it when you look at me. And why can't you sleep in the living room?"

Matthew listened in silence. He couldn't speak if he wanted to.

"I can't wait for you to get out of here. Oh and just so you know, that little sexcapade of ours last night meant nothing. I did that for me. I know you think you're the only one around here with needs, but I've got needs, too."

Matthew couldn't take any more of her mean comments, so he got up and went into the bathroom.

Racquel stormed behind him.

"I need some money."

"What does that have to with me?" he said, turning on the vanity faucet. He didn't look at her, though.

"Everything."

"Whatever, Racquel," he said.

"Are you gonna give it to me?"

"For what? So you can blow it on a fifth of liquor?"

"If that's what I choose to do with it."

"Well, I don't have any money. I'm the only one who works around here, remember?"

"You're the only one who *should* be working. I took care of your child for a whole year, *remember*?"

Now Matthew turned and looked at her. "You mean *our* child, don't you?"

"Look, are you gonna give me the money or not?"

"Nope."

"I knew I never should have married you. You're such a weakling. You make me sick."

"Why don't you go back to bed, Racquel? Or maybe turn on one of those pathetic reality shows of yours. I'm sure some rerun is on."

Matthew cast his eye at her through the mirror, and she looked as though she wanted to kill him.

"You know what I wish?" she said. "I wish you would drop dead. I wish I never had to see you again."

"You're sick," he said.

"I'll show you sick," she yelled and knocked his head to the side with her hand.

"Why do you keep putting your hands on me, Racquel?"

"Because you deserve it. You *and* that tramp you call a mother."

"Why are you doing this?"

"Because I need money. I told you that already."

"And I told you I don't have any."

"You're such a loser," she said and walked away.

Just then Matthew heard MJ talking—his kind of talk, anyway—and when Matt went into his room, MJ was sitting in the middle of his crib, playing with a toy, but when he spied his father, he pulled himself up by the rail.

"Hey little man. Good morning. You hungry?"

MJ smiled and bounced excitedly when he felt Matthew lifting him up. Matthew looked at his son, something he did all the time, but today he truly looked at him. Then he made a decision. He and MJ were moving out.

Chapter 20

Dillon stared through his front windshield, completely dazed. He'd replayed every word his aunt Susan's friend had told him, but he couldn't believe she was gone. She was actually dead, and he would never see her alive again.

He sat in his truck, still parked at the side of the road, and finally he picked up his phone. If there were ever a time he needed his dad's love and support, it was now, so he called him.

"Hey son," he said right away.

"Hey."

"So how's it going?"

"Not good. My aunt Susan just passed."

"Oh no. I'm so sorry to hear that. What happened?"

"I don't know. Her friend Tina called me, but I was too upset to ask any questions."

"Had you spoken to her lately?"

"Just last night."

"Really? And she was fine?"

"She didn't say anything was wrong."

"Gosh, I tell you... I really am sorry to hear this."

"I'm still stunned."

"Are you planning to leave for Atlanta today?"

"No, I was thinking first thing in the morning. I'll need to meet with the funeral home as soon as possible."

"I understand."

Dillon wondered when his dad was going to offer to go with him. Surely, he wasn't planning to let him travel all the way to Georgia by himself.

"And you don't have any other aunts or uncles, right?" Curtis asked.

"No, and with the exception of a couple of cousins, I'm her only living relative."

"I hate you have to go through this, son, but God will give you strength. He'll comfort you in your time of need."

All this biblical and spiritual encouragement was fine and well, but Dillon needed more from his father. He needed him to get on a plane and stand by his side until he buried his aunt. Since it didn't sound as though he thought that kind of support was necessary, however, Dillon decided to flat-out ask him.

"Can you go with me?"

Curtis paused for a few seconds. "Of course. I'll be glad to."

Dillon swallowed tears for as long as he could, but soon they streamed down his face. He was terribly hurt over losing his aunt, but he was happy out of this world about his father accompanying him to her funeral. He needed someone to be with him more than ever.

"Dad, I really appreciate this."

"It's not a problem, and I'll ask Lana to have one of her assistants check on flights and a hotel for the three of us."

"That would be great, Dad," he said, wondering who the third ticket was for. Surely not that witch, Charlotte, because he didn't want anyone infringing on their time together. "This really means everything to me, and I won't forget it. Also, who else are you getting a ticket for?"

"Melissa. She is going, isn't she?"

Dillon leaned his head onto the back rest and shut his eyes. How was he going to explain to his dad that he didn't want her going anywhere with them? He didn't want to be bothered, but he knew he had to pick and choose his words because he didn't want his father knowing how much he despised Melissa. For now, he wanted his dad to believe he had the utmost respect for his fiancée and that he couldn't live without her.

"I'll have to check with her. She's starting a summer class at the university, so she may not be able to go," he lied.

"Oh, I didn't realize that. Well, just let me know."

"I will."

"You take care, son, and be strong. I know you're hurting, but things will get better every day."

"Thanks again, Dad."

"Anytime."

Dillon hung up and sat a few minutes longer, thinking about his childhood and how happy he'd been—how his aunt truly had loved him like a son. He thought about the time she'd taken him to this huge amusement park and how he'd had the time of his life. He'd only been in second grade, and Aunt Susan had gotten on every ride he asked her to—even the ones she'd been frightened of. Then there was the time two of his third-grade classmates, Jason and Timothy, had bullied him and his aunt had come to his rescue. Not in the way one would have expected, though. Unlike most parents of a child who was being bullied, she hadn't said a word to Dillon's teacher or to the boys' parents. Instead, she'd asked the parents if the boys could come over for a belated birthday party she was giving Dillon. Dillon remembered how strange he'd thought that was because he'd already celebrated his birthday three months before. Still, she'd invited them and when they'd arrived, she'd sat them down in the dining room, alongside Dillon. Then she'd set one blank piece of paper in front of each of them and asked them face-to-face why they didn't like her nephew. They'd both seemed terrified and as if they were afraid to speak, and this was when she'd told them, "Maybe it'll be easier if you just write it down." They'd seemed dumbfounded, but his aunt had been serious. "Go ahead. Number your papers from one to five and write down all the things you don't like about Dillon. Then, when you finish that, I want you to write down at least one thing he's done to hurt you." The boys had sat there in silence, not knowing what to do. So Aunt Susan had taken things a step further. "Let's move on to spelling."

Now, Dillon had wondered if his aunt had maybe lost her mind because he hadn't understood how spelling words was going to help his situation. Little did he know, though, his aunt had known exactly what she was doing.

"Spell *aunt*," she'd told them, and finally Jason had said, "A-n-t."

"No, I mean like your mom's or dad's sister," she explained. "That kind of an aunt."

"I know," Jason said. "That's how you spell it."

"Is that how you'd spell it, too, Timothy?"

"Yep."

"Then you're both wrong," she said, staring at them. How about *bottom*? Can you spell that?"

This time Timothy smiled, clearly confident that he could get this one right. "B-o-t-t-u-m."

"That's wrong, too. You wanna try that one, Jason?"

Jason had shaken his head, no.

"Really? And you boys are in third grade? That's interesting, because Dillon knew how to spell these little baby words a whole year ago. But let's try one last one. *Dumb*."

"That's easy," Timothy said. "D-u-m."

"Do you agree, Jason?"

"Yes."

"Wrong again. But you know what? Maybe we should try some kindergarten words instead. Because I would hate for Dillon to tell everyone at school that neither of you could spell anything at all."

"I wanna go home," Timothy had said, and then he'd started crying.

But Jason, the leader of the two, had surrendered. "I'm really sorry, Miss Whitfield. We didn't mean all that stuff we said to Dillon, and we want to be friends with him now. We like Dillon."

Needless to say, Jason and Timothy had never bullied Dillon again, and third grade had turned out to be one of his favorite school years—all because of his wonderful aunt, who'd been willing to do anything to protect him and make him happy.

Dillon sighed deeply, drove to the intersection, and headed back to his house. As soon as he rolled into the driveway, though, he saw Roger and he was glad he'd slipped his sunglasses back on. Roger was a little slow, maybe even illiterate, but Dillon still didn't want any man to see that he'd been crying. As he pulled into the garage, Roger spoke to him, and thankfully he kept working on the yard and never looked Dillon's way again.

When Dillon got inside, he went straight up to the bedroom but he cringed when Melissa almost ran into him. She'd been coming out of the room just as he'd walked in.

"Oh, I'm sorry, baby. I didn't know you were back. I was just about to take your clothes to the cleaners."

Dillon walked around her and didn't say anything.

"Is everything okay?"

He dropped down in the chair and leaned his head back. "My aunt passed away."

"Aunt Susan?"

"How many aunts do I have, Melissa? Even Country Roger out there wouldn't ask such a dumb question."

"I'm really sorry, baby. What happened?"

"I don't know, but I'm heading to Atlanta to find out," he said, but then he thought about something. "And if you'd taken my clothes to the cleaners before today, I'd have them back by now."

"I'm sorry. I didn't know you'd—"

Dillon raised his hand in front of him. "Just save it, Melissa."

"So when are we leaving?" she asked.

"My dad and I are leaving in the morning."

"But what about me?"

"You're gonna stay here and take care of what I told you."

"But I can start calling private investigators today and hire one while we're gone."

"No."

"But, baby—"

"Melissa, please. When I say, no, that's what I mean. You're not going with me, so just get over it."

He didn't dare waste his time looking at her, but he still heard her sniffling. It was too bad, though, because no one was going to tag along with him and his dad to his aunt's funeral. Not a soul—and that was all there was to it.

Chapter 21

Matthew hadn't been to a bowling alley since he didn't know when, but he was glad Jonathan and Elijah had wanted to come. It was only Thursday night, but for some reason, it was packed the way it once had been on Fridays and Saturdays. Matthew was sure that this was a result of all the college students being home for the summer. He did see a few high school "youngins," as Jonathan would call them, but for the most part, everyone else looked to be somewhere between eighteen and twenty-two, and Matthew was having a good time. He'd sort of felt bad about leaving MJ with Aunt Emma, especially since she'd already kept him while he'd been working, but she'd basically insisted that he go enjoy himself with his friends.

"Man, I'm goin' on record right now," Jonathan said matter-of-factly, checking out a tall, stallion-looking girl with short, brown hair. "That'll be mine before the night is out."

They all leaned against the wall facing the direction

of the bowling lanes, and Elijah and Matthew cracked up laughing.

"What?" Jonathan said.

Matthew shook his head. "Man, you haven't changed a bit. Still chasin' girl after girl."

"You mean woman after woman, because there's nothin' girlish at all about that fine thing over there."

Now Elijah shook his head. "Matt, man, can you imagine what it's like dealin' with this fool every single day? I even gotta live with him."

Matthew forced a smile on his face, but it was hard not to envy the kind of life Jonathan and Elijah were living. College life...and they were also playing football. He loved his friends like brothers, something he could never say enough, but he couldn't help wishing things had turned out differently for him. All three of them had gone off to college, Jonathan and Elijah to the University of Illinois in Champaign and Matthew to Harvard, yet Matthew had returned home a long time ago. It seemed so unfair, too, because during their senior year in high school, Matthew had been named "Most Likely to Succeed," and he had certainly done much better than Jonathan and Elijah when it came to their grades. He'd been a star football player, too. Interestingly enough, though, it was the two of them who'd completed their second year at U of I, and they were making their parents proud. Matthew, on the other hand, was a total failure.

"Wow," Jonathan said, eyeing another girl up and down. She scanned his body from head to toe and back up, too. "Maybe I spoke too fast. Maybe she's the one I should get to workin' on."

"Man, will you cut it out," Elijah said. "Forget about these girls. We're supposed to be cheerin' up our boy."

"Well, now that I've heard the whole story," Jonathan said. "I don't see where Matt has any choice. Divorce is the only option. You can't help someone who don't wanna be helped."

When they'd stopped for pizza a couple of hours ago, Matthew had gone ahead and told them everything—not about Racquel hitting him, of course, because the two of them would see him as a feeble punk—but he'd shared everything else. He'd been so full inside, slightly depressed and confused, that he hadn't held back. Now, though, Jonathan acted as though Racquel was the worst mother and wife he'd ever heard of, and Matthew was sort of sorry he'd told them anything.

"It's not that simple," Matthew said.

"I don't know why not," Jonathan declared. "You said you tried to talk to her. Her parents even tried to make her get help. And on top of that, she wants nothin' to do with little MJ, *and* she's goin' out gettin' drunk? What else is there to do?"

Matthew looked at him and then toward the couple of lanes in front of them. He knew that when Jonathan formed an opinion about anything, there was no changing his mind, so Matthew didn't try to.

"Matt, if I were you," Elijah said, "I'd do what I thought was best for my family."

"Divorcing her *is* what's best," Jonathan said. "Something's wrong with that girl, and if she won't try to help herself, then there's nothin' Matt can do about it."

"Let's talk about somethin' else," Matthew said. He hated hearing Jonathan's rants, but mostly it was because he knew Jonathan might be right. If Racquel wouldn't get help, and no one could force her, then his hands were tied. He certainly wasn't planning to take MJ around her again either, not with her acting so violently. He didn't want to believe she'd ever lay a hand on MJ, but when he'd been away in Boston, he'd seen a news segment about a woman who'd drowned her eight-month-old baby and had never shed a tear. The experts had talked a lot about postpartum depression, but for some reason Matthew hadn't thought about that story again until this morning. He'd picked up his son, looked at him, and the thought of that woman had hit him like a bulldozer. It was then that he'd decided it was time he and MJ moved out. He wasn't sure when he was going to pack their things, because he knew he had to do it when Racquel wasn't around, but for now, MJ would stay with Aunt Emma. Aunt Emma had thought this was best, too, and tomorrow he would tell his in-laws about it.

Matthew, Elijah, and Jonathan laughed and chatted like old times, and soon Matthew felt much better. His marital problems still lingered in the back of his mind, but at the moment, they weren't consuming him and he was able to enjoy himself for a change.

"Uh-oh," Jonathan said, and Matthew and Elijah

looked in the same direction. "Here comes Stacey," he sang.

Elijah smiled but Matthew could tell he was trying to keep a straight face so as to not egg Jonathan on.

Jonathan kept on, anyway. "Dang, Matt, she still wants you, man. After all this time."

Matthew pursed his lips. "Man, you're crazy."

"Hmmph, whatever you say."

"Hey fellas," Stacey said, walking up with two of her girls and smiling. "Long time, no see."

"Long time indeed," Jonathan said.

"How's it goin'?" Matthew finally said.

Stacey smiled more than she had before. "Wonderful. Especially now."

Jonathan raised his eyebrows and winked at Matthew. Then he turned to Stacey's friends. "So, you two not speakin'?" he asked.

"Hello," they both said together.

"You ladies must be from Stacey's school."

"They are," Stacey said, laughing. "So just leave them alone, Jonathan, because I know how you are."

"What?" he said, smiling slyly. "I'm as innocent as they come."

All six of them laughed. Even Stacey's two friends had already figured out how forward Jonathan was.

Stacey folded her arms. "Well, we won't hold you guys. We just wanted to say hello...and, of course, it was good seeing you, Matt."

"Good seein' you, too. You take care."

Jonathan barely waited for them to leave. "Man, that

Stacey is just as fine as ever, and don't pretend you didn't see how she was lookin' at you. I thought she was gonna throw you down right here on the ground in front of all of us."

"You're sick," Matthew said, laughing.

Elijah laughed, too. "That he is, Matt, but I'm with Jon on this one. That girl still has it bad for you."

Matthew hadn't thought about Stacey Martin in a long time, but before he'd started dating Racquel they'd become pretty close. Now Matthew wondered how things might have turned out for him had he stayed with Stacey and never hooked up with Racquel. He felt bad just thinking about it, but it was hard not to wonder. He also felt bad about something else: the reason he'd stopped dating Stacey. She'd made it clear that she wasn't going to have sex with him or anyone else while in high school. He remembered how his mom hadn't liked her, the same as she hadn't liked Racquel, thinking Stacey was only trying to trap him with a baby; but little had his mother known, she'd been wrong about her. Stacey had been one of the good girls, and Matt had been fine with it; that is, until Jonathan and some of their other teammates had poured on the pressure. They'd worked on Matthew until they'd finally convinced him that any girl who wasn't giving it up wasn't worth his time or money, and it hadn't been long before he'd succumbed to their comments like a dummy. He'd broken up with Stacey, started a relationship with Racquel, and now he was a twenty-year-old husband and father.

Boy, had he made a lot of mistakes, and the more he stared at Stacey, standing a few feet away, the more he regretted them. She stared at him, too, and that only made things worse. From the time he'd been old enough to understand what the word *infidelity* meant he'd promised himself he would never be like his mother or father. He would never commit that kind of sin against God or his wife, but just for a quick moment, he ignored his long-held Christian values. What he thought about instead was how happy his life might've been had he continued dating Stacey. God forgive him, he wondered what it would feel like to be with her now—tonight even.

Chapter 22

As soon as the doorbell rang, Dillon looked at Melissa and she dragged herself into the entryway to open the door. If only she would listen to him she wouldn't have to walk around with a black eye or have to feel embarrassed. He didn't know why she made him do these kinds of things, and in all honesty, it had been a couple of years since she'd made him lose it to the extent he had last night. But she just hadn't wanted to give up on traveling with him to Atlanta. He'd told her once, twice, three times even, but she'd kept crying and begging him to let her go. This was when he'd warned her about pushing him too far, but lo and behold, she'd asked him a fourth time and then she'd told him how she had every right to go to his aunt's funeral because she'd been the one to call to check on her all the time, anyway. Dillon barely remembered what had happened after that, but all he knew was that this morning when he'd gotten up, he'd found her sleeping in the den on the sofa and he'd noticed how strange her eye looked. Maybe now she would listen when he told her something once and for all and she'd accept it.

When Melissa opened the door, the driver looked at her and seemed uncomfortable. "Uh, hi. I'm Carlisle, and I'm here for Mr. Whitfield."

"Hey, how's it goin'?" Dillon said, rolling his suitcase toward the door.

Carlisle took it from him. "I'm fine, thank you. I'll be right outside, sir."

As the driver walked away, Dillon had to admit he liked this kind of service. He certainly had more than enough money to hire limos whenever he wanted, but since he never left town he never needed transportation to O'Hare, which was an hour away. This limo was very special to him, though, because his father had paid for it. His dad had also told him that whenever they ordered a car, they always requested Carlisle because he was the best.

Dillon grabbed his black blazer, slipped it on, and looked back at Melissa. Tears filled her eyes. He wished he hadn't gotten so upset last night, but she was so doggoned hardheaded. The whole thing had been her fault, and he sort of resented her for making him punish her like this. He figured the least he could do was say good-bye, though.

"I'll see you later."

Tears flowed down her cheeks. "Bye."

What a pitiful sight, Dillon thought, and walked outside.

Once Carlisle closed Dillon's door, he got back in the

car and drove out of the subdivision. Dillon was glad to be leaving Melissa behind, which made him happy, but suddenly he thought about his aunt. He hated feeling sad and helpless, though, so he tried to think about the happy times they'd shared. Then, the closer they drove to his dad's house to pick him up, the more content Dillon felt again. His dad lived closer to the interstate, so that was the reason he'd requested that the car swing by to get Dillon first.

Dillon stretched his legs all the way out, looked at cars passing by them, and sort of got tickled. He could barely contain himself because he was finally getting what he'd wanted—time alone with his father, and on top of that, they were traveling out of town together. They would spend days in Atlanta, just the two of them, and miles away from everyone else—Charlotte the Harlot, Curtina, Alicia, Phillip—folks who didn't matter or mean squat to Dillon. He also no longer had to worry about Matthew easing his way back into the picture, at least not for now, anyway. Dillon still hadn't learned whether Matthew had gone to visit his parents that day he'd seen him or not, but today Matthew didn't worry him—today, his dad would think only about one of his sons, his firstborn child, and that was all that mattered.

It was funny how even though his aunt had always told him that for everything bad, something good happened, he'd never believed her, yet now he knew she'd been right. Who would have thought that losing his aunt could lead to spending such quality time with his father? Losing Aunt Susan was the worst, but being with his dad was the best, and he knew the latter would alleviate his pain with each passing day. He felt as giddy as a small child, and now that Carlisle was waiting for the gate to open so he could drive up his father's lengthy driveway, he wanted to laugh out loud. Dillon almost didn't like the way he was feeling because most grown men would never feel this kind of emotion. It was actually embarrassing, so Dillon calmed himself down so his dad wouldn't see him acting this way. He manned up—but then he spotted his dad walking outside, all lovey-dovey with Charlotte. They acted as though they'd just met maybe a month ago, and that they had no idea what they were going to do without each other. It was enough to make Dillon ill. Down to the very last minute, this woman was still getting on his nerves, and he couldn't wait for his father to get in the car.

Carlisle opened the door, and Curtis kissed Charlotte. Then he hugged her.

"I'll call you as soon as we get to the airport," he told her.

"I love you," she said.

"I love you, too, baby. Kiss my baby girl for me when she gets home from school."

"You know I will. Be safe."

Dillon looked straight ahead, refusing to as much as glance at Charlotte, and his dad made himself comfortable inside the limo.

"Good morning, son."

"Good morning."

"How are you feeling?"

"Okay, I guess. Still a little shocked about my aunt, though."

"That's to be expected, but I've been praying for you."

Carlisle drove around the circular drive, and Dillon glanced at the fountain displayed in the center. He wasn't sure why exactly, but he'd always admired it. Maybe it was because it screamed wealth and elegance, and that excited him. Actually, he wondered if his dad might let him move in with him once he kicked Charlotte out. Dillon didn't see why not because this was simply the way most well-off people lived, specifically those wealthy people who had lots of bedrooms and tons of square footage. In those cases, adult children lived with their parents for as long as they wanted. He knew this because he'd seen the new version of *Dallas*, which was a spin-off of the old one that had aired back in the eighties when he was just a toddler. On *Dallas*, the adult children never moved out, and when they got married their spouses moved in, too. When they had children, they built nurseries for them right inside the mansion.

As Carlisle exited onto the interstate, Curtis's phone rang and he pulled it out of his blazer pocket. He looked at the display, smiling, and Dillon wondered who it was.

"So we're ten minutes away from the house and you're missing me already?" he said, laughing.

Was that Charlotte? Why couldn't she leave his dad

alone? She saw him every day, so wasn't that enough? But Dillon knew she was only calling as a way to irritate *him*. She knew Dillon had been trying for such long while to spend time alone with his father, and this was her rude way of interrupting it. She was secretly taunting him again, the same as always, but that was okay because he would get her back soon enough. In the end, she would beg him to forgive her. She would plead for mercy, but all he would do is laugh at her.

Chapter 23

Finally. No fiancée he despised, no irritating half sisters or brother, no evil stepmother. Life just didn't get any better than this. As far back as Dillon could remember, he'd dreamed about having a dad. He'd fantasized about it, and now all that he'd hoped for was reality. He'd met his dad last year, but today was the first full day he'd been able to have him all to himself. They'd arrived in Atlanta yesterday, early afternoon, rented an SUV, and then driven to the Ritz-Carlton downtown. Then when they'd gotten settled into their room, they'd gone straight to the hospital to release his aunt's body to the funeral home. After that, they'd both been a bit tired, so they'd gone back to the hotel, eaten dinner in the restaurant, and gone up to their room to watch the NBA playoffs. At first, when his dad had told him that one of his secretaries would make the hotel and flight arrangements, he'd wondered if they would book two separate rooms. So he'd been thrilled when he'd learned that his father had requested one room with two double beds. He'd been ecstatic because he knew that no father would share a hotel room with a son he didn't love. No father would pack up at the last minute and hop on a plane for a son he didn't want to be there for, and Dillon couldn't be more grateful.

When the valet pulled the black SUV around to the front entrance, Dillon gave him a ten-dollar bill and drove away. It was only half past nine in the morning, and it was also Saturday, so thankfully there wasn't much traffic. They didn't have too far to go, at least not by Atlanta standards, since his aunt's home was just over in Lithonia. It was maybe twenty miles away at the most.

"So, do you miss Atlanta?" Curtis asked him.

"Sometimes, but not really."

"It's a huge change of pace. Mitchell is at least ten times smaller. Especially if you count all the suburbs here."

"True, but I've never done a lot of socializing or partying, so living in a smaller town doesn't bother me."

"Well, I've lived in both Atlanta and Chicago, and sometimes I miss big-city life."

"But Chicago is so close, you could drive there daily if you wanted to," Dillon said.

"That rarely happens, though, because I'm always too busy. And don't get me wrong, I love Mitchell. I'm just saying that sometimes it would be nice to take Curtina downtown to some of the larger plays for children. It would be great to see other attractions, too."

Dillon cringed. The conversation had been going exceptionally well, so why did he have to bring up that little brat? Why couldn't he just forget about them? At least while they were down here for his aunt's funeral.

Dillon changed lanes and tried to act as though nothing was wrong. He didn't speak, though.

So they drove another couple of miles, but now his dad's phone rang. Dillon cringed again.

"Hey baby girl," he said.

Dillon didn't know whether it was Alicia or Curtina calling, because his dad regularly referred to both of them as his "baby girl," but that was beside the point. Dillon didn't want him talking to either one of them.

"So what are you and Phillip up to this weekend… really…sounds like a nice time. You can never go wrong spending the day on Navy Pier. Especially since it's pretty hot there today. I saw on TV this morning that it was gonna be eighty-two in Chicago. So you can imagine how hot it is here."

Dillon wanted to yank his dad's phone away from him. He and Alicia weren't even talking about anything important, so why couldn't he talk to her later? Better yet, why couldn't he call her when he got back home?

"We're headed to his aunt's house now. Her friend is meeting us there, and then we're going to the funeral home…We're not sure yet, but we found out from the hospital that her cause of death was heart failure. We don't know the official reason yet, though…Okay, I'm glad you called, baby girl, and I'll make sure to tell him. Love you much," he said and ended the call. "Alicia sends her best and says she's praying for you."

Yeah right. She didn't even like him, so why would

she care one way or the other about his aunt dying? People did this all the time, telling others they were going to pray for them, even though they knew they weren't. They said this only because it sounded good and because it made them feel better about themselves.

"Are you okay?" Curtis asked.

"I'm fine," he said, trying to settle his temper.

"Why are you so quiet?"

"No reason," he said dryly.

Curtis looked out his window and didn't say another word. Now Dillon worried that maybe his dad had picked up on his anger and he was annoyed by it. Dillon couldn't have his dad upset with him, though, not when they'd bonded so perfectly last night, so he did what he could to fix things.

"I was just thinking about my aunt. I still can't believe she's gone, and Dad, it hurts."

"I know. Losing someone you love is the hardest thing anyone has to go through. I remember how I felt when I lost my mother. I was devastated. It also didn't help that I hadn't been in touch with her for years. I still regret that to this day, and sometimes the guilt tears me apart."

Dillon felt the same way about his aunt, but he tried not to think about it. He tried telling himself that he couldn't call her as much or fly back and forth to Atlanta and also get to know his father the way he needed to. He was sure she'd understood that, though. Of course, she had.

But Dillon did wonder why his dad hadn't spoken to his mom. He knew his grandmother had passed away a few years back, but that's all his dad had told him.

"So why hadn't you seen your mom?"

"It's a long story, son, but mostly it was because of how selfish I was. I didn't realize how important family was, and I went on with my life without them. But like I said, I regret it, and I can never change the way I treated her."

Dillon drove a few more miles and turned into his aunt's driveway. When he looked in his rearview mirror, he saw a stocky woman with brown hair walking toward them. It must be Tina.

Dillon opened his door and got out.

She smiled brightly and hugged him. "It's so good to finally meet you. Susan talked about you all the time. She thought the world of you."

"It's nice meeting you also. And this is my dad."

Curtis walked around the vehicle and shook her hand. "Very nice to meet you."

"Likewise."

"So how long have you known Aunt Susan?" Dillon asked.

"Only about nine months. After my divorce, I moved in next door," she said, pointing across the way, "and your aunt and I became fast friends. She was such a kind spirit."

They made small talk while walking up the sidewalk. Tina unlocked the door, opened it, and disarmed the security system. Dillon wondered why she even knew the code, and that made him wonder if his aunt had been sick for a very long time. The attending doctor had listed her cause of death as heart failure, as his father had just told Alicia, but Dillon had assumed it was the result of a sudden heart attack. That had to be it because had she been ill for months, there was no way she wouldn't have told him.

"Susan had everything in order, and it's all right over there in the dining room. We can have a seat if you want."

Dillon walked through the living room and down the short hall, reminiscing about his childhood. After all these years, the house still looked the same, and it still felt like home. It was amazing how comfortable he felt in only a matter of minutes when he hadn't been there in more than twelve months.

As they sat down at the table, Dillon looked at the wall of photos, smiling, but then he choked up when he saw the one where his aunt was holding the back of his little red bike. It had been taken the day she'd taught him how to ride it without training wheels. This was more proof that his aunt had been there for him every step of the way, and he could kick himself for not coming to see her every time she'd asked him.

"So had she been sick very long?" Curtis asked, and Dillon almost hated to hear the answer.

"She had. For more than six months. She actually lived longer than her doctors expected."

Dillon frowned. "What was wrong with her?"

"She had pancreatic cancer."

Dillon leaned back in his chair. "What? How? And why did the hospital tell us she'd died from heart failure?"

"Because she did. But it was still a result of complications relating to her cancer."

"Why didn't she tell me?"

"I tried to get her to, but she wouldn't. All she'd say was that she didn't want to burden you."

"Had she been sick before she was diagnosed?" Curtis asked.

"No, and when they discovered what she had, she was already in her final stage. This is common with pancreatic cancer, though. No symptoms until it's too late."

Dillon was speechless. Why hadn't she told him so he could have come back to Atlanta to take care of her?

"I just don't get it," Dillon said. "When I spoke to her the other night, she sounded a little tired, but she seemed fine."

"That's because all that day, she'd seemed better than ever. Almost like she was well. It was as if she got better to leave here."

Curtis nodded. "I've heard that many times before, so I believe it."

Dillon had tried to forget about all the messages she'd left him before he'd finally called her a couple of days ago. Actually, ever since learning of her death, he'd pushed those phone messages out of his mind. He could no longer pretend that she hadn't tried to call him, though, and that there was a chance she might have told him she was dying—if she'd had a chance to talk to him.

"Here's a list of everything she wants for the service, and she also asked me to give you this." Tina passed Dillon a sealed envelope.

Dillon was almost afraid to take it, but he knew he didn't have a choice. He wasn't sure when he would read it, though. Not when there was no telling what Aunt Susan had written.

They sat discussing the church home-going and burial services, and then prepared to head over to the funeral home. Dillon wasn't looking forward to picking out caskets, flowers, or anything else relating to his aunt's death, and he couldn't wait for this to be over. It was too painful to deal with, but more than anything, he was drenched with guilt and it tore him apart. He'd managed to keep a straight face, but he wasn't sure how long that would last because what he wanted to do was run outside, screaming at the top of his lungs. He wanted to beg, plead, and bargain with God—anything to bring his aunt back. But sadly, it was much too late. He'd chosen to not come see her, and she was gone. He'd been sure he had plenty of time, but now he knew that not even the next minute was promised to a person—not even the next second.

Chapter 24

Matthew opened his eyes, trying to focus them, and realized he'd slept on the sofa—again. He certainly wasn't doing it because it was comfortable or because he wanted to, but he also couldn't take Racquel. Thursday night when he'd gotten home from the bowling alley, she'd been passed out drunk on the bed and then last night when Matthew had gotten home from spending the entire evening with MJ and Aunt Emma, she'd stumbled in after eleven, trying to seduce him. Her advances hadn't worked this time, though, and he couldn't remember ever feeling more disgusted. She'd looked and smelled like a drunken streetwalker, and he'd pushed her off of him. He'd expected her to react violently, but instead, she'd laughed at him, wobbled into their room and fallen onto the bed.

He was so tired of this, and though he'd decided it would be best to wait until she wasn't around, he knew it was time he set a date to move out. It was amazing, too, how he'd seemed to find more courage to do so after seeing Stacey at the bowling alley. He'd tried not to think about her, because he knew he was a married man, but the truth of the matter was, he'd found himself sitting at work yesterday daydreaming about her. He'd visualized himself picking her up and taking her out on a date, and then he'd imagined what it would feel like to be with her romantically. He knew his thoughts were sinful and that his fleshly desires were wrong, but he couldn't shake them. Maybe it was because he hadn't tried and because fantasizing about Stacey gave him a warm feeling and placed a natural smile on his face.

Matthew tossed the blanket away from him and stood up. He went into the bathroom, and though seeing an almost-comatose Racquel was the last thing he wanted to do, he pushed the bedroom door open and looked at her. She still had on every stitch of clothing that she'd worn out to the club, and the room stank like a brewery. He wondered what the heck she'd been drinking and how much of it because this was worse than what he'd smelled those times his mom had gotten drunk. Not to mention, Racquel was still driving around endangering people. This bothered Matthew more than anything, and he'd called her parents yesterday morning to tell them about it. They were worried sick, but like him, they didn't know how to stop her. Matthew had suggested that maybe they needed to try another intervention, but when they'd both gotten quiet, he'd realized they weren't all that interested in hearing her scream at them and blast them for all their past mistakes.

He closed the door all the way shut, went back into the living room, and picked up his phone. He turned on the television so that there would be background noise, just in case Racquel woke up. Then he dialed Stacey. As he, Jonathan, and Elijah had prepared to leave the bowling alley, he'd debated asking her for her number, but after talking to her during his full lunch hour yesterday, he was glad about his decision. He'd also spoken to her for another hour once he'd left work. So now his daydreams about her had intensified.

"Hey," he said as soon as she answered.

"Hey."

"Were you up?"

"Not really," she said, sounding as though she were stretching. "I'm still on college hours, and on Saturday mornings I'm usually never up before noon."

Matthew chuckled. "I can imagine."

"Are you alone?" she asked.

"Might as well be. She's passed out again."

"I'm really sorry, Matt."

"Yeah, well, it is what it is."

"I was never friends with Racquel, but I knew her well enough to know she never drank in high school. Mostly, she was quiet and laid-back."

"You don't have to tell me. I started dating her three years ago, and there were times when she used to criticize people who drank or did drugs."

"It really must be postpartum depression like you were saying."

Matthew had shared with Stacey what he and his in-laws thought, and though he didn't want everyone to know his and Racquel's business, he felt like he could trust Stacey. Actually, he knew he could trust her because she sounded more sympathetic toward Racquel than he did.

"She hasn't been diagnosed, but she has a lot of symptoms," he said.

"Who I really feel bad for is your son. I know he's only one, but I've heard that babies can feel rejection and the absence of their moms right out of the womb."

"I wish Racquel realized that, because believe it or not, she hasn't even asked me where he is. He's stayed with my aunt Emma for two nights straight, and she couldn't care less."

"That's too bad."

"It is, but at least he has me and Aunt Emma, and Racquel's parents are gonna keep him for a couple of days, starting this afternoon. They've been wanting to spend time with him, anyway."

"I'm glad he has all of you, too. Poor little thing."

"So what do you have up for today?" he said, flipping the TV channels.

"My mom and I are supposed to be going shopping, but I'm not doing anything later."

Matthew heard her response but the word *later* was what he focused on. It almost sounded like an invitation.

"Maybe I'll call you after I leave my in-laws. I'm gonna take MJ over there and then have dinner with them."

"Sounds good to me. Do you wanna go somewhere maybe?"

Matthew wasn't totally against the idea, but surely she wasn't expecting him to come to her home. Her parents would never be okay with their daughter spending as much as a few minutes with a married man.

Still, he said, "Where?"

"I dunno. We could just hang out. Drive around and talk."

Matthew didn't mind doing that, but he also wasn't in the kind of financial position where he could burn unnecessary gas. He'd worked out their budget so that he always had just enough to make it to and from work every day and then a few other places, but that was it. Although, since Aunt Emma had already gone out and bought baby supplies, he wouldn't have to spend as much on that over the next two weeks.

"We can just decide when I call," he said.

"That's fine."

"Are you sure about this, Stacey? Because let's be honest. I'm married, I have a small child, and you're still in college."

"Matt, I already know all that and if that bothered me, I wouldn't have given you my number. I'm not saying I'm gonna sleep with you, but I won't lie, I'm still attracted to you and I wanna see you. Just to talk and have some fun."

Matthew felt that warm sensation again, the one he experienced just about every time he thought about her.

"I just wanted to make sure you knew what you were dealing with. None of what I'm going through is pretty, and things are likely gonna get worse. Especially when I move outta here."

Matthew switched his phone to his other ear, but panicked when he heard the bedroom door opening. Racquel walked out with bloodshot eyes and her hair scattered all over her head.

"Why are you looking at me like that," she said, frowning. "You must be guilty of something. And who is that you're talkin' to?"

Matthew's heart pounded. "Hey, I'll talk to you later, okay?"

"Call me when you can."

Matthew pressed the End button, and Racquel walked closer to him.

"Who were you on the phone with, Matt?"

"None of your business."

"Excuse me?"

"Racquel, not today, okay. I'm not in the mood."

"I wanna know who you were talkin' to. And don't say it was Jonathan or Elijah, because you looked like you'd been busted for something."

Matthew flipped the channel again, trying to act normal. "Actually, it *was* Jonathan. Satisfied?"

"You're such a liar, and not even a good one."

Racquel stared at him, and he stared back at her. They watched each other until Racquel rushed toward his phone, but Matthew snatched it up from the sofa before she could get her hands on it.

"Let me see it, Matt!"

"No! Do I ask you to see your phone?"

Racquel lunged toward him again, and this time they tussled off the sofa and onto the floor. Matthew stretched his arm away, keeping the phone out of reach, but that only made Racquel angrier. She struggled with him, but then she stopped and got herself up—and kicked him in the head.

Matthew lay there for a few seconds, gathering his faculties and trying to clear his blurred vision. But it was only for a few seconds because now he grabbed her by both her legs, tripping her to the floor. Then he leaped on top of her.

"Oh my God," she screamed. "Stop it, Matt! You're hurting me."

Matthew grabbed her by her throat, squeezing with all his might. He hadn't even realized what he was doing until he saw water oozing from her eyes. He gazed at her, released her, and rolled onto his back, breathing heavily, and she coughed nonstop and went into the bathroom. He'd never felt more devastated or broken. Still, though, regardless of all of the commotion and heartache he was feeling, he'd come to a major conclusion. He had to move out today. That was all there was to it, because if he waited any longer, he would end up in jail.

But just as he'd settled on his decision, Racquel came at him again—like a madwoman.

Chapter 25

No matter how scenic the brick building appeared or how manicured the landscaping was, this funeral home gave Dillon the creeps. He hated anything that had to do with death, funerals, and cemeteries, and he was glad his aunt had asked that her services be held as quickly as possible. Thankfully, it was happening the day after tomorrow, on Monday.

Dillon, his dad, and Tina walked through the glass double doors, and a scary-looking gentleman greeted them with a smile. He almost looked dead himself, and Dillon wondered if this came with the territory. He didn't know very many funeral directors, actually none at all, but the sooner he left this place and the likes of Mr. Lawrence, the happier he would be.

"I'm very sorry for your loss," he said.

"Thank you," they each responded.

"If you'll follow me to my office, we can get started with the arrangements."

They strolled down a long carpeted corridor, and

Dillon scanned his surroundings. He knew it was silly, but it was almost as if he expected one of the closed doors to fly open and he'd have to see dead people. Or worse, he'd be forced to see his aunt when he wasn't ready for that either. The hospital staff had offered to let him see her yesterday, but Dillon had declined. He wanted to remember the beautiful, kind, and very vibrant aunt he'd known since childhood, so seeing her once at the funeral would be enough.

Mr. Lawrence took a seat behind a shiny, huge wooden desk, and the three of them sat in front of him. Tina laid the plastic garment bag that contained his aunt's clothing on her lap.

"You mentioned an insurance policy?" Mr. Lawrence asked her.

"Yes," she said, pulling it out and passing it to him.

The funeral director looked it over and though Dillon wasn't sure, Mr. Lawrence seemed to sort of smile.

"Everything looks to be in very good order here, and I'll contact the insurance company first thing Monday. What I'd like to do now, then," he said, standing up and giving each of them a colorful brochure, "is go over the various options and prices we have. You can choose just about anything you want for your loved one, and since Miss Whitfield has such great coverage, your choices are infinite."

Dillon frowned, and if his father and Tina hadn't been sitting there, he would tell this man something. Mr. Lawrence was consumed with greed and glad to be working with a chunk of money worth fifty thousand dollars. But Dillon was going to set him straight before he drooled any further.

"My aunt was a very frugal woman who didn't like a lot of flashiness or expensive worldly possessions, so we're going to keep the cost of the funeral at a minimum. We're going to put her away nicely, but we won't be buying anything over-the-top or unnecessary."

Curtis and Tina passed on commenting, but Dillon could tell they agreed with him.

Mr. Lawrence grinned a nervous grin, trying to figure out what to say. "Of course, son. We offer all levels of price ranges, so please choose only what you're comfortable with."

Dillon and Tina answered all of Mr. Lawrence's questions regarding next of kin, where Aunt Susan had gone to school, where she worked, what organizations she was a member of, etc., etc., etc. Sadly, her obituary would be short and to the point because once she'd graduated high school, she'd immediately gone to work for a company that she'd remained with until her passing, and with the exception of Dillon she had no close relatives. Dillon had considered including the names of her two cousins, but they'd never really come around much, anyway, so he decided against it. They did list his grandparents and his mom in the predeceased section, and they also included the name of her church, along with the church auxiliaries she was a member of, but that was it.

Mr. Lawrence printed out the information he'd typed in, read it out loud for accuracy, and then set it to the side of his desk. "We have an array of casket colors and styles, so if you'll come with me, I'll show them to you."

They all strolled back down the hallway and went into an oversized room. There must have been twenty caskets displayed. Black, white, bronze, dark blue, silver blue, brown, off-white, tan, and multiple shades of wood. Dillon had no preferences at all and hoped Tina and his dad would choose something fast and in a hurry, so they could get out of there.

"If you'd like, I can explain some of the features and tell you which of these are top sellers."

Dillon held his tongue, but what he wanted to ask Mr. Lawrence was whether he thought this was some sort of furniture store.

"Dillon?" Tina asked. "Do you wanna choose?"

"Not really. You go ahead."

"Well, if it's okay, I like the shiny wooden one over there. I know it's a little pricey, but..."

"This one?" Mr. Lawrence asked, pointing to the shiny, medium-stained oak and already walking toward it. Dillon could only imagine what the funeral home's markup was on something like this. Dillon wouldn't make a fuss, though, only because he wanted this to be over, but if he had time he would search online and purchase the casket wholesale. He'd be willing to bet the same brand and quality would be much lower than forty-five hundred dollars.

"Yes, that's the one," Tina answered.

Curtis nodded. "I like that one, too."

Dillon didn't know how anyone could *like* a casket, but whatever.

"We'll go with that one then," Tina said.

Mr. Lawrence smiled, of course. "Great choice. Now, all we have to do is select a vault."

Dillon had no idea what a vault was until Mr. Lawrence explained that the cemetery required it and that it would be placed in the ground. That way the casket could be lowered inside of it. This would protect the casket, and there were various price points for those, too. Dillon didn't have an opinion on this subject either, so Tina chose one mid-range.

When they went back to the funeral director's office, they went over a few more items, and Tina pulled out the crimson red suit she'd brought for Aunt Susan.

"This is what she said she wanted to wear."

Mr. Lawrence took it from her. "Wonderful. She'll look very nice in this."

"I think we'll choose red roses for the flowers as well," Tina added. "But only if you're okay with that Dillon."

"That'll be fine. My aunt loved roses. It's the one thing I hope you don't cut any corners on."

"You can go with me if you want."

"No, I'll just let you handle that," he said.

When they walked outside, Tina hugged Dillon and his dad and left. Curtis sat inside the SUV, but then realized he'd left his sunglasses on the edge of Mr. Lawrence's desk.

"I'll be right back."

Dillon watched as his dad strolled back inside and couldn't help smiling. This had been a tough day, but having his father there had made all the difference. His father's love had never been more evident, and this gave Dillon peace. As a matter of fact, he felt so good right now, he opened the armrest console and pulled out the envelope Tina had given him yesterday. He'd been hesitant about reading it, but now he felt like he could handle it because no matter what his aunt had written, his father was going to be there with him until the end.

Dillon carefully tore the letter open.

To my dear nephew, Dillon:

If you're reading this, it can only mean two things. I am gone, and I never got a chance to tell you that I was dying. I debated writing you this letter, but when you finally called me, it was then that I realized you were never coming back to see me before I passed on. I'd wanted to tell you, and then again, I hadn't wanted to burden you with my illness. But when I called you several times and you never called back, I decided that maybe it really wasn't meant for you to know. I was even a little sad about it because what I couldn't understand was how a young man I'd raised up from the time he was a newborn could forget about me. It has been more than a year since you moved to Illinois, and although I know how happy you are to be with your father, I never imagined that you would go months without calling me or that I would never lay eyes on you again. I spent many nights wondering what I'd done wrong, but I never came up with anything. Then I wondered if maybe being only an aunt to you hadn't been enough. I loved you like I was your mother, I made sacrifices for you, and I would have given my life for you if I'd had to. But in the end, what I finally had to accept was that, regardless of all of that... I still wasn't really your mother. Then I thought about the fact that maybe it was me who expected way too much. I'd never considered that one day you would grow up, desperately wanting to know your father and that having a father would trump having been raised by some needy old auntie. The reason I say "needy" is because what I never told you was that just before your mom died, I was six months' pregnant and had gone into early labor, and I lost my baby. I'd only been married to my husband for one year and was devastated. But then when your mom died and I took you in, I was finally able to go on. I was happy. I even saw you as God's way of giving me a child again. There was one problem with that, though. My husband never sat well with the idea of bringing you to live with us. He complained a lot and said we couldn't afford more than one child, because he still wanted to have a child of his own. He even demanded that I give you over to a foster care agency, but I told him I couldn't. I refused, and the very next day he walked out and I never saw him again. Then I never saw you again, Dillon, either. I do hope, though, that you and your dad eventually become closer and that his love grows stronger for you every day because I realize now that it is your father's love and acceptance that means more than anything to you. I also want you to know, Dillon, that I have always loved you the same as if you were my biological son, and that I pray only the best for you. More than anything, though, I want you to know that I forgive you.

Aunt Susan

Dillon read the last line again, and his heart crumbled. What had he done, and how could he have been so selfish? He'd been so caught up with trying to bond with his dad that he'd ignored his beloved Aunt Susan. But he hadn't meant to hurt her. He would never purposely do that, and he truly did love her like she was his mother. But now he could never tell her that or make things right with her. Dillon folded the letter and saw his dad coming back outside. He fought back tears as best as he could.

Curtis hurried to the SUV and opened the door. "Dillon, Matt has been rushed to the hospital, so we've gotta get back to the hotel as soon as possible. I have to get back home."

"What? Why?"

"He was stabbed, and I need to take the next flight out of here. Charlotte already has Lana working on my reservation."

"But what about the funeral?"

"I'm sorry, son, but I can't stay here knowing Matt's life is in danger. I hope you can understand that."

Dillon glared at his dad and then turned away from him. His father was never going to change. His other children were always going to be his priority no matter what. Dillon hadn't wanted to believe his aunt when she'd told him his father would never love him the way he loved the others, but now he knew she was right—he knew his father had only pretended to love him and be there for him. He didn't care about all the pain Dillon was feeling or that Dillon had no other family to lean on. But starting this very second, things were going to change. Dillon was done playing nice. He was finished being made a fool of. He would make every one of them sorry.

Chapter 26

Matthew took a couple of deep breaths and tried forcing his eyes open, but then gave up. Beeping monitors and several different voices surrounded him, and it took him a while to realize where he was. He was at the hospital, and soon he remembered why: Racquel had stabbed him multiple times.

He coughed a couple of times and frowned. He wasn't sure what they'd had to do to him, but he was groggy, and he felt a little pain in both his abdomen and his right arm.

"Matthew?" a female voice called out. "I'm Mary, and I'll be taking care of you while you're in recovery. How are you feeling? Can you open your eyes for me?"

He coughed again and then squinted at the woman.

"Do you know where you are?" she said. "You just had surgery, and you're in the recovery room. Are you having any pain?"

Matthew nodded yes.

"We'll see what we can do about that, okay?" she said.

Matthew opened his eyes a bit further, focused them, and he saw her squirting something from a needle. He guessed maybe she was adding something to his IV. He'd seen a nurse give his dad medication that way when he'd been in a car accident a couple of years or so ago.

"That should kick in pretty quickly," she said. "We're going to keep you here for a little while longer, and then we'll send you to a room. Oh, and your sister has been here the whole time."

Now, as he thought back, he remembered the paramedics bringing him into the emergency room, and how he'd given one of the hospital staff members Alicia's number. He'd been in so much pain, though, he hadn't been sure they'd understood him. He was glad Alicia was there because he needed her. Sadly, he also needed his parents and wished they were there, too. He knew he was a grown man, but he was afraid and he couldn't help the way he was feeling.

He lay there thinking until...

"Oh no!" he yelled, struggling to raise his body from the gurney.

"Honey, what's wrong?" the nurse hurried to say.

"My son! I have to go check on him."

"I'm sure he's fine, so please try to settle yourself down."

"No, I have to make sure he's okay. I have to make sure my wife hasn't tried to take him. I need to call my aunt Emma."

"Why don't we ask your sister to check on him for you?"

"No," he said, raising his body and flinching in pain.

The nurse grabbed his shoulders and forced him back down. "Honey, you've got to calm down. You just had surgery and you can't move around like this. You have to take it easy."

"Somebody, please give me a phone," he said, raising his body again.

"Please get his sister," the nurse said to another.

"I need to get out of here. I need to check on MJ."

Matthew rustled back and forth, steadily trying to get up until Alicia walked in.

"Matt, I'm right here," she said. "MJ is fine. He's still with Aunt Emma, so there's nothing to worry about."

"So you talked to her?" he asked, out of breath.

"Yes, she called to check on you."

"And you're sure he's okay?"

"I promise."

Matthew relaxed a little more, but he wouldn't be content until he saw MJ. He wouldn't be at peace until he knew Racquel was nowhere near him.

Matthew closed his eyes and replayed what she'd done. He'd been sure she'd left the living room for a while, and that's when he'd decided he was moving out right away. But then, when he'd looked up, he'd seen her storming out of the kitchen with a huge butcher knife. He hadn't even heard her come out of the bathroom, so by the time he'd seen her, it had been too late for him to jump up, but he'd rolled away from her.

She'd rushed toward him again, though, and drew the knife back, and when he'd thrown his hand up to block it, she'd slit his fingers. Blood had spewed everywhere, but when he'd tried taking the knife from her, she'd slashed his arm and then his abdomen and he'd fallen to his knees. It had all happened so fast, but what he couldn't believe was how he'd allowed her to cut him three separate times. Had he been that caught off guard and unable to stop her, or had he been naïve enough to think he could actually block a sharp butcher knife with no problem? Had he maybe not wanted to fight back because deep down, he'd worried that if he got control of the knife he would hurt Racquel even worse? He didn't know what to think but this whole thing was sick and crazy, and he was ashamed. It was bad enough that Racquel had slapped him and kicked him in the head, but now she'd stabbed him?

Matthew closed his eyes again, hating that his big sister had to see him like this. He was so embarrassed.

"Are you okay?" she asked.

Matthew didn't say anything.

"Matt?"

"I'm fine," he said, opening his eyes and lying to her.

"I'm so sorry this happened," she said with tears streaming down her face and holding his hand. "I'm so, so sorry."

Matthew tried to smile but felt groggy again.

"Matt, I'm gonna let you rest, but I'll be right outside. I'll come back when they get you a room."

"Okay, sis."

"I love you so much," she said, leaning down, kissing him on the forehead.

"I love . . ." he said, but drifted off before he could finish his sentence.

When Matt woke up, he scanned the room and saw a different nurse than before standing at the side of his bed.

"How are you?"

"Okay, I guess."

"I'm Janet, and I'll be your nurse for the next few hours."

"What time is it?"

She looked at the wall in front of him. "A quarter to eleven. I'll be here until seven a.m., though."

"Is my sister still here?"

"Yes, I was just about to go get her. But how's your pain? Do you have any?"

"Not really."

"Well, just let me know if you do, and here's your call button," she said, passing the large handheld pad to him, which also housed buttons that controlled his television.

"Thanks."

"I'll get your sister," she said.

Matthew turned on the TV and searched for ESPN until he found it. They were showing highlights from tonight's playoff games. Normally, watching anything sports related would excite him, but the more he watched and listened now, the more depressed he became. His life was in total shambles, and he was a disappointment to so many people.

He lay there, thinking, until Alicia walked in.

She smiled. "Hey Matt."

"Hey."

"How are you?"

"About the same. Have you checked on MJ again?"

"I just spoke to Aunt Emma a few minutes ago. Everything's fine."

"I don't trust Racquel at all, and I can't wait to get outta here."

"Matt, what happened? Why did she do this? She could've killed you."

"Why did they have to do surgery?" he asked trying not to talk about his wife.

"To stop the bleeding in your abdomen. Thank God she didn't damage any of your organs, but she certainly could have."

"I just wanna put this whole thing behind me."

"I don't know how you can do that. Not without getting full custody of MJ and divorcing her."

"Whatever I have to do. But hey, did you call Jonathan and Elijah?"

"I did. They're out in the waiting area and so are your grandparents," she said. Still, she seemed nervous and had a strange look on her face, and Matthew wondered why.

"What's wrong?" he asked.

"I have something to tell you. And I hope you don't get mad at me."

"What?"

"I was really scared, Matt...so I called Daddy and Charlotte. I couldn't help it."

Matthew stared at her but didn't comment.

"They're worried sick, Matt, and they wanna see you."

Matthew still didn't say anything. He wanted to see them, too, but now that the opportunity had come, he wasn't sure he could face them.

"Matt, please," she said. "You know you need them, and so does MJ. They're outside waiting."

Matthew's stomach churned, and he swallowed hard. Finally, he said, "Will you stay in here with me?"

"Of course," she said, pulling out her phone. "I'll text Daddy now."

Matthew debated stopping her, but when he saw the door ease open he knew it was too late. He also realized they must have been waiting right outside his door.

His heart palpitated, but he kept a straight face. As they walked closer, he looked from his father to his mother and then at his father again.

"Hi, son," Curtis said.

"Hi, Dad."

"Hi, sweetheart," Charlotte said, already crying.

"Hey Mom."

Now a flood of tears fell from Curtis's eyes. "Thank you for letting us see you."

"We're so sorry this happened," Charlotte said. "We're sorry for everything."

Matthew stared at his mom and dad, replaying the

many awful things they'd done to him. Mostly, though, he thought about how much he loved his parents and how he would never let anything or anyone come between them again. Never. Not under any circumstances.

Chapter 27

"Twenty-year-old Matthew Black, son of world-renowned Pastor Curtis Black, was stabbed earlier today in Mitchell, Illinois," the short-haired TV news anchor said. "One of the neighbors in the apartment complex where Black lives has stated that after hearing loud arguing and scuffling late this morning, she decided to call the police. We have also learned that Black's wife, Racquel Black, was arrested on the scene."

Dillon paced back and forth across his hotel room, watching the news broadcast and getting angrier by the second. Even the Atlanta affiliates were already airing the story, and he'd heard it on CNN also. Too many people were trying to ruin Dillon's life, and it was time he got even—specifically with Matthew for being such a selfish idiot and cutting off their dad in the first place and Charlotte for insisting that his dad fly home immediately. Had Matthew not ended his relationship with his parents, his dad wouldn't have felt as obligated to rush back home to see about him. And had Charlotte not wanted to spoil Dillon's trip, she never would have blown this whole stabbing thing out of proportion. Dillon didn't doubt that Matthew had been assaulted, but he was also sure Charlotte had been hysterical and had thrown in extra theatrics, just so she could make something minor seem more like a life-threatening catastrophe. She'd been looking for a reason—any reason at all—to spoil Dillon's time with his father, and she'd succeeded. He wouldn't let her get away with it, though.

It was true that, at first, he'd blamed his dad, but over the last few hours, he'd done a lot of thinking, and now he realized this wasn't his dad's fault at all. His dad couldn't help that he'd raised a couple of ungrateful brats—three if you counted his baby sister, Curtina—so Dillon knew that the only way to fix this was to turn his dad against them. He would start primarily with Matthew because it was pretty evident that no father could be close with two sons, and he would continue with his plan to eliminate Charlotte, too.

Actually, this made Dillon wonder how far along Melissa had come with her research. During his time in Atlanta, he'd expected her to call harassing him every hour on the hour, but so far, she hadn't contacted him once. Not Friday, Saturday, or today, so maybe she was finally planning to move out, and he wouldn't have to deal with her silly behind any longer. He wouldn't *let* her move out until she'd helped him destroy Charlotte, though, so he hoped she knew that.

Just to be sure, he called her to confirm things. Her phone rang until it went to voice mail, though, and Dillon frowned. It was almost midnight, so there was a chance she was asleep, but she knew better than to ignore his calls. So he tried her again, and this time she answered.

"Hello?" she said, sounding wide awake.

"Why didn't you answer the first time?"

"I was in the bathroom."

Dillon wasn't sure he believed her, but he didn't dwell on it, because no one lived a more boring life than Melissa. So whatever she'd been doing didn't matter.

"Did you find a good investigator?"

"I found three."

"And?"

"They all have a lot of experience with this kind of thing, so I'm sure any of them will work."

Dillon frowned. "Then what are you waiting on? Why haven't you hired one of them?"

"I wanted you to decide on which to go with."

"And how am I supposed to do that, Melissa? I'm all the way here in Atlanta, remember?"

"I just thought— "

Dillon cut her off. "You just thought nothing. I told you to hire someone as soon as possible. So why would I need to authorize anything?"

"I'm sorry. I'll get it taken care of."

"Can't you do anything right?"

"I said I was sorry, Dillon."

"I'm hanging up now," he said.

"Baby, wait. How are you doing? I've been praying for you because I know this is a tough time."

"How do you think I'm doing, Melissa? I mean, honestly? How would you feel if the only person to ever really love you passed away and you didn't get to say good-bye? Huh?"

"I'm sure she understood why you never called her."

"Yeah, well, I guess we'll never know, will we? And anyway, what did you mean before I left?"

"What?"

"When you said you were the one who called to check on her, what did you talk about?"

"Not much. I would just ask her how she was doing, she would ask how we were doing, and that was it."

"And she never told you she was sick? She never said she was dying?"

"No."

"You'd better not be lying to me, because if I find out you knew something..."

"I didn't, baby. I wouldn't keep something like that from you."

"Like I said, you'd better not be lying to me."

"I didn't know."

"Whatever. I'll talk to you later."

"Okay, but how are things going with your dad?"

Every muscle in Dillon's body tensed up. Her question made him just that angry. "He's gone."

"What do you mean?"

"Supposedly that stupid brother of mine got stabbed. Haven't you seen the news?"

"No. Oh my God, when?"

"Sometime today."

"Have you spoken to your dad since he left?"

"No."

"Maybe you should call him, baby."

"For what? So I can hear how happy he is to see his bratty little golden boy?"

"No, so you can let him know you're worried about him."

"But that's just it, I'm not. He could die for all I care."

"I'm talking about your dad. Maybe you should call to see how he's doing."

Dillon was done with this tired conversation. "I have to go. Good-bye, Melissa."

He pressed the End button on his phone and tossed it onto the bed. She must have been out of her mind if she thought he was going to waste his time calling his father while he was probably still sitting at the hospital. He did want to hear his dad's voice, but the last thing he wanted was for his dad to think he was calling to get an update on his brother. Because it was like he'd just told Melissa, he didn't care about Matthew. He never had, he never would, and there was no changing that. He hated him. With the exception of seeing him in a few photos and then last week when he'd passed him on the street, Dillon had never laid eyes on Matthew. But just the idea that he existed was enough. Just knowing that Matthew held a solid, loving place in their father's heart unnerved Dillon. It was the reason Dillon had to put an end to this sham of a relationship that his father and brother thought they had. Although what if Matthew still wanted nothing to do with his parents? Maybe it hadn't mattered that he'd been stabbed and had been rushed to the hospital. Maybe his father had tried to see him, and Matthew had thrown him out of his room. Dillon smiled at his thoughts and wondered if he could be so lucky. It was hard to say what was going on, so maybe Melissa was right. Maybe calling his dad was a good idea.

He picked up his phone and dialed his dad's cell. It rang three times, but just as Dillon prepared to leave a message, Curtis answered.

"Hey son, how are you?" he said, and Dillon heard the excitement in his voice. "I'm so glad you called. We're in with your brother now, and he's gonna be fine. They had to do surgery, but they're releasing him tomorrow. We're taking him home."

Dillon stared into space, not knowing how to respond.

"Son, are you there?"

"Yeah," he finally said. "I saw on TV that his wife was arrested. Is that true?"

"It is, and that's why Matt and MJ are coming to stay with us. We don't want him going back to that apartment."

Dillon wanted to curse the way he used to before he'd met his father. He'd been very good at it, but he'd also known that using four-letter words wasn't what folks expected to hear from a minister's son. He hadn't wanted his father to think lowly of him either, so he'd given up cursing. He'd done it cold turkey, but right now he wanted to relapse.

"Well, I guess I'll let you go," Dillon said.

"Thanks again for calling, son. Oh and I'm really sorry I had to leave so quickly. I really wanted to be there for you."

"I'll talk to you later," Dillon said.

"I'll check on you in the morning, and I'm praying for your strength," Curtis said.

Dillon ended the call but didn't say good-bye. What good was prayer going to do? If it wouldn't bring his dad back to Atlanta or stop Matthew from moving back into his dad's home, what difference would it make? Dillon didn't want prayer, and he wished his father would stop praying about anything that had to do with him. Although this whole prayer thing did make him think about his dad's church and how he'd been practically begging Dillon to come work for him. Dillon had always shied away from it, but now that Matthew was moving back home, Dillon didn't see where he had any other options—that is, if he wanted to be near his father and see him every day the same as Matthew would be. This was also the only way he'd be able to see Charlotte on a regular basis, something that was about to become more and more necessary. And it wouldn't hurt to learn the inner workings of the ministry, either, because there was no telling how Dillon might benefit from that in the future. So, yes, that's what he would do. He'd bury his aunt on Monday, do a final review of her will with her attorney on Tuesday, and then he'd fly back to Illinois the day after. He almost couldn't wait to get there.

Chapter 28

A whole twenty-four hours had passed since Racquel had slashed him with a knife, yet he still couldn't believe it. His own wife, the woman he'd loved and given up everything for, had nearly killed him. It just didn't make sense, and though Matthew did believe she was ill and that maybe she couldn't help herself, it was hard for him to find sympathy for someone who was so violent. As it was, she'd slapped him and kicked him, but this butcher knife drama had beat it all. For her parents' sake and hers, too, he was sorry she'd been arrested, but maybe being locked up would make her think. Maybe being handcuffed and driven off to the county jail would snap her back to a normal mental state.

He lay there watching one of the local ministers on television, wondering why this had happened. Was it because he'd sort of broken his vows? All he'd done was talk to Stacey, but he couldn't deny the lustful thoughts he'd had about her. So maybe this disaster with Racquel was God's way of punishing him. He at least wanted Stacey to know he was all right, though, and he would call her just as soon as he could. After being rushed to the hospital by ambulance, he hadn't had a chance to get his phone, and he hadn't as much as thought about it until now.

Matthew thought about calling Alicia, but someone knocked at his door.

"Come in," he said.

His in-laws pushed open the door and walked in, and Matthew smiled at them.

"Oh Matt," Vanessa said. "I'm so glad to see you smiling. I was so afraid you were going to be upset with us."

"Why?"

"Because of Racquel. We're so very sorry, Matt."

"It's not your fault."

"We know, son," Neil said, "but she's our daughter and we can't help but feel responsible for her. We're just sick over what she did, and now we wish we'd done something."

Matthew raised himself higher in the bed and frowned. He didn't have a lot of throbbing pain like he'd experienced in the middle of the night, but the soreness had definitely started to set in, both in his abdomen and his arm. His hand was bandaged up, too, but it didn't hurt as much as the other two areas.

"How are you feeling?" Vanessa said, resting her leather tote down onto the chair.

"Okay. I'm a little sore, but the doctor said I'll be fine."

"That's good to hear," Neil said. "Thank God for that."

"Also," Vanessa said, "I hope you don't think we forgot about you yesterday, because after we came from checking on Racquel, we came straight to the hospital. But when we saw your mom and dad walking inside, we decided to wait."

"I understand," Matthew said. "My sister called and told them what happened. They would have seen it on the news, anyway, though."

"Did you see them?" Vanessa asked, and Matthew could tell she half expected him to say no.

"I did."

"Good," she said, but Matthew knew she didn't mean it, at least not when it came to his mother because she still couldn't stand her. "Oh and we went by your aunt's and saw MJ. We thought about taking him home with us, but we wanted to go see Racquel again today and also come see you."

"How was he?"

"Fine. He really does love his aunt Emma, and we're very glad about that."

"So is the doctor releasing you today?" Neil asked.

"Yes."

"Maybe you should come home with us, so we can help you with MJ. At least until you're feeling better."

Matthew hated having to break the news to them, but he didn't have a choice. "MJ and I are moving out of the apartment for good."

Vanessa sighed. "Well, we figured you might, and no one can blame you. So will you be staying with your aunt Emma?"

"No, I'm moving back with my parents."

Matthew watched his mother-in-law cringe. He wasn't surprised about her reaction at all.

"I know you still love them, Matt, but I really don't want MJ living with your mother. Not after that stunt she pulled."

"I know my mom was wrong, but she would never hurt MJ."

"I'm not sure about that. Your mom is an awful woman, and if you want, you and MJ can come live with us."

Neil didn't say anything and barely moved.

"I really appreciate the offer, but it's time I work things out with my parents. I'm actually relieved to be going home."

"But you know how controlling your mother is," Vanessa reminded him. "She only cares about herself, and she'll make life miserable for you. Not to mention, she's a terrible example for MJ."

Matthew looked at her, and it was funny how even though he knew his mother-in-law was telling the truth about his mom, he didn't want to hear any more of her comments. They were making him uncomfortable.

"And what about Racquel?" Vanessa said. "Are you going to be there for her? I know it's a lot to ask, but she needs you, Matt."

"I'm sorry, but I can't. Not after what she did."

Vanessa's face fell somber. "I'm not trying to excuse her actions, but she needs help. She'll be arraigned tomorrow, and we're going to ask the judge to send her to a psychiatric facility. We want her to be evaluated."

"I'm glad she's gonna get some help, but I can't be with someone so abusive. I can't subject MJ to that kind of thing either."

"But she wasn't herself," Neil finally added. "She's been very depressed, but I believe she'll be so much better once she gets treatment."

Matthew felt bad for Racquel, but he wasn't sure what else to say. Then, if things weren't awkward enough, his parents walked in. Tension flooded the room like a tidal wave, and Matthew wished he could crawl under his bed. He prayed there wouldn't be any drama.

"Good morning," Curtis said, shaking Neil's hand.

"Good morning. Good to see you."

"How are you, Curtis?" Vanessa asked, hugging him.

"I'm good."

Matthew waited for his mother and Vanessa to speak, but they ignored each other. Actually, this was probably a good thing because no words meant no arguing.

"Hey Curtis," Neil said, "we've already apologized to Matt, but we're really sorry about Racquel."

Curtis nodded. "Thanks."

The room fell silent, and everyone pretended to watch television. Matthew loved his in-laws, but he hoped they would leave soon. If they stayed, there was no telling what might happen.

"Well, I guess we should get going," Neil said, and Matthew was grateful.

Vanessa walked over and picked up her handbag. "Are you sure you won't reconsider, Matt?"

"No, I don't think so."

Vanessa looked sad again, and though Matthew felt bad, his decision was final. There was just no other way.

"We'll be checking on you, son," Neil said, smiling.

"You take care of yourself," Vanessa said. "You, too, Curtis."

"Take care, both of you, and we'll be praying for Racquel."

When they left the room, Matthew exhaled. He was surprised his mom hadn't already started asking questions, wanting to know what his mother-in-law had wanted him to reconsider, but she didn't. Matthew knew, though, that she didn't want to anger him, so this was likely the only reason she kept quiet.

"How are you feeling, son?" Curtis asked.

"Okay. Ready to get out of here."

"Now you know how I felt the last two times I was in the hospital."

Charlotte laughed. "But that's only because you're such a bad patient. Such a busybody."

Matthew couldn't help smiling because his mom was right. His dad hated being confined or told he couldn't do certain things because of an illness.

"When we dropped Curtina off at Aunt Emma's, we saw that beautiful grandson of ours," Charlotte said.

Curtis folded his arms. "He's definitely a handsome little thing. Looks just like his grandfather."

"You're a trip, Dad."

They all laughed.

"Well, he does. He looks like you, and you look like me, so what do you expect?"

Matthew smiled, and though he never imagined he would be this happy to be with his parents, he was thrilled. He was plowing his way through a major life storm, but his mom and dad made him feel better about things. Their love and support gave him hope, and he felt a strong sense of peace. There was nothing like family, and from now on, Matthew would never forget that.

Chapter 29

Baby, I am so, so sorry," Racquel said. "I don't know what came over me. It was almost like I was having an out-of-body experience. But you know I didn't mean it."

Matthew listened as his wife apologized and pleaded, but he regretted answering her call. Actually, the only reason he'd taken it was because she'd caught him off guard, and he'd hit the Send button by accident. It was only one in the afternoon, so he certainly hadn't expected to hear from her anytime soon. He'd known she was being arraigned this morning, but he'd assumed the judge would honor her parents' request and would transfer her to a treatment center. He could tell from her conversation, though, that she was nowhere near any mental facility.

"Matt, I really need to see you. I need to talk to you."

He walked into MJ's nursery and picked him up. MJ smiled happily, the same as always. "Racquel, I really don't want to do this right now."

"Why?"

"Because there's nothing to say."

"I know you're upset, but if you'll just let me explain things to you. Baby, I really am sorry. Ever since MJ was born, I've been under a lot of pressure, and I wasn't myself. For months now, I've felt like I was having a nervous breakdown, but I didn't know what to do about it."

"Really?" he said. "Well, what finally made you realize that today?"

"Matt, I spent two nights in jail, and then I had to go before a judge this morning. I had two full days to think about everything."

"And he let you out? Just like that?"

"No, my parents had to pay five thousand dollars."

"That's all?"

"My bond was fifty thousand, but the judge allowed them to post ten percent of it. You sound like you're disappointed. Like you wanted me stay locked up."

"Racquel, how would you feel if I'd treated you like a dog for more than a year and then physically abused you? What if I'd stabbed you with a knife? Would you be happy I was out of jail?"

She didn't say anything.

"That's what I thought. You'd be doing everything you could trying to make sure I was sent to prison."

"I would never want that for you."

"Yeah, right."

"Matt, I'm really gonna get help. I wanna be a better

wife and good mother to MJ. There's something wrong with me, and I can't help what I did. I'm really, really sorry."

"I'm sorry, too, but I'm done, Racquel."

"What do you mean?"

"Our marriage is over."

"What?"

"I hope things work out for you in court, but I'm getting a divorce."

"Baby, you're just upset, and I don't blame you. But things won't always be like this."

"You're right. Eventually, you'll move on and so will I, and that'll be that. We never should have gotten married in the first place. We were way too young last year, and we're still too young now."

"I can't believe you're doing this."

"I don't know why. Just last week you were hanging out at bars, drinking, and offering me a divorce. And you were planning to leave this fall for school."

"I told you I wasn't myself. I wasn't thinking straight, and I'm finished with all that."

"Good for you, Racquel. But hey, I have to go. MJ's hungry."

"I can't believe you moved back with your parents. After all the trouble your mother caused us. After all the horrible things she did to me."

"She's still my mother, though."

"Well, I don't want my son around her. I don't want her poisoning his mind the way she's already doing with you."

"Excuse me?"

"Matt, please. The only reason you're talking about all this divorce stuff is because of her. I know she's the one who's pushing you to do this. She couldn't wait to turn you against me. She tried and tried before, but this time she's going to do everything she can to make sure it happens."

Matthew walked down the stairs and into the kitchen. His mom looked at him strangely, and he could tell she knew who he was talking to. "I'll talk to you later, Racquel."

"Whatever," she said and hung up.

"You wanna hold him while I pull out some baby food?" he asked.

"Of course," Charlotte said, reaching for him. "Hi, sweetie. So did Nana's baby have a good nap? Huh?"

MJ smiled at her and pulled at her necklace.

"Where's Dad?" Matthew asked.

"In his study. You need something?"

"No, I'm fine."

"You don't seem to be as sore as you were yesterday."

"I'm not."

"I'm glad. This could have turned out so much worse, Matt."

"I know, but let's not talk about that, Mom, okay?"

"I'm not trying to upset you. I'm just grateful is all."

Matthew knew she meant well, but he was so used to her controlling attitude and negative comments that he couldn't help analyzing everything she said. He guessed he was afraid she would return to her old ways, and he didn't want that.

"I can feed him if you want," she said.

Matthew passed her the jar of green peas and a bottle filled with apple juice, but then his phone rang. It was his mother-in-law, and he debated answering it. If he didn't, though, she would leave a message, expecting him to call her back, so it was better to talk to her now and get it over with.

"Hello?"

"Hey Matt, how are you?"

"Good, and you?"

"Well, I was doing fine until Racquel came into my office crying her eyes out."

Matthew wasn't sure what she wanted him to say.

"I know you're upset," she said, "and you have every right to be, but Racquel really is very sorry. We've known for a while that she was depressed, but I believe her when she says she never meant to hurt you. She just needed help."

"Well, why didn't the judge send her to a facility then?"

Vanessa paused but finally said, "She called us last night from jail and begged us not to do it. Being arrested really traumatized her, so she just wanted to come stay with us for a couple of days. Then, she'll go wherever we want her to."

"So the judge doesn't know about her being depressed and how she hasn't had anything to do with her own son for over a week?"

"Our attorney didn't mention any of that to him. We decided it was best to get treatment for her on our own, and then when it's time to go back to court we'll be able to document her progress."

Matthew didn't respond.

"The reason I'm calling you, though, Matt, is because Racquel really needs to see you. She wants to talk things over."

Matthew looked at his mom, who was staring straight at him, so he left the room.

"It's like I told Racquel when she called," he said. "Our marriage is over. We tried to make it work, but we couldn't."

"But you can. All marriages have problems, and you know yourself that your mom didn't help things. She made life very hard for you and Racquel before you were even married."

"Yeah, but that's all in the past, and my mother didn't make Racquel stab me with a knife."

"Maybe you just need some time."

"I don't think so."

"Well, can you at least think about not pressing charges?"

Matthew raised his eyebrows. It wasn't as though he was dying to see the mother of his son go to prison, no matter what she'd done to him, but he was shocked to hear his mother-in-law's request.

"I know it's a lot to ask," she continued. "But Racquel is practically a baby, Matt. I know she's an adult, but she's way too young to be locked up."

"I'll have to think about it," was all he said, hoping this would get her to hang up.

"Even if you do drop the charges, the prosecutor can still charge her and try her in court, but it won't look as bad. Our attorney has also advised us that, as the victim, you can sign an affidavit of nonprosecution. This can make a huge difference, and there's a chance that Racquel won't have to serve any time. She could get probation."

Matthew didn't know much about the law, and he certainly had never heard about any nonprosecution affidavit, but he could tell Vanessa knew was she was talking about. Racquel had only been out of jail for a couple of hours at most, but it sounded like they'd come up with a well-thought-out plan.

"I'll have to talk to my parents."

"We really need you to work with us, Matt. We'll do anything you ask. Just please don't send our daughter to prison," she pleaded.

"I have another call," he lied.

"Please think about everything I said, okay, Matt?"

"I will."

"You take care."

Matthew walked back into the kitchen and looked at his mother, but he didn't say anything. She would go ballistic if she knew what Vanessa was asking him to do, and he didn't want to upset her. His dad, of course, would be more understanding because that was just the kind of man he was, but Matthew wasn't even sure how he felt about things himself. On the one hand, he did want Racquel to pay for what she'd done, but on the other, he didn't want her doing time in prison. More than anything, he just wanted this whole mess to go away. What he wanted was to just be a normal young person with normal problems, period.

Chapter 30

Dillon was finally only twenty minutes away from Mitchell. It had been a rough few days, but he had made it through the funeral and was almost home from the airport. He hadn't realized his aunt knew so many people. She didn't attend a large church, but there must have been at least two hundred people who'd come to pay their respects, and it was mostly her church members and coworkers who'd filled the sanctuary to capacity. It was clear that she was loved by many, and Dillon was happy about that. Everyone who'd approached him, both during the visitation period and after the funeral, had spoken very kindly about his aunt, so she had certainly touched a great number of people in a very special way. One woman had told him how Aunt Susan had been her greatest confidante and that she'd come to love her like a second mother. Then there'd been a young single mother who'd told Dillon that the only reason her children had Christmas was because Aunt Susan had bought all three of them clothes and toys for three years straight.

Dillon had listened to one story after another, but after a while, all they'd done was make him feel guiltier. How could he have walked away from such a wonderful woman and acted as though she didn't exist? He'd tried his best to justify his actions, but in the end, he knew he'd been wrong for the way he'd treated her and that it would likely haunt him for the rest of his life. He just wished he could have another chance, a few moments even, just so he could tell her how much he loved and appreciated her. No one had ever loved him as unconditionally as she had, but he'd still packed up his things and moved to Illinois like it was no big deal. He hadn't thought anything about it, because he'd always figured that once he built a great relationship with his dad, he'd be able to spend all the time he wanted with his aunt. Sadly, though, that would never happen.

Dillon gazed out the limo window and was glad he had on sunglasses because his eyes were watering. It was bad enough that Aunt Susan had loved him and done everything she could for him, but even in death, she was still looking out for his best interest. Yesterday, Dillon had gone to meet with her attorney to review her will, and that was when he'd learned that she'd made him the sole beneficiary of two insurance policies that totaled one hundred fifty thousand dollars. Her funeral expenses would be deducted from the fifty-thousand-dollar one, but the rest would be sent to him. She'd also willed him her home, which she owned outright. Dillon would never sell it, though. Her house—his childhood home—was the only real thing he had left of her, so he would keep it and stay there whenever he visited Atlanta.

As the driver continued west on I-90, Dillon leaned his head back and closed his eyes. He so wanted a different kind of life than the one he was living. In a perfect world, his father would love him more than anything, he would have grown up side by side with Alicia and Matthew, and he would have gotten to know Curtina as soon as she'd been born. All three of them would have loved their big brother, and he would have loved them back and protected them from everything. His mother would also be alive, and she would never have stooped low enough to be a stripper. She would have been a woman of integrity and one who'd had a lot more respect for herself. Dillon didn't think on this level often and he'd certainly never shared his true feelings about his mother with another living soul, but this was the real reason he had very little respect for women. To him, they were all tramps who flaunted their bodies and slept around with as many men as possible, and he'd never trusted one woman he could think of—that is with the exception of Aunt Susan. Other than that, he tended to expect the worse of all women, and he wasn't sure any woman could ever make him feel differently.

Dillon's phone rang, and when he saw that it was his father, his spirits lifted. His dad had called to check on him Monday, a couple of hours before the funeral, and then again that night. He hadn't spoken to him yesterday, though, so he was glad to hear from him now.

"Hey Dad."

"Hey. So you landed safely I see."

"I did, and I'm almost home. Maybe another ten minutes or so."

"Good. And how are you doin'?"

"As well as can be expected. What about you?"

"Well, son, I tell you. I haven't felt this good in a long while. Matthew and MJ are home, and I'll finally be able to get all my children together at one time. Since Memorial Day is next Monday, Charlotte and I are thinking about having a cookout. It'll just be for family. You don't have any plans, do you?"

"No," he struggled to say because the last thing Dillon wanted was to spend hours watching his dad having the time of his life with his other children. He'd invited Dillon, but when it was all said and done, Dillon knew he'd be treated like an outsider.

"Great. I'll keep you posted on the time, and I can't wait for you to meet your brother and nephew. I'm sorry it has taken as long as it has, but thank God Matthew is back with us."

Dillon thought about telling his dad that he'd finally decided to come work at the church, but he chose to wait for a better time—such as a few days from now when maybe his dad wouldn't be so ridiculously focused on Matthew's return. Dillon was only taking this job as a way to carry out his plans of destruction, but he still wanted his dad to be happy about his decision, and he wanted him to be proud.

After Dillon and Curtis chatted a few minutes longer

and ended their call, Carlisle pulled the limo into the driveway. Roger, Dillon's lawn-care guy, was working away. Normally, he came on Thursdays, so Dillon wondered why he'd come a day early.

Carlisle got out, opened Dillon's door, and removed his luggage from the trunk.

"Hey, Mr. Whitfield. I'm glad you back, but I'm really sorry 'bout your aunt."

"I appreciate that, Roger. How come you're here today?"

"I need to get some dental work done, and they closed on Wednesdays. So, I figured I would come today instead so I could go to my appointment tomorrow. I cleared it with Miss Melissa, and I hope you don't mind."

"No problem at all." Dillon had always wondered why he wouldn't do something about his mouth, because those missing teeth definitely looked awful. Implants were costly, though, so maybe he wasn't getting those taken care of at all. He was probably getting more teeth pulled or just a filling.

Roger smiled. "A man just can't keep runnin' 'round here like some snaggletoothed first-grader. Not if he wanna catch him a good woman."

Carlisle laughed as he carried the luggage up to the front door and Roger laughed even louder, but Dillon was embarrassed for him. Roger was so country and uncultured, but Dillon could tell he didn't know it.

Dillon pushed the luggage farther into the entryway and closed the door. He walked through to the kitchen, skimmed through a stack of mail, and then went upstairs. Melissa was in the den, sitting at the computer. She looked up when she heard him walk in, and the first thing Dillon noticed was that her eye had already healed. Either that or she'd covered it with makeup.

"Hi," she said.

"Hey."

"So how was your flight?"

"Okay. So did you hire an investigator?"

"Yeah, he started yesterday. So far, he hasn't found anything we don't already know about, though."

"He will, so just tell him to keep searching. I also want him to follow her if he has to."

"I'll call him."

"You can do that later," he said, moving closer to her, but she stared at the monitor.

"It's been almost a whole week."

Melissa didn't move or say anything, but Dillon forced himself to stay calm.

"I'm asking you nicely," he said. "I always try to ask you nicely, but when you don't do what I tell you, Melissa, it makes me angry. Now, take care of me the way I like it. Or else."

Chapter 31

Four. That was the number of days Matthew had been back home, and he couldn't be happier. He hadn't been this content in months. More than anything, though, MJ was safe, and Matthew didn't have to worry about what Racquel might do to either of them. She'd only been out on bail for two days, but she'd called him at least twenty times. Whenever the phone rang, Matthew checked to see who it was and then hit the Ignore button. He hadn't seen where they had anything to talk about, and he certainly didn't want to discuss their getting back together, because he didn't want that. He also didn't want his mother-in-law pressuring him about signing any documents. For whatever reason, his father-in-law hadn't tried to contact him, and Matthew was relieved.

"I'm so glad you're home, Matt," Curtina said, sitting next to him in the family room and leaning her head against his arm. She also played with MJ, who was sitting on Matthew's lap. "Hi, MJ," she said, touching her nose to his, and he giggled.

MJ was only one, but he and his six-year-old auntie had taken a huge liking to each other, and that made Matthew smile. Curtina had always been fond of MJ, ever since he'd been born—she'd sometimes played with him over at Aunt Emma's when she spent the night there—but now that the two of them were able to see each other daily, they'd bonded even more.

Charlotte and Curtis walked into the room and sat down on the loveseat.

"So what's on, son?" Curtis asked.

Matthew picked up the remote control. "Playoffs are starting in a few minutes."

"Sounds good to me."

Charlotte pulled her feet onto the loveseat. "The pizza should be here soon. I ordered enough for Jonathan and Elijah, too. Didn't you say they were coming by?"

"Yep," he said, smiling because it truly did feel like old times. Most of his life, his parents had ordered pizza at least once every week because they knew how much he liked it. They also did it because Curtina loved it as well. He was sure they'd love to have something different, but they never complained. They did what they thought would make their children happy. This was the kind of parent Matthew wanted to be to MJ. His parents had made a lot of mistakes and caused him a lot of pain, but they'd also made Matthew a priority on many occasions. They'd made sacrifices pretty regularly, and he was thankful.

Matthew's phone rang, and although he didn't answer it, he stood up. "Mom, can you take MJ?"

"Of course. You bring my little sweetheart right on over here."

Matthew passed him to her and went upstairs to his bedroom. He dialed Stacey back as fast as he could.

"Hey, I'm sorry I couldn't answer."

"No problem. Whatchu doin'?"

"Watchin' the game with my parents. My boys are comin' by, too."

"Sounds like fun."

"What about you?"

"Just sitting here, doin' nothin'," she said.

"I wish you could come over here, but..."

"I know. So have you heard from Racquel again?"

"Yeah, but I never answer. Hopefully, she'll just give up."

"But what if she doesn't? Because it sounds to me like she really wants to get back together."

"Maybe, but only because she wants me to help make her case go away. Nobody changes overnight the way she has. Last week she hated me, and now this week she loves me and wants us to stay married? I don't think so."

"What are you gonna do?"

"I'm really getting a divorce."

"Are you doing it soon?"

"That's the plan. I have a doctor's appointment early next week to get my stitches out, so once I go back to work, I'll get it taken care of."

"How do your parents feel about it?"

"They support me a hundred percent."

"Well that's good at least."

"My mom never liked Racquel, anyway. She never wanted me to marry her."

"Well, if you and I end up together, I hope she likes me!"

Matthew laughed. "Do you mean that?"

"What?"

"That you wanna be together."

"Is that what *you* want?"

"I do, but it's like I told you before. You're still in college, and I have a son."

"And it's like I told you, I know all that."

"Yeah, but how will your mom and dad feel about it?"

"They'll be fine."

"Somehow I don't think so. Dating someone who's divorced is one thing, but a teenage father?"

"Well it's not like you're a teenager anymore. And anyway, you let me worry about them."

"Whatever you say."

"So when can I see you?" she asked.

"Maybe this weekend."

"Okay."

"Well, hey," he said, "that's the doorbell, so I'd better get going."

"Call me before you go to bed?"

"I will. Later."

Matthew headed back downstairs, but the faster he walked the more nervous he got. Was that Racquel he heard?

When he landed at the bottom of the stairs, he

rushed toward the front door. He saw his dad barricading it with his arms.

Matthew frowned. "Girl, what are you doin' here?"

"I came to get my son, and I'm not leaving here without him," she said, barely able to stand up.

"You're drunk, Racquel," Matthew said.

"Mom, take MJ upstairs."

Racquel pushed against Curtis's chest with both hands, screaming, "Don't you take my son anywhere, you crazy lunatic! Please move, Pastor Black. I'm not leaving here until I get my son."

Matthew dialed his father-in-law, hoping he didn't have a late surgery.

"Hello?" he answered.

"Dr. Anderson, can you please come and get Racquel? She's over here trying to force her way in. And she's drunk."

"What? Oh my God. I'm only a few miles away. I'll be right there."

Matt set his phone on the table.

"I hate you, Matt!" she spat, still trying to push Curtis out of the way. "I hate you, and I should have stabbed you until I got tired."

Curtis grabbed both her arms. "Look, that's enough, Racquel. Either you settle down, or we're calling the police. This is ridiculous."

"No, your wife is the one who's ridiculous. She's the one who messed up everything. She ruined all of us, and now I'm the one who has to stand trial. I'm the one who might go to jail."

Matthew stared at her and shook his head.

"Why are you doing this, Matt?" she said, now crying. "Why won't you let me see my son? Why won't you give me another chance?"

Matthew still didn't say anything. He just stood there trying to figure out what was wrong with her. He was angry with her for drinking the way she was and causing all this trouble, but he also felt sorry for her. She was truly messed up emotionally, and if she didn't get help soon, he wasn't sure what would happen to her. For the life of him, he couldn't understand why his in-laws hadn't told the judge about her history so he could order that she be admitted to a treatment facility. Why wouldn't they want their own daughter to get help? It didn't make any sense, especially since Dr. Anderson was a physician.

Finally, Racquel dropped down on the front step, weeping loudly. But then Matthew's phone rang. It was his mother-in-law.

"Hello?"

"Matt, I am so sorry," Vanessa said. "Neil just called me, and I'm on my way, too. I thought she was still upstairs. I laid down to take a nap, and I guess she snuck out. And Neil said she was drunk?"

"Yep."

"I don't know what to say, but I promise you this won't happen again."

Matthew would believe that when he saw it. Racquel was a loose cannon, and if her parents didn't do something soon, either she or someone else would end up dead. He also had to rethink his decision about waiting to divorce her, because now she was demanding to see MJ—and she was doing it while she was drunk. He didn't want to take MJ away from Racquel, at least not legally, anyway, but he would do it if he had to. If she forced him, he would file for full custody and she would never see MJ again. He would do everything he could to make sure of it.

Chapter 32

It was Memorial Day, and although he and Melissa had just arrived at his dad's, Dillon already dreaded being there. He wasn't sure if it was simply because he didn't care for most of the people he knew he was about to see or if it was because his no-good sister Alicia had been the one to answer the door.

"I'm so glad you guys could make it," she beamed, all while decked out in what looked to be an overly expensive pure white maxi dress. "Everyone's out on the patio, so just follow me."

Alicia acted as though she lived there and as though Dillon and Melissa were nothing more than outside guests. It was true that they were in fact visitors, but Alicia treated them as though they weren't even family. She spoke to them as if they were no different than church members or friends, and this made Dillon want to light into her.

Ever since meeting her, Dillon had tried tolerating Alicia as much as he could, mostly for his father's sake, but he was getting to the point where he couldn't stand the sight of her. He wished he could feel differently, but he couldn't. *He* was the eldest child and not her, and it was time he did whatever he needed to do to make everyone realize it.

Dillon and Melissa followed Alicia down the shiny marble hallway, through the family room, and out to the elegant, spacious patio. Everyone who'd been invited was there: Phillip; Charlotte's parents; Charlotte's aunt Emma; and her daughter, Anise; and, of course, Matthew and his son, little MJ. And who could forget that tiny brat Curtina? Curtis had told Dillon that today's gathering would include only family, but his dad's assistant, Miss Lana, and Elder Dixon were there as well. Dillon liked Miss Lana, though, so he was actually glad to see her, but he could certainly do without Elder Dixon. Dillon didn't care much for the elder, mainly because he was about as country as Roger and he also didn't have any tact. The only reason Dillon pretended to like him was because his father seemed to love and respect him to the utmost. Curtis saw him as the father he didn't have, so Dillon went along with it. Actually, it wasn't much of a problem, anyway, as long as Elder Dixon continued to mind his own business and stay out of his way.

"Hey son," Curtis said, smiling and walking in their direction.

Dillon forced a smile back but didn't say anything. He was also glad he still had on his sunglasses because he didn't want his dad to see his true feelings.

"Glad you both made it," Curtis said, hugging him and Melissa.

"Thank you for inviting us," Melissa said.

"Of course."

Dillon tried to stay focused on his dad and what he was saying, but he couldn't help noticing how all the other adults were outrageously obsessed with little MJ, and Dillon could barely stomach it. Here it was, he'd already had to spend the last few days plotting and trying to figure out exactly how he was going to drive a new wedge between Matthew and Curtis, not to mention how he was going to end his dad's marriage to that trifling Charlotte, yet now he had this awful baby to contend with. Everyone acted as though MJ were the most precious thing in the universe, and needless to say, all this did was provide Curtis with a whole other reason to push Dillon to the side. First it had been his dad's children, but now there was this grandson of his to compete with.

"Are you okay?" Curtis asked him.

"Huh? Oh yeah, I'm fine. Just hungry."

Curtis laughed. "So am I. But before we eat, I want you to meet your brother."

Dillon stared at his dad, trying to mask his rage. Why couldn't his dad do him a favor and leave things as is? Until now, Dillon had never met Matthew, and Dillon was fine with that.

"Hey son," Curtis yelled out to Matthew. "Come here for a minute."

Matthew set his bottle of water down and walked over.

"Son, this is Dillon... Dillon, this is Matthew."

"How's it goin'?" Matthew said, reaching his hand out.

Dillon grabbed it and forced another smile on his face. "Good, and it's nice to finally meet you."

"And you must be Melissa," Matthew said.

"Yes," she answered, cheesing like a Cheshire cat, and Dillon wanted to slap that smile of hers across the patio. "It's a pleasure to meet you."

Curtis sighed loudly with total pride and placed his arms around both his boys. "Now, this is the kind of thing that really makes me happy. Both my sons together for the first time. Talk about a huge blessing this is."

Curtis went on and on about how happy he was, but the atmosphere couldn't have been more awkward. It was clear that neither Dillon nor Matthew had anything to say, and actually, Matthew kept looking over at the rest of the family, where everyone was still making a big deal over MJ. Finally, though, Curtis decided it was time to eat. Before he did, however, everyone else spoke to Melissa and Dillon—that is, all except Charlotte, who graciously spoke to Melissa but pretended she didn't see Dillon. This was just one more reason Dillon couldn't wait to annihilate her.

When Curtis finished saying grace, everyone filed together in a single line, leading toward the food tables, and although Dillon truly didn't want to be there, he couldn't deny how awesome everything looked. He'd heard a lot about Aunt Emma and her cooking, and just based on the way she kept positioning and repositioning all the dishes and making sure nothing was missing, he could tell she'd likely prepared the entire meal, and it smelled heavenly. Barbeque ribs, chicken, bratwurst, macaroni and cheese, seven-layer salad, potato salad, cole slaw, and baked beans. Then there were so many desserts to choose from, he wasn't sure which he'd have first. This entire layout sort of reminded him of all the many holidays he'd spent with Aunt Susan. She'd never had to prepare as much food as this, but she'd still fixed most of the same items, and Dillon remembered how he would eat and eat and eat until he made himself sick. Aunt Susan was a down home, Southern cook, and he'd never eaten anyone else's food that tasted better. Boy did he miss her, and it was all he could do not to slip into some dreadful state of depression. He would never let these people see him that way, though.

Dillon filled his plate with everything he could, but just as he turned to look for his father, his heart dropped. The round table Curtis was sitting at was already full. Charlotte, Matthew, Alicia, and Phillip had plopped down around him, and they'd even pulled MJ's high chair into the mix. At the other table sat Charlotte's parents, her aunt Emma, her cousin Anise, and Curtina. Not one person in his family had offered him a seat, clearly not wanting to be bothered, and it took everything in him not to make a scene.

Finally, Dillon went over to one of the empty tables, but as soon as he and Melissa sat down, Curtis said,

"Son, you and Melissa okay over there? I hope you brought your appetites!"

"We're fine," he said, secretly fuming.

"Good."

Dillon relaxed in his chair, Melissa did the same, and he guessed Miss Lana and Elder Dixon must have felt sorry for them, since they took seats at the same table. Either that or it was simply the fact that they didn't want to sit at another table by themselves. What Dillon wanted to do was stand up, storm over to both the other tables, and explain to every one of them, point blank, how he couldn't stand them—that is, with the exception of his father.

But what calmed his nerves a great deal was the plan he'd been working on, the one that was going to make everything all right. The plan that would prove to his dad his worth as a son. The plan that would also confirm that neither Charlotte, Alicia, nor Matthew cared about Curtis as much as he did. He would demonstrate hands down that all they wanted were the financial benefits and social prestige his dad had afforded them.

Miss Lana and Elder Dixon made a lot of small talk with Dillon and Melissa, but mostly Dillon kept his attention focused on his dad's table. Matthew's phone rang, but all he did was look at the screen, frown, and ignore it.

"Was that her again?" Dillon heard Alicia say to Matthew.

"Yep. She's called four times today already, and she

sounded drunk in all four messages. She's really starting to get on my nerves."

Alicia drank some of her lemonade. "You need to file for a divorce. Then you need to get full custody of MJ."

"I've been trying my best to stay out of this," Charlotte added. "But you really don't have a choice, Matt. Racquel is getting worse instead of better."

Matthew sighed and ate more of his food. It was clear he didn't want to talk about his wife or the problems they were having, but Dillon's interest had been piqued and he wanted to hear more.

Unfortunately, however, Alicia glanced over at him, realizing he'd been listening to their conversation, and she changed the subject. But that was okay with Dillon because for the most part, he'd heard all he needed to. He even wondered if maybe he could use this Racquel disaster to his advantage. He wasn't sure how exactly, but he had a feeling Racquel might be instrumental in helping him ruin Charlotte...and Matthew, too, for that matter. There was a chance she knew things and would be glad to tell him about them. It was certainly worth finding out. And he would.

He also had another surprise for his dad and everyone else who was here. He'd still planned on waiting for the right time to tell his dad that he was ready to work for the church, but given the way everyone was treating him this afternoon, like he didn't belong, he now realized there was no better time than the present. At first, he'd settled on taking whatever position his father chose for him; that is, until about two minutes ago, when he'd taken yet another glance at his dad's table and noticed all the attention Curtis was practically drowning his *other* children with—so because of that, *he* was going to decide what position he would hold at the church. Whether his dad realized it or not, Dillon wanted some attention, too. He needed it, and it was for this reason that he'd made up his mind about what he had to do.

Dillon stood up. "I'm sorry to interrupt everyone's meal, but Dad, there's something I need to say. I've been struggling with this and struggling with this. I've tried my best to ignore it, but I just can't do that anymore."

There was total silence and no movement from anyone. Finally, Curtis said, "What is it, son?"

Dillon sighed loudly and paused for a few seconds, trying to seem genuine. "Well, Dad...the thing is...God has called me to preach. He wants me to deliver His Word and minister to His people."

Everyone stared at Dillon in shock. Even his dad seemed stunned, but Dillon knew they'd all get used to the idea soon enough. It wasn't as though they had a choice, anyway. Whether they liked his news or not, there was in fact a new reverend in town and his name was Dillon Whitfield—soon to be Dillon Whitfield Black, with no hyphen, once he moved forward with legally changing his name. He'd been planning to do just that right before his aunt had passed away, but now he would take care of it immediately.

Dillon loved the way his new name and title sounded

already. Minister Dillon Whitfield Black, eldest child of *the* Pastor Curtis Black. After all these months, Dillon had finally discovered the perfect way to bond with his father, and he was sorry he hadn't thought of it sooner. His dad's other children would never be able to compete with something like this, and Dillon could barely contain his excitement. But then as he gazed over at Charlotte, his emotions calmed down a bit, and he focused on his original plan. Working for the church was one thing, but this phony calling from God that he'd concocted would also afford him the kind of reputation, credibility, and access he needed to obtain critical information about his stepmother. Plus, the other benefit, too, was that he'd be able to learn more about his dad and the church as a whole. This last-minute idea of his would change everything for the better, and Dillon couldn't wait to see the fruits of his labor. More than anything, he couldn't wait to hear his father say, "Son, you did good. Job well done."

Chapter 33

Matthew drove into Jonathan's driveway, turned off his car, and shook his head. He wasn't sure why he'd made the grave mistake of answering his phone, but he had, and Racquel was driving him nuts. She just wouldn't go away, and he wondered when she would leave him alone.

"Matt, baby, please," she said. "I really need to see you."

"Why?"

"So we can talk. So we can fix this problem we have."

"Hmmph, you pretty much fixed everything when you stabbed me, Racquel. And if that wasn't enough, you came over to my parents' last week making a huge scene. You were as drunk as a skunk."

"I know, and I'm so sorry for that. I don't know what got into me, but I didn't mean it."

Matthew switched the phone to his other ear, wishing she'd hang up.

"Are you there?" she asked.

"Yeah, but I really need to go now."

"Why can't you just talk to me? Why won't you give me a chance?"

"I gave you lots of chances."

"When?"

"All this last year. I gave up everything for you and MJ. Even when you treated me like crap, I stayed faithful to you and I tried to be the best husband I could. But it never mattered to you."

"I was sick, Matt, and you know that."

"And I tried to talk to you about getting help, too. You didn't want it, though."

"I realize that, but that was then. Now I'm willing to do whatever you tell me. I'll do whatever it takes to make things right between us. I want you and MJ and me to be a family again."

"It's too late for that."

"What about for better or worse? What about in sickness or in health?"

"I really have to go."

"Matt, I'm really trying. I even went by the church to see your dad this afternoon, and he said he's already forgiven me. He said he's praying for both of us."

"That's nice to hear, but Racquel, I've already told you...I can't do this with you anymore."

"But what about the vows we took before God?"

"I've thought about all that, but our marriage is over. I'm done, Racquel. I loved you with all my heart, but I'm moving on."

"You selfish, evil idiot!"

Matthew had wondered how long it would be before

Racquel nixed this noticeably calm demeanor she'd been portraying and ultimately turned into a crazed maniac. It had taken her all of three minutes at the most.

"Look, this whole conversation is pointless. So let's not do this anymore, okay?"

"Where's my son?" she shouted.

"Don't worry about it."

"Excuse me?"

"You weren't worried about it a couple of weeks ago, so what difference does it make now?"

"I wanna know where my son is, Matt."

"He's safe and away from you."

"You're gonna be so sorry."

"So now you're threatening me?"

"Take it any way you want, but if I were you I'd see it as a promise."

"Good-bye, Racquel."

"Payback can be vicious, so I suggest you watch your back."

Matthew pressed the End button on his phone, took a deep breath, and leaned his head back. He'd told himself that he would no longer allow Racquel to upset him, but he just couldn't seem to help it. Maybe it was because they had so much history and because they had a child together. Maybe it was simply because they despised each other for different reasons. Matthew had no idea, one way or the other, but he prayed things would get better for him and her. He prayed that they would someday make amends and find happiness. They would never be able to do that as long as they stayed married, but Matthew hoped that eventually they could be friends. He hoped they'd be able to get along for MJ's sake because no matter what Racquel had done to him, he didn't see her as an enemy. He didn't have a lot of experience with relationships, but what he now believed was that not every couple was meant to be together. Not every man was right for every woman. He wished things had turned out differently for him and Racquel, but sadly, the damage was done and nothing would change that.

Matthew finally found the strength and will to step out of his car and head toward the front door. Jonathan opened it and walked outside to meet him.

"Man, what's up? Why you lookin' all upset?"

"Guess."

"Racquel?"

Matthew nodded.

"Man, I keep tellin' you it's time to get rid of that girl. She's nothin' but trouble, and if you don't divorce her, you'll regret it from now on. And that's real talk."

"I hear you, Jon, but man, it's just not that easy. I'm definitely gonna divorce her, but these things take time."

"Have you even contacted an attorney?"

"No, but I will."

"What're you waitin' on?"

"I dunno. I guess deep down I feel bad about it."

Jonathan laughed out loud. "Man, you must be kiddin' me. That girl stabbed the mess outta you, and you're the one who feels bad? Man, please."

Matthew's phone rang, but as soon as he pulled it out of his pocket he pursed his lips. It was Racquel again.

Jonathan sighed loudly, acting as though he'd been the one to get the phone call. "Is that her?"

Matthew hit Ignore and slipped the phone back inside his jeans pocket.

"I'm tellin' you, man, you need to end this. And you need to get a restraining order. I don't trust that broad for a minute."

Matthew looked at him in silence. He was at a loss for words, and although he knew Jonathan was right about at least some of what he was saying, he didn't feel like talking about this any longer.

Jonathan looked past Matthew and down the street. "And anyway, if you want things to work out with this one right here, I suggest you take care of that Racquel madness quick."

Matthew turned around and saw Stacey driving up. Since Jonathan's parents were out of town for the week, Jonathan had offered his house as a place for Matthew and Stacey to meet up and spend some time together. At first, Matthew hadn't known if this was a good idea, but now that she'd arrived, he was glad he'd agreed to it.

Stacey parked in front of the house and got out. She had on a fitted, royal blue maxi sundress, and Matthew couldn't stop staring at her. Apparently, Jonathan couldn't either.

"Man, you'd be a fool to mess up somethin' like that. Stacey is hot, smart, and without issues. Good thing you got those stitches out on Friday, too."

Matthew rolled his eyes. "Whatever, Jon."

"I'm just sayin'."

"Hey guys," she said, smiling and hugging both of them.

"Hey yourself," Jonathan said. "But you know I'm not too happy with you right about now."

"Why?"

"You didn't bring one of your girls with you?"

Stacey shook her head, laughing. "You're too much."

"I'm just kiddin' with you. I'm on my way to see this honey I met the other night, anyway. So I'm outta here. Oh and you guys can eat and drink whatever you want. The house is yours."

"Thanks, man," Matthew said.

"We really appreciate this, Jonathan," Stacey added.

"Just make me proud," he said, smiling. "And my bedroom is upstairs if you need it."

Matthew had been best friends with Jonathan since childhood, yet he still couldn't believe some of the things he said and did. He was such a free spirit, and mostly all he concerned himself with were girls and sex. It was all he seemed to care about.

Matthew and Stacey went inside and made themselves comfortable on the plush tan sofa in the family room. For some reason, Matthew's stomach churned a bit and he felt a little awkward. So he turned on the television. The channel was already set on ESPN, but he turned it to the Lifetime Movie Network for Stacey's sake.

They sat at opposite ends of the couch, and just as Matthew prepared to make small talk, his phone rang again. He dreaded pulling it out, but he also didn't want to ignore it just in case his mom was calling about MJ. She was babysitting for him. Sadly, though, when he looked at the screen, Racquel's number was displayed; he hit Ignore and set it on the table in front of them.

"So what did you do today?" he asked.

"Not a lot. Mostly I just sat around watching TV, and that was it. What about you?"

"Took a nap, played with MJ, got something to eat, and then came over here."

Matthew looked at the television, but then he heard his phone vibrate and he checked the screen. Now Racquel was texting him.

I hate you, Matt, and I hope somebody kills you!

Matthew reread the line three different times and set his phone back down.

"Was that Racquel?" Stacey asked.

"Why do you say that?"

"Just a feeling."

"Yeah, it was," he said, getting up and walking over to the large picture window. He placed his hands in his back pockets, sighed, and wondered when this would be over. He wondered when Racquel would stop speaking so violently to him and get on with her life. He'd tried to hold off with filing for the divorce, but now he knew it was time.

Stacey walked over to where he was standing, and to his surprise, she wrapped her arms around his waist and leaned the bottom of her chin against his back.

"Are you okay?"

"Not really."

"I'm sorry you're so sad, Matt. I hate that this is happening to you."

"I wish I'd done things so much differently. I wish I'd never gotten married to her."

"We all make mistakes, but you're a good person and you'll be fine."

She held him tighter, and though Matthew wanted to turn around and face her, he was too afraid of what might happen if he did. His nerves were shot, but at the same time, he hadn't felt this comfortable with a woman since he began dating Racquel, and he wanted to hold her back.

"Thank you," he finally said.

"For what?"

"For being so understanding and for still wanting to be here even with all this drama. My life is so messed up right now."

"Yeah, but it won't always be this way. Things'll get better real soon."

"I hope so, but I still appreciate you being here for me."

"I'm here because..."

"Because what?"

"Nothing."

Matthew finally turned around and gazed into her eyes. "Because what?"

She gazed back at him. "I know it might sound crazy to you, but Matt, I'm so in love with you I can barely stand it."

His heart beat wildly, and while he'd been trying to deny his true feelings for her for days, he knew he felt the same way.

Matthew pulled her closer. "Baby, I love you, too."

They stared into each other's eyes again, and Matthew kissed her. She kissed him back, and Matthew wished he never had to let her go. They kissed ravenously, but suddenly, even with as wonderful as Stacey made him feel, he worried about where things were headed. No matter how much of a decision he'd made about ending things with Racquel, he was still married and he didn't want to commit adultery. He didn't want to commit yet another sin he'd have to pray about.

But God forgive him, he couldn't help himself. He couldn't stop kissing Stacey, and in a matter of minutes, he found himself lying on top of her on the sofa. They were still fully clothed, but the passion between them was so deeply out of control that Matthew could hardly think straight.

Stacey slightly pushed him away, barely able to breathe. "Matt... please make love to me."

Matthew stared at her, now winded himself. "Are you sure?"

"Yes."

Matthew swallowed hard, thinking about his marriage and little MJ, but in the end, he led Stacey upstairs to Jonathan's bedroom. He knew it was wrong, but the truth of the matter was he wanted Stacey just as badly as she wanted him. He wanted to feel good for a change, so he decided that he'd just have to deal with the consequences. It was simply the way things were.

Chapter 34

Dillon almost wanted to laugh out loud at how easy this all had been. This morning, he'd gotten up bright and early, left the house to run a few errands, and then he'd actually gone by the church to see his dad. He had dropped by unannounced, and as usual, his dad had been too busy to talk to him and had hurried into some staff meeting—but not before introducing Dillon to Matthew's wife, Racquel. Now, lo and behold, she and Dillon were in bed together. They were at a suburban Chicago hotel, recovering from the best sex Dillon had experienced in his life. This girl had done things to him that women in their late twenties and early thirties had never been able to accomplish, and although he normally had no respect for any woman who slept with him this quickly, there was something special about Racquel. There was something mesmerizingly attractive about her, and he couldn't get enough of her.

As it was, they'd only been together for two hours, yet they'd already had sex three times. Maybe it was the liquor she'd drunk that had her so turned on. Dillon didn't drink, but he certainly hadn't had a problem buying a bottle of brandy for her prior to their meeting at the hotel. Racquel had made it pretty clear that she wanted something to calm her nerves and that she wanted to have a good time—especially once he'd asked her what she knew about Charlotte and even more so once he'd told her that he couldn't stand Charlotte either.

So now, here they were, lying in bed, butt naked, like they were longtime lovers.

"I can't stand that tramp," Racquel said matter-of-factly while slurring her words. "She's so not who everyone thinks she is. Such a phony trick."

"Wow, you must really hate her."

"I do. She took my son away from me and ruined my marriage. Don't you know about that?"

"Bits and pieces."

"Well, long story short, she paid some people to say my mom and I were abusing my son, and they took him from me. Then she got away with it. When she got caught, they locked her up, but she never went to prison. That's what having money will do for you, though."

"That's too bad," Dillon said. He'd known Charlotte was a snake, but taking someone's baby was low even for her.

Racquel slipped from under the covers, lifted the bottle of brandy from the nightstand, and poured herself a drink. "Charlotte is the reason I'm so messed up in the head. She's the reason I became depressed and ended up stabbing Matt. And, of course, now he wants nothing to do with me."

Dillon wasn't sure what to say, so he didn't say anything.

Racquel took a long swig of her alcohol like it was water. "I've done my best to apologize to him, but he won't listen. I even called him late this afternoon, but all he did was dismiss me. That's when I decided to call you," she said, getting back under the covers. She turned on her side and faced him. "I'm so glad I finally met you, Dillon."

"I'm glad, too, but I'm sorry you've got so many problems right now."

"And then some. This court thing really scares me because there's a chance I could get time over this."

"Well, let's just hope you don't."

"My parents hired me a really good lawyer, but who knows what will happen."

"You haven't been in any trouble before, have you?"

"No."

"Then, I'm sure it'll be fine. Especially since it's not like you killed anyone."

"Matt isn't making things any better. He won't even let me see my son. I mean, who does something like that?"

"I'm sure that witch, Charlotte, is behind it, though. And hey," Dillon said, realizing that this might be the right time to find out what Racquel knew about her. "Do you think Charlotte has more skeletons she's hiding? Some huge secret that still hasn't been exposed?"

"Hmmph. Trust me. If there is, I'm not aware of it, because I would have already used it against her. I would have done that a long time ago."

"I can imagine."

"There is one thing, though."

"What's that?"

"This whole last year, I've made sure to stay in touch with one of the assistants at the church. She doesn't care all that much for Charlotte, because of how full of herself she is, so if Charlotte ever does do something she shouldn't, my friend will definitely tell me about it. I know Charlotte has more secrets, though. She's too sneaky not to."

Dillon just listened as Racquel continued.

"I hate that woman. Charlotte is by far the most evil woman I've ever known, and she's also the reason I've been so out of it. I even have to take medication now."

Dillon raised his eyebrows. "And you're drinking alcohol?"

"I haven't taken anything in two days, so I'm fine."

Dillon wondered if that was a good thing or a bad thing—good maybe, because clearly no one on antidepressants should be drinking liquor, but bad because if she'd been diagnosed with depression, she likely needed to take her medication on schedule. The thing was, though, she didn't seem depressed to him at all, not even earlier when he'd first met her at the church. She seemed pretty normal.

Racquel went on and on about Charlotte and Matthew, but then Dillon's phone rang. He hoped it wasn't Melissa, but he doubted that it was because he'd told her not to call him. She had, of course, wanted to know where he was going, and after telling her it was none of her business, he'd gotten in his truck and left.

Interestingly enough, though, it was his father.

"Hello?"

"Hey son. I know it's late, but I just left a ministers' meeting and before I knew it, it was almost eleven o'clock. Anyway, I wanted to apologize again for not being able to talk to you today."

"No problem," Dillon said.

Actually, it was a problem, but he didn't want Racquel to know he was having issues with his dad.

"Why don't you come by the church tomorrow around ten o'clock."

"Works for me. I'll see you then."

"You have a good night, son."

"You, too, Dad."

"So tell me," Racquel said, sitting up and pouring herself another drink. "What was it like meeting your dad for the first time?"

"Weird. Scary. Strange. You name it."

"Matt never talked much about you, but then he never really got to meet you either."

"No, we just met yesterday at my dad's."

"Are things going well for you?"

"For the most part. I wish I could see my dad a lot more than I do, but it'll happen."

"I'm sure Charlotte can't stand you, though, right?"

"Nope. Hates everything about me."

"I'm not surprised. She doesn't like any outsiders, and although you're Pastor Black's son, she'll never see you as family."

"I can tell."

"What about Alicia and Curtina? Are you close with them?"

"Not really."

"Even when Matt and I were just dating, Alicia was always very nice to me. She's a really good person."

Dillon didn't bother telling her that just yesterday Alicia had been the one advising Matthew to get rid of her. He didn't like Alicia, and nothing would make him feel better than turning Racquel against her, but right now he didn't have the energy to focus on his sister.

"You know..." she said, scooting closer to him. "I really like you, Dillon. I like you a lot."

"I like you, too," he said, caressing the side of her face.

But it wasn't like he had to do anything more, because Racquel was already showcasing her skills again. She was good, and Dillon lay back, letting her do whatever she wanted.

He wasn't sure why exactly, but sleeping with his brother's wife gave him a certain sense of satisfaction. Matthew didn't know about them, but Dillon still saw this as the perfect way to get back at him for stealing his dad's attention. Before Matthew's stabbing, everything had been going so well. Curtis had flown to Atlanta with Dillon for his aunt's funeral, but Matthew had been the reason his dad had hurried back home, leaving him to mourn all alone. So *what* if Matthew had been rushed to the hospital? Dillon had lost the only mother he'd known, and that should have counted for something, too. But it hadn't, so again, this was all Matthew's fault, because had he been a better husband to Racquel—a man who had the guts to stand up to that slut of a mother of his—Racquel would have never had a reason to stab him in the first place. If Matthew had defended his wife from the very beginning—before they'd ever gotten married—they'd be living happily ever after the way they should, and Curtis would be free to focus a lot more on Dillon.

But that was okay because sooner or later Dillon would get everything he wanted. Even right now, he wasn't doing too badly. Just yesterday, he'd become a minister, and today, here he was sleeping with his very talented and attentive sister-in-law. She'd already proven that she knew how to take care of a man, so to him life was good. For the moment, he had absolutely no reason to complain about anything.

Chapter 35

It was well after eight a.m., yet Matthew hadn't slept more than a couple of hours. For the life of him, he just couldn't shake this guilty feeling of his. On the one hand, he couldn't have been happier about making love to Stacey, but on the other, he was consumed with regret. He'd also been shocked to learn that she was still a virgin, so he felt bad about that as well. In high school, she'd always insisted that she didn't want to have sex until she got married, yet now he was the reason she'd changed her mind about it. There was no doubt that most guys his age would feel very proud of themselves, but Matthew felt nothing more than confusion.

There was one thing, though, that he was sure about and that was the fact that he had fallen in love with Stacey. He hadn't planned on it, and he wasn't sure how it had happened so fast, but he definitely loved her. They were so good together, he could talk to her about anything, and the chemistry between them was incomparable.

Matthew went down the hall to check on MJ and smiled. He wasn't in his crib, but just looking at the beautiful nursery that his mother had built gave Matthew peace. He knew she hadn't built it with the right intentions, but now that he and MJ were back home, he appreciated it a lot more.

Matthew walked back into the hallway and went down to his parents' room, and of course MJ was sitting in the middle of their king-size bed, playing with one of his toy trucks. Charlotte sat against a stack of pillows admiring her grandson.

"I'm surprised you're not holding him," Matthew said, teasing her.

"Don't worry. I'll be holding him soon enough, and I won't feel bad about it either."

They both laughed.

"You know you're spoiling him, though, right?"

Charlotte nodded. "Yep, and I'm not going to apologize for that either."

"Very sad, Mom. Pitiful."

"I know," she said, her tone turning serious. "But, Matt, I'm so glad you and MJ are here. I missed you both so, so much, and I will never fully forgive myself for what I did to you."

Matthew sat on the edge of the bed, and MJ chuckled with joy. He was certainly a daddy's child. He knew how much his father loved him, and Matthew was very proud of that. He guessed maybe it was a generational thing, because no matter what had happened in the past, no matter what terrible thing his own father had done, he knew Curtis had always loved him. It was the reason Matthew had been more of a daddy's child as well.

"It's okay, Mom. A lot of mistakes were made, a lot of hurtful things were said, but now we have to move forward."

"You're right, son, but I just want you to know how sorry I am, and that I take full responsibility for my actions. I've done some truly horrible things in my life, but lying on Racquel and having little MJ taken away from her was the worst. It was completely uncalled for, and I hope you can forgive me."

"I already have, Mom. It took me a very long time, but you're my mother and I love you."

"I love you, too, honey, and I hope you never forget that."

Matthew smiled.

"And I'm so proud of you. You were always a good child, but to see how great of a father you are to MJ makes me even prouder. Especially since I know things haven't been easy for you."

"MJ is everything to me, Mom, and so are you and Dad."

Charlotte's eyes welled up with tears. "So," she said, wiping her face and changing the subject. "Did you enjoy yourself with Jonathan and Elijah last night?"

"I did," he lied.

The one thing Matthew rarely did was lie to his parents, but there was no way he could let them find out he was spending time with another girl. His marriage to Racquel was practically over, but he also knew he shouldn't be seeing anyone else until he divorced her. What he was doing behind closed doors was dead wrong, and the guilt he felt was overwhelming. He also thought about his vow to never become like his parents. He'd promised God, Racquel, and himself that he would never be unfaithful to her, yet he had done exactly that. He was so ashamed of the choice he'd made, and although for years he'd never understood how either of his parents could sleep around on the other, he sort of understood it a little better now. There was still no excuse for it, but for the first time, he saw how desire and temptation could consume a person and how it could cause them to do things they shouldn't. Not only had Matthew committed an awful sin, he'd broken one of God's commandments, and he was very sorry about that. What worried him, however, was that although he'd already repented and asked God to forgive him, he couldn't guarantee he wouldn't do it again. He knew his thinking was selfish and sinful, but he couldn't help the way he felt about Stacey.

Matthew thought he heard his phone ringing and sprinted down to his bedroom. "Oh boy," he said when he saw that it was his mother-in-law.

"Hello?" he answered.

"Hey Matt, how are you?"

"I'm good. You?"

"So-so I guess," Vanessa said, sounding sad. "Racquel is still very upset, and she really misses you. She misses you and MJ, and Neil and I do, too."

Matthew wasn't sure what she wanted him to say.

"Then there's this whole court situation, so I was just wondering if you'd thought more about trying to help her."

"Not really."

"Matt, I know you're upset, but if you could just sign that affidavit we talked about, it could really make all the difference. At least then the prosecutor will realize you've forgiven her and you don't blame her for what happened."

But that's just it, I do blame her. Matthew would never say what he was thinking, but he was sort of having a hard time understanding why his mother-in-law thought it was okay to ask him to do something like this. He knew Racquel was her daughter and she loved her, but Vanessa was acting as though Racquel hadn't snapped and tried to kill him. She'd inflicted him with serious bodily harm, yet Vanessa didn't seem to think it was important. All she wanted was for her daughter to walk away with no punishment.

"Matt, please say something."

"What I want is for Racquel to get some help."

"She is. She started seeing a doctor the day after she showed up at your parents'. We told her that driving around drunk and causing a scene was the final straw, and she agreed. She's also on medication, and she's doing a lot better."

Matt didn't see where she was doing better at all, but he kept his thoughts to himself.

"She really is very sorry for what she did, Matt. She's

sorry for everything. So, please... I'm begging you to give her another chance. Do it for little MJ, because he needs both his parents."

Matthew wanted to tell her that this was never going to happen, but she kept talking.

"I was also hoping that maybe we could come get MJ for a visit."

"I don't think that's a good idea."

"We really miss our grandson, honey, and you know we'll take good care of him. And it would be good for Racquel to spend some quality time with him."

Matt didn't want to be rude, so he said, "Maybe once Racquel has been on her medication a little longer, because just yesterday, she called me and said some really awful things. She even threatened me again."

"What? I can't imagine why she would do that. Although she really is hurting right now. She doesn't wanna lose you and MJ. That's why I keep pleading with you to take her back."

Matt heard his phone beep. "Mrs. Anderson, one of my coworkers is calling, so can I get back to you?"

"Sure, but please think about what I said."

"I will," he said and then answered his other call. "Nicole?"

"Hey Matt, how's it goin'?"

"Pretty good. So what's goin' on with you?"

"Same ole same ole. I hadn't checked on you since last week, so I thought I'd see how you were doing."

"I'm glad you did. I'm planning to be back on Monday."

"That's great. I sort of wondered if maybe you were gonna quit. You know, since you're back with your parents."

"No, my son is still my responsibility, so I wanna keep working."

"Wow, I'm impressed. But then again, I'm not surprised. I've always admired you because even though your parents are very wealthy, it hasn't changed you as a person."

"Thanks for saying that."

"I'm serious, and if you wanna know the truth, I'd do anything to be with a guy like you."

"Thanks for saying that, too," he said, laughing. "You're just full of compliments."

"Look, Matt, I know this might sound strange and sort of out of left field, but I may as well tell you. I've been attracted to you since the first day you started working here."

Matt was stunned. He wasn't blind or oblivious to her good looks or the way she subtly flirted with him from time to time, but he also wasn't aware that she was seriously interested. Or at least that was how she sounded, anyway.

"I know you're going through a tough time right now, but I really would like to get to know you better—outside of work and on a more personal level."

Matt wasn't sure how to respond. Nicole was a lot older than him, so he'd never imagined she'd be interested in dating a twenty-year-old. He had to admit, he'd be lying if he'd said he wasn't proud to know that an older woman wanted to be with him, but at the same time, he'd already fallen in love with Stacey.

"I guess I don't know what to say," he said.

"Don't say anything, because like I said, I know you're going through a tough time right now. Just think about it, okay?"

"I will," he said, wondering why he hadn't just told her thanks but no thanks. He guessed, though, he didn't want to hurt her feelings. As it was, she'd already been traumatized by her abusive husband, and Matthew didn't want to add even the slightest disappointment to that.

"Okay, well, I won't keep you," she said. "I'm glad you're doing great, and I'll see you on Monday."

"See you then, and thanks for calling."

Matthew set his phone on his dresser and hoped this conversation of theirs wouldn't make things awkward at work. He pushed the whole thing out of his mind, though, when his phone rang again. This time it was Stacey, and he could barely contain himself. Just seeing her number gave him a warm, peaceful feeling. As a matter of fact, whether he spoke to her on the phone or saw her in person, she brought him much hope and contentment. It was the reason he had to start his divorce proceedings as soon as possible. His mother wanted that, so did Alicia, and so did Jonathan, and now Matthew wanted it more than all of them. He needed to move on and plan for his future. More than anything, he wanted to start a new life with Stacey.

Chapter 36

After Lana gave him the okay, Dillon walked toward his dad's office and eased open the door.

"Hey son," Curtis said.

"Hey."

"Have a seat. And again, I'm really sorry I couldn't talk yesterday. My day was full."

"No problem. I know you have a lot to do here."

Dillon didn't think anything should come before a man's oldest son, but he faked like he understood it.

"So, I'm guessing you wanna talk about that big announcement you made at the cookout."

"Sort of. I'm excited about it, and I can't wait to get started."

"Well, actually, it's going take a little more than just getting started."

"Meaning?"

"Well, for one thing you need to ask yourself a lot of questions, and then you need to answer them for me. This isn't a formal requirement of any man who says he's been called into the ministry, but they are questions I ask all new ministers who are planning to serve at Deliverance Outreach."

Dillon didn't like any of what his father was saying, but he went along with it. "What kind of questions?"

"For one, have you truly accepted Jesus Christ as your Lord and personal Savior? Do you recognize and worship the Trinity as the Father, the Son, and the Holy Spirit? Do you fully understand what it means to be called by God to preach? Do you understand the responsibilities that come with it? When you say God called you, did He truly speak to your heart and mind or is this something you've chosen to do on your own?"

"I can answer yes to every question, and yes, He spoke to my heart and mind. I would never choose something like this just because."

"That's good to hear."

Dillon didn't know why his father felt the need to grill him this way, and he wished he'd move on to something else.

"What about your situation at home?" Curtis asked.

"I don't know what you mean."

"Melissa and the fact that you live together. Surely, you don't plan to keep shacking up like that if you've been called into the ministry?"

His dad was going too far with all these questions and borderline demands. It was as if he wanted Dillon to be perfect.

"I hadn't thought about that. I'll figure out something, though."

"You don't plan to marry her?"

"Maybe. I just don't know. It might be best if she just got her own place for a while. That way I can focus on what I need to do as a minister."

Curtis looked at him strangely, and Dillon wasn't happy about it.

"Look, son, I know these aren't questions you want to answer, but as a man of God and because I'm your father, I can't help but feel a certain level of responsibility toward making sure you understand what will be expected of you."

"It's not a problem," he said, but what irritated him was the idea that his father wasn't being very supportive of his *call* to the ministry.

"This is very serious, and the reason I know that is because of my own experience. I was called at a very young age, too, but I did things no minister should ever do. I did whatever I wanted, no matter how sinful, and I've reaped every bit of what I've sown. So much responsibility comes with being a minister, and even more so once you become a pastor. When that happens, you end up leading innocent people who are sometimes very hurt, very vulnerable human beings. So again, saying that you've been called is very serious, and I just want you to be sure that God really has spoken to you."

His father sounded as though he was lecturing him instead of encouraging him, and Dillon was offended.

"Dad, I'm not sure what you want me to say. I'm not some child trying to play games with you. I'm not a dummy."

"I know you're not, and I'm not trying to discourage you. I don't want to doubt you either, but I also need to be honest with you."

"About what?"

"Well, for one, son, I rarely see you open a Bible. You don't even carry one or have a Bible app on your smartphone. On Sunday mornings, when everyone is flipping through pages of scripture, all you do is sit there. You don't even seem all that interested. And you almost never attend Bible study on Wednesday nights."

"I read my Bible all the time at home," he said. He knew that wasn't true, but he was telling his father what he wanted to hear. "And as far as Bible study, Melissa and I have our own sessions. We do that at home, too."

He was lying again, but he did what he had to do.

Still, Curtis didn't seem to be buying it, and if anything he seemed less supportive of Dillon than he had been a few minutes ago.

"Maybe you should spend a few days praying about all this. Go into deep prayer, just to make sure this is really what God wants you to do."

"So you think I'm lying?" Dillon said, frowning. "You think I made all this up?"

"That's not what I'm saying. I just want you to spend some quality time with God, both down on your knees in prayer and also by reading the Word."

"How long do I have to do this?"

"Until you hear confirmation."

"And when I do—when I get confirmation again, that is, since I already have it—then what?"

"We'll get you enrolled at a seminary. There are a lot of good ones out there, all over the country, so we'll sit down together to choose one. We'll figure out which one is best for you."

Seminary? Good ones all over the country? This meeting wasn't going nearly the way Dillon had planned for it to, because the last thing he wanted was to leave Mitchell. The whole point of putting on this call-to-ministry charade was so his father could assign him an office near his and so he could add him on as an assistant pastor. That way he could work side by side with his father and see him every day. Apparently, his father didn't want that.

"This really is very serious, son. I'm telling you from experience."

Dillon wondered how many more times he was going to say that.

"I really thought you'd be happy about my call from God," he finally said.

"I just want you to be sure, and I'm here for you either way."

Dillon stared at him with anger and disappointment.

"Trust me," Curtis said. "You'll be glad you took your time with this."

Dillon heard everything his dad was saying, but he wasn't happy in the least. Especially since he was pretty sure that if his father's golden boy, Matthew, had announced that he'd been called to preach, his dad would have shouted to the heavens. The other thing that infuriated Dillon was the way his father sat there judging him. So *what* if he never read his Bible or saw a reason to attend Bible study? What did that have to do with anything? What mattered was that he was planning to start studying his Bible *now*.

Dillon listened as his dad went on and on with more boring, self-righteous suggestions, but mostly he couldn't wait to get out of there—mostly he wanted to forget about this whole plot to become a minister altogether. The reason: it was time to concentrate on plan B—or even C if he had to. It was time to do whatever was necessary.

Chapter 37

What a morning. It was almost noon, and Dillon was sorry he'd ever gone to see his father. Their meeting had been a disaster, and Dillon was livid. Then, when he'd pulled into his driveway, he saw Roger trimming the edges of the grass and that irritated him, too. Yesterday, Roger had called to say that because of another dental appointment, he'd be coming on Wednesday again, but Dillon wasn't in the mood for seeing anyone.

As Dillon drove into the garage, Roger grinned like he had perfect teeth, but Dillon hurried to close the garage door so he wouldn't have to speak to him. He just couldn't be bothered with any of Roger's country bumpkin chatter today, and he wasn't going to apologize for it either. His dad had certainly enraged him with all his doubts and questions. For months, Dillon had blamed Charlotte and his siblings for the distance that existed between him and his father, but now he blamed his father for it, too. Dillon loved Curtis and he was trying to do everything he could to win his approval, but he was slowly but surely losing his patience. He was tired of begging and pleading with his dad and then getting nowhere. It just didn't make sense to him, and it wasn't fair. Here his dad had humiliated Dillon's mom many years ago, he'd disowned Dillon as soon as he was born, and now after all that, he still couldn't do right by him?

It took everything in Dillon not to explode—it took everything in his whole being not to add his dad to the top of his revenge list.

Dillon threw his keys across the kitchen counter and went upstairs. He'd been hoping Melissa would pretend he wasn't there, but no such luck.

"Hey baby," she said, walking into the bedroom behind him. "Is everything okay?"

"Why wouldn't it be? And instead of asking a bunch of dumb questions, where's my information? What have you found out about that trick, Charlotte?"

"The investigator is still working on it, and he's even had her followed a few times. But he's found nothing."

"Why not?"

"He just hasn't."

Dillon stepped closer to her and grabbed her by her arm. "This is all your fault. You can't do anything right, can you? But I've got news for you. If you don't get me what I need, then I want you out of here."

"Baby, you're hurting me. And what else can I do?"

"You do what I told you, Melissa!" he said, staring her down and pushing her away from him.

She tried to steady her balance. "But the investigator

can't find anything. He's tried and tried, but everything he's come up with is the stuff we already know about."

"I hope he's not expecting to be paid. And, anyway... why haven't you contacted a different investigator? If this one can't do his stupid job, why haven't you hired another one?"

"I don't know. Jasper Davis is one of the best, and I just don't see where we'll be able to find anyone better."

Dillon tossed the lamp from the nightstand and brushed by Melissa so forcefully, she lost her balance again.

Still, she followed him downstairs. "Baby, what's wrong? Why are you so upset?"

Dillon plopped down on one of the chairs in the family room. "Just leave me alone."

"But baby, what is it? Tell me what to do, and I'll do it."

"I already did, but you couldn't even handle that."

"I'm so sorry. I really tried, and it's not like the PI is gonna give up. Maybe he'll come up with something soon."

"You know what? I'm sick of you, my dad and everybody else I can think of right now, so just leave me alone. I already told you that."

"Why don't we go upstairs," she said.

Dillon scrunched his forehead. "For what?"

"To make love. That always makes you feel better."

"Well, not today. Today, I just wanna be left alone. This is my third time telling you that."

"But—" she said before he cut her off.

Dillon squinted his eyes and spoke through gritted teeth. "I told you to leave me alone. Now, get your stupid behind out of here."

Melissa backed away in tears and finally left.

When she did, Dillon grabbed his keys, went back out to his SUV, and called Racquel. All this morning, he'd tried to push her out of his mind, but here, hours later, he was still thinking about her. This was totally new territory for him since he'd never *needed* to be with any woman, but he knew why he felt the way he did. Racquel made him feel good, and he wanted more of her. Not tomorrow, not next week, or next month. He wanted her today, and he would have her.

Matthew had told himself he wouldn't see Stacey right away again today, but here they were, sitting next to each other at Jonathan's.

"I'm really confused," he said. "I mean, so much is happening so fast. Here I am about to go through a divorce, but I'm also in love with you...and the guilt is killing me, Stacey."

"I get that, but it's not like we can help the way we feel, Matt. We didn't purposely go looking for this. We saw each other at a bowling alley, but we didn't plan it."

"Still, what we're doing is wrong."

"I know that, too."

"I just wish my divorce was already final."

"So do I. I know that probably sounds terrible, but

that's just the way I feel. I'll wait for you as long as I have to, though."

Matthew pulled her into his arms so that her back rested against his chest. "Hopefully, it won't take long at all."

"Even if it does, I'm not going anywhere."

"You say that now, but what about when it's time for you to go back to school?"

"I'll still be waiting."

"I could kick myself for breaking up with you in high school. Just because you wouldn't have sex with me."

"You were young and dumb back then, so I forgive you," she said, laughing.

Matthew chuckled, too. "I guess I was."

"But now you're much older," she said sitting up and turning toward him. "And I'm in love with you."

Matthew wished she wouldn't look at him this way. What he'd hoped was that she would simply be content lying in his arms and watching television. But now they stared at each other like animals, and Matthew grabbed both sides of her face and kissed her.

A whole minute passed, but then Stacey pulled away. "Make love to me again."

Matthew gazed into her eyes, admiring how beautiful she was and wishing he could deny her. But he couldn't, because the truth of the matter was, he wanted her, too. She was almost like a drug that he didn't want to wean himself from, and that scared him. It alarmed him because the love he'd had for his own wife had never been this intense. It hadn't as much as come close, and the chemistry he'd shared with Racquel couldn't compare either.

Nonetheless, he still knew that what he was doing was wrong and that he was committing another terrible sin. But he couldn't stop himself. Likely because he didn't actually want to.

Chapter 38

This is the day the Lord hath made, so let us rejoice and be glad in it," Curtis said, standing behind the podium in the pulpit.

It was Sunday morning, and as Dillon sat listening to his dad preparing to give his weekly sermon, he glanced down the pew at his wicked stepmother. He just knew there had to be at least something—anything would do—that he could learn about Charlotte the Harlot, and he was sorry that this worthless investigator Melissa had hired hadn't come through for him. Actually, he still blamed Melissa for every bit of this because had she made this Charlotte thing her top priority, Dillon would now have all the damaging information he needed, and Charlotte wouldn't be sitting a few feet away from him, all decked out in some overpriced outfit. He was sure her suit and shoes had set his father back close to a thousand dollars or more.

Melissa had been trying his patience for a while, but as of last Wednesday, he'd become flat-out sick of her. He'd even gone these last few days without saying more than five words to her, and he'd also made her stay home this morning. Then, there was the fact that he'd spent the last five days straight with Racquel. Dillon hadn't wanted much to do with Melissa for months and months, but now that he'd found a real woman who willingly gave him what he wanted without being asked, Melissa was the least of his worries. And to think Racquel was only twenty, and nine years his junior, yet she could run circles around Melissa. He wasn't sure where she'd learned all her tricks, but he loved those tricks just the same. He was actually a bit surprised at how experienced she was, given her age, and also because she'd gotten married so young. But Dillon had learned a long time ago that some seemingly nice, quiet women were, well... well, they were just born with a little freak in them. Church girls, well-educated girls, rich girls, it didn't matter. It was simply a fact, and Dillon loved it.

Dillon looked up at his father and then glanced down the pew again, this time paying attention to Matthew, MJ, Curtina, Alicia, and Phillip. They were all such a joke, and Dillon wished they would somehow disappear. He wished none of them had been born, period.

"Today," Curtis said, turning pages in his Bible, "I want to talk about the prodigal son, so if you would, please turn with me to the Book of Luke, chapter fifteen, verse eleven. I know I've preached from this particular chapter more than once, but because my son Matthew and my little grandson are back home with us,

I believe this is the reason God has laid it on my heart to share this message again."

Dillon listened and watched, and although his father had been right about his rarely spending any time reading the Bible, this was the one chapter Dillon had paid attention to. He remembered last year, the first time he'd heard his dad speak about the prodigal son, how upset he'd gotten. Like a sick puppy, his father had delivered part of his message in tears, all because he missed his precious Matthew, and this had persuaded Dillon to read this story multiple times on his own.

Curtis looked across the congregation. "As most of you know, I sometimes read scripture from the King James version, the New Living Translation, and also from the New International Version. Today, I'll be reading from the NIV, and it reads as follows:

> [11]*Jesus continued: There was a man who had two sons.* [12]*The younger one said to his father, "Father, give me my share of the estate." So he divided his property between them.*
> [13]*Not long after that, the younger son got together all he had, set off for a distant country and there squandered his wealth in wild living.* [14]*After he had spent everything, there was a severe famine in that whole country, and he began to be in need.* [15]*So he went and hired himself out to a citizen of that country, who sent him to his fields to feed pigs.* [16]*He longed to fill his stomach with the pods that the pigs were eating, but no one gave him anything.*
> [17]*When he came to his senses, he said, "How many of my*

father's hired servants have food to spare, and here I am starving to death! [18]I will set out and go back to my father and say to him: Father, I have sinned against heaven and against you. [19]I am no longer worthy to be called your son; make me like one of your hired servants." [20]So he got up and went to his father.

But while he was still a long way off, his father saw him and was filled with compassion for him; he ran to his son, threw his arms around him and kissed him.

[21]The son said to him, "Father, I have sinned against heaven and against you. I am no longer worthy to be called your son."

[22]But the father said to his servants, "Quick! Bring the best robe and put it on him. Put a ring on his finger and sandals on his feet. [23]Bring the fattened calf and kill it. Let's have a feast and celebrate. [24]For this son of mine was dead and is alive again; he was lost and is found." So they began to celebrate.

[25]Meanwhile, the older son was in the field. When he came near the house, he heard music and dancing. [26]So he called one of the servants and asked him what was going on. [27]"Your brother has come," he replied, "and your father has killed the fattened calf because he has him back safe and sound."

[28]The older brother became angry and refused to go in. So his father went out and pleaded with him. [29]But he answered his father, "Look! All these years I've been slaving for you and never disobeyed your orders. Yet you never gave me even a young goat so I could celebrate with my friends. [30]But when this son of yours who has

squandered your property with prostitutes comes home, you kill the fattened calf for him!"

[31] *"My son," the father said, "you are always with me, and everything I have is yours.* [32] *But we had to celebrate and be glad, because this brother of yours was dead and is alive again; he was lost and is found."*

Dillon watched his father walking back and forth in the pulpit, and he had to admit, he did tend to like the very last part of what his father read; particularly the line that stated, "and everything I have is yours." Dillon liked it because he believed his father was saying that, since Dillon was the eldest of his two sons and he had never left Curtis, it would be Dillon who would inherit Curtis's final fortune. After all, just last year, his father had already proven that he considered him to be an important heir, right when he'd given him that large sum of money. His father had felt bad about the way he'd disowned Dillon for nearly thirty years, and recognizing Dillon as his primary heir was likely Curtis's generous way of making things up to him.

So as it had turned out, hearing his father read from Luke 15 had ended up being a blessing, and Dillon felt a lot better. Things hadn't gone well between him and his father over the last week, but maybe the reason his dad had chosen this topic was because he felt guilty about their last meeting. Maybe his dad was sorry for doubting his call to the ministry.

Curtis spoke for another forty minutes, and although he was just about finished with his sermon, suddenly the tone and meaning of his message changed drastically. So much so that Dillon thought he would pass out when he heard him say, "So as I prepare to close, I just want to say how enlightening this story has always been for me. More so now than before, though, because it represents what happened between my son Matthew and me. The only difference is that Matthew never went out and squandered my money or slept with prostitutes, and he's still just as much of an heir to my estate as the rest of my children. Actually, because of all the problems his mother and I have caused him over the years, I feel like we owe him even more."

Dillon didn't like what he was hearing, and his heart pumped a little faster.

"As a matter of fact," Curtis said, reaching his hand out to Matthew, "son, why don't you bring my beautiful little grandson up here so everyone can see him. Let 'em see that he's just as good-lookin' as his grandfather."

Everyone laughed, and when Matthew walked up the steps and passed MJ over to Curtis, they applauded. Even MJ seemed tickled by all the commotion, but Dillon wanted to tear Matthew's head off.

Dillon tried to calm his nerves and mask his anger, but as soon as Matthew and MJ took their seat, things got worse.

"I would also like to ask all of you to pray for my other son, Dillon. On Memorial Day, he shared with us that God has called him to minister."

There was loud applause again, and this time folks

stood up. Had his father not just made it clear that Matthew was still his golden boy and also the son he loved more, all this attention from the church would have made Dillon feel special. But the most he could do was force a phony smile onto his face, pretending to be happy.

"Dillon has assured me that God has given him confirmation, but I've asked him to go into deep prayer. I want him to be totally and completely sure about this."

Lots of amens filled the sanctuary.

But Dillon had never been more humiliated. Whether his father realized it or not, what he was doing was telling everyone that he didn't believe his own son. He was telling a church full of people that his son was a big liar.

Dillon couldn't imagine anything worse happening than that, at least not today. But sadly it did.

"And then if you'll allow me to keep you just a little longer," Curtis said, smiling and beckoning for Phillip to join him. "I have one final announcement."

Dillon looked down the row at Alicia. She seemed just as curious as he did.

"First, I just wanna say what a happy day this is for me," Curtis continued. "A few years ago, Phillip married my daughter, and although they're divorced now, I've never stopped loving him. I know he was my son-in-law, but I never saw him that way. I've always loved and respected him like a biological son. Anyway, he and I had a long talk yesterday, and he has something he wants to say to all of you."

Phillip hugged Curtis, and Dillon cringed. Didn't he have his own father? Although, now that Dillon thought about it, he remembered hearing something about Phillip's father being dead. Still, as far as Dillon was concerned, Phillip needed to go find someone else's father to latch on to, because Curtis had enough of his own children to worry about.

"First of all," Phillip began. "I just wanna say how much I still love every one of you. When I served as an assistant pastor here at Deliverance Outreach a few years back, those were some of the best days of my life, and it is because of my love for this church that I've decided to accept my former father-in-law's offer. I've done a lot of praying and soul searching, and I know coming back here to serve is the right decision. I know this is where I'm supposed to be."

Practically every parishioner got to their feet again, smiling and applauding in a way that Dillon had never seen them do before.

But Dillon couldn't understand why there was so much excitement, and his heart thumped so hard he felt it against his chest. He couldn't believe his father would betray him this way. How could he ask Phillip to come back to the church but then totally disregard Dillon's calling to the ministry? Dillon had decided to forget about being a minister, anyway, but his dad didn't know that. So, to Dillon, his father should have been doing everything he could to support him, and it should have been him his father was offering that assistant pastor position to.

"Thank you all so much," Phillip said, smiling. "Thank you for everything."

Dillon glared at Phillip, wishing he could do bad things to him. He'd never cared for his tagalong behind, anyway, but now he hated him.

"And that's not my only news," Phillip said, looking directly at Alicia. "Baby, I know our marriage didn't end well, but for three years now, you've gone completely out of your way to prove just how much you love me. You've shown me time after time how committed you are, so baby... will you marry me? Will you be my wife again?"

Alicia covered her mouth, as tears flowed down her face. "Oh my God," she said. "Yes, yes, yes."

She left her seat, and Phillip walked down the steps and hugged her. They held each other for what seemed like a century, and Dillon wanted to hurt somebody. He was so taken aback by all of these newsflashes that his body went numb. *I'm the one who's been here for my father, yet he wasted a whole freakin' sermon on Matthew? I'm the one who told my dad that God has called me to preach, yet he's giving Phillip a full-time pastor position? Then, as if that wasn't enough, he just told everyone here that Phillip has always been more a son to him than a son-in-law?*

Dillon broke into a cold sweat and wondered if he was dreaming. He must have been, because there was no way he could make himself believe his father would dismiss him and ignore him so publicly. He was reminded again of Aunt Susan's words when she'd told him that his father simply couldn't love him the way he loved his other children. It was the most painful reality, one he now had to accept, and he wished he'd never moved to Illinois. He wished he'd never gotten to know his dad at all, and since his father had done him so dirty, he was now glad his father's ex-wife, Mariah, had gotten two thugs to beat him nearly to death. Dillon was also happy that he'd exposed his father's sinful little secret on local television last year—by telling that awful story about his mom and the way his dad had treated her. To Dillon, this had been the ultimate payback, but he would pay his father back again, too. Curtis was great at quoting scriptures, but there was one in particular that Dillon loved. He wasn't sure where it was located in the Bible, but it went something like, "Vengeance is mine; I will repay, saith the Lord."

Dillon tossed those words back and forth in his mind, and then he got up and walked out of the church. He had tried with all his might to love his father and build a relationship with him. But now Dillon knew Curtis didn't care a thing about him, which meant Dillon didn't have any choice but to get even—and he would use that scripture he loved to help him. He knew these were God's words, but in this case, vengeance belonged to Dillon...and vengeance he would get—against his father and anyone else who had wronged him.

Chapter 39

As soon as Dillon left the church, he called Racquel, asking her to meet him at their usual hotel outside of Chicago. It was only a fifty-minute drive, and though that wasn't just around the corner, he was glad Racquel didn't mind taking it. He'd come to enjoy her company a great deal, but today he didn't just want her, he needed her—he needed someone to hold him, comfort him, and assure him that everything would be fine.

"You have no idea how hurt I am," he said after partially filling her in on what he'd experienced at church earlier. "My father treated me like I was nothing, and I'm done with him."

Racquel held him and caressed the back of his head. "I'm so sorry this happened to you."

"All this time, I'd thought my father was a better man than this, but he's just as selfish as that witch, Charlotte. They deserve each other."

"I'm a little shocked about Pastor Black, too, because

he always stood up for me when it came to Charlotte. He never treated me badly."

"Well, he certainly treated *me* badly. But that's okay, because he'll never get a chance to hurt me again."

"I hear you, and maybe we can work together to get what we want from them."

"I agree. I hate things turned out like this, but I'm not leaving here until I get some sort of satisfaction."

"Well, I already tried to work things out with Matthew, but since he wants nothing to do with me, I want my son back, I want child support, *and* I want alimony. He doesn't talk about it much, but I know he has a trust fund."

"Tomorrow, I'm gonna file to have my last name changed to Black. I don't plan to have anything else to do with my father, but I deserve to have his name just like the rest of his children. Then, since I haven't been able to destroy Charlotte the way I wanted, I've decided to take my dad for everything he has. Or at least most of it. That way, I'll be ruining Charlotte at the same time."

"At this point, they deserve whatever they get."

Dillon leaned back on the bed, and Racquel curled up next to him. He still couldn't get over the way his father had boasted about Matthew and MJ and also Phillip to the entire church. He'd even invited all three of them up to the pulpit with him, but not Dillon.

Dillon tossed out one thought after another, sighing deeply, and Racquel hugged him tightly.

"I know this is hard," she said. "But this too shall pass. You won't always feel so hurt."

Dillon lay there but didn't say anything. Still, he thought about his aunt, and his pain turned to rage. His dad was the reason he hadn't been there for her the way he should have been. He'd thought about this before, but now the reality of it all was almost too much to bear. Dillon had left his aunt behind and moved to Mitchell, hoping he'd have the best relationship ever with his father, but it hadn't happened. Needless to say, Dillon was furious and someone would have to pay.

Racquel grabbed both sides of Dillon's face and kissed him. It was amazing how awesome she made him feel, and not ever would he have thought any woman could satisfy and console him the way Racquel was doing. He was even to the point where he didn't want to be without her. She did have a bit of a drinking problem—he'd smelled alcohol on her breath again as soon as she'd entered the room—but she understood him, she never judged him, and she seemed to care about him. They also both had it in for Charlotte and Matthew, and he liked that, too. She didn't have anything against his dad, but she also didn't seem to mind that Dillon was planning to take him to the cleaners.

Maybe once they ruined all of them and Racquel got her divorce from Matthew, she would move to Atlanta with him. They might even be able to get married someday, something Dillon had never considered doing with any woman. When it came to Racquel, though, it was just that they connected so well and they had so much in common. Dillon wasn't sure if she felt the same way as he did or not, but he guessed time would tell. Deep down, he hoped for the best.

It was after midnight, and Dillon almost hated coming home anymore. Mainly because he didn't want to deal with Melissa, but of course, here she was standing and waiting for him as soon as he walked inside the condo.

"Baby, where have you been?"

Her tone sounded a little curt, and Dillon raised his eyebrows. "You must be losing your mind. Have to be if you're questioning me about anything."

"Why didn't you come home after church? That was hours ago."

Dillon pushed past her, but like a rodent he couldn't get rid of, she followed him upstairs.

"Are you seeing someone?" she asked, looking pitiful.

Dillon removed his blazer. "Look. If you know what's good for you, you'll leave me alone."

"Baby, I just wanna know what's wrong. Why you're doing this. Why you haven't been the same lately."

Dillon unbuttoned his shirt and ignored her.

She leaned against the dresser. "You know how much I love you. You know I'll do anything for you, so why isn't that enough?"

Dillon shook his head at her, removed the rest of his clothing, and slipped into his pajama bottoms. He climbed into bed and relaxed against two pillows, turned on the television, and pretended she wasn't there.

Still, she wouldn't go away, and instead, she sat down next to him on the bed.

"Let me make love to you," she said. "Let me make things right."

Dillon gazed at her, completely sickened by all her groveling, and went off.

"Didn't I ask you to leave me alone? Didn't I?" he yelled. "I don't love you, Melissa. I never have, and you know why? Because you're worthless. You're one of the most naïve, spineless women I've ever met, and the only reason I started dating you when we lived down in Atlanta was because you gave me money. You paid my car note, and bought me clothes. You did whatever I wanted. You were a total doormat, and nothing's changed."

Tears streamed down Melissa's face, but Dillon had no sympathy for her.

"Look, Melissa, this isn't working. It hasn't worked for a very long time, and I want you outta here by the end of the month. Today is the second, and I want you gone by June thirtieth."

Melissa sniffled, seemingly in shock. "You don't mean that."

"When have you ever known me to say anything I don't mean? And if you don't have all your junk out of my house by the thirtieth, it'll be tossed in the street."

Melissa wiped her tears but finally got up and walked away.

"Dumb broad," Dillon said, flipping the TV channel. "That's why I slept with your best friend. I got with her every chance I could. Although, maybe she really wasn't your friend after all."

Melissa turned and looked at him in horror. "What are you talking about?"

"How many best friends did you have in Atlanta? Venus, that's who."

"Venus would never do something like that."

"She would and she did."

"Why are you telling me this now? Why are you being so cruel?"

"Because I feel like it, and because you didn't get me what I needed from that investigator. Now get outta here, Melissa."

Tears poured down her cheeks, but soon she left the room. When she did, Dillon pulled out his phone and called Racquel.

Chapter 40

Matt pulled into the parking lot of the bank. It was his first day back, and although he'd rather be back in school or working somewhere different, he was sort of glad to be there. He loved spending time with and taking care of MJ, but he also didn't like sitting around the house and not being responsible.

As he turned off his vehicle, Nicole got out of her car and walked toward him. Because of their conversation the other day, he couldn't help feeling a bit uneasy, but he rolled down the window to speak to her.

"How's it goin'?" he said.

"Good. Can I talk to you?"

"Yeah, but we only have about fifteen minutes."

"This won't take long," she said, already making her way around the car and getting in.

"It's really good to have you back, Matt."

"It's good to be back."

"So, did you think about what I said?"

Matthew didn't want to hurt her feelings, so all

he said was, "I'm really going through a lot right now."

"I understand, but I can help you with that. I can be here for you."

Matthew didn't have the heart to tell her that even if he weren't in love with someone else, he still wouldn't be attracted to her in that way.

"You are still filing for a divorce, aren't you?"

"I am, but I'm not looking forward to it."

Nicole rubbed her hand against the side of his face, but as soon as she did, Racquel slammed her hand against his window.

Nicole jerked her hand away from him. "Oh my God, is that your wife?"

Matthew never bothered answering, but he opened his car door and got out.

Racquel squinted her eyes in anger. "So, is this the reason you keep blowin' me off? Is this the tramp you're sleeping with?"

"Racquel, why are you even here?"

"Because you're my husband, and I have a right to be."

"You need to leave before security comes out and calls the police."

Racquel took a step back, glaring at him. "Do I look like I'm afraid of the police? And anyway, as soon as I explain how you were sitting in your car, drooling over some whore, I doubt they'll be arresting anybody. Especially once they find out I'm your wife."

Matthew sighed loudly. "I'm going inside."

Nicole finally found the courage to get out, but as she hurried away she looked back at Racquel.

"What're you looking at? And if I catch you with my husband again, you'll regret it for the rest of your life. Either that or you'll be dead."

Nicole walked faster, and Matthew locked his car door.

"I know you're sleeping with her, Matt."

"Nope."

"Yep," she said, mocking him. "You think I'm stupid."

"You must not've taken your medication this morning."

"What? Who told you I was taking anything?"

"Just forget it," he said, walking past her.

"You dirty snake. You've been sleeping with that whore all along, but that's okay, Matt. Every dog has his day. Just watch."

Chapter 41

Dillon strutted across the street, got into his SUV, and started it up. He'd just left the courthouse, and the application for his name change was complete. He wasn't planning to ever be a part of his father's life anymore, but he was certainly planning to use the Black name whenever necessary, which was the reason he'd confirmed again with the clerk as to how long this process would take. He needed to know because as soon as he received the official paperwork, he would use his last name in multiple ways. He was even considering whether he should sue his dad for a lot more money than he'd already given him. He honestly didn't see why not, since he was in fact the good reverend's eldest son, and he hadn't gotten nearly what belonged to him.

Until now, all Dillon had wanted was his father's love, but today he wanted his fortune. It was the least his father could do for him, what with the awful way he'd handled things, and Dillon planned to get it.

Dillon drove away from the curb but soon stopped at a red light. When he did, his phone rang and he saw that it was his father. Actually, Curtis had called him three other times, too, but Dillon hadn't answered. He wouldn't answer now, either, because he didn't want to talk to him. When the phone stopped ringing, however, he dialed Racquel.

"Hey, baby," she said. "I was just about to call you."

"So what's up?"

"Not much. Where are you?"

"Just leaving the courthouse."

"Oh yeah, that's right. I have to go there this afternoon with my parents, and I'm not looking forward to it. Something about a preconference hearing, but whatever."

"It's good you're going, so you can put this behind you."

"I guess, but hey, are we getting together today?"

"I have a few errands to run, but I'll see you this evening for sure."

"Sounds good. Oh and I got those dates and cities for you."

Right before they'd left the hotel last night, Dillon had come up with a genius plan, and he'd asked her to get whatever information she could from her friend who worked at his dad's church.

"Do you want it now? Otherwise, I can just bring it tonight."

"I'll take it now," he said, pulling a pen and notepad from the console between his two front seats.

Racquel recited dates, times, locations, and reasons for travel.

"Is that it?" he asked when he wrote the last of what she'd told him.

"That's all she gave me."

"Thanks so much for this."

"I just hope it helps. And what are you gonna use it for, anyway?"

When the light changed, Dillon drove through the intersection. "I'll tell you when we meet."

"Okay, see you then."

Dillon drove a few more blocks and turned left onto Brockton Street. He immediately saw Sasha, the woman he'd spotted last night while driving home from the hotel. She was wearing a bright red dress that was easily one size too small, and it barely covered the middle of her thighs. It was tighter than tight, shorter than short, and she wore five-inch red sandals to match it. What was interesting to Dillon, however, was that she sported her own hair, which was beautiful, and she didn't wear excessive makeup. Sasha was clearly a professional hooker, though, and Dillon was glad he'd connected with her, especially since he'd devised the perfect scheme and Sasha had agreed to help him—that is for the right amount of money.

She'd even charged him two hundred dollars just to talk because she said her time was very valuable, but Dillon hadn't minded paying her. Not when Sasha was going to get him everything he wanted from his father.

Dillon pulled over and parked, and Sasha got in the vehicle.

"So you got my money?"

"Sure do," he said, readily passing her an envelope with another two hundred dollars in it.

She counted the four fifties and slid her payment into her shoulder bag. "I'm sorry to have to charge you again, but normally I don't come out during the day like this. Normally, I'm asleep."

"I understand, and this won't take very long."

"I'm listening."

"A videographer will be recording your full confession, and he'll be doing it day after tomorrow."

"Do you want me to say something in particular or just something like, 'world-renowned Reverend Curtis Black has been paying me a large sum of money for years to have sex with him.' "

"Yeah, I definitely want you to mention that, but I also want you to mention every one of these dates and cities," he said, passing her the information he'd written down. "That way folks will know you've traveled with him as well. I also want you to mention what church events, conferences, or book signings he was in town for. That information is listed also. Oh, and these are all trips that his wife didn't travel with him on."

Sasha scanned the piece of paper from top to bottom.

"Then I want you to talk about all the jewelry he's bought for you."

"What kind?"

"Anything you wanna say will be great. Just make something up, but make sure the items you name are expensive. I also want you to practice this over and over, so that people will believe you. I want them to have no doubts about whether you're telling the truth."

"Not a problem."

"We'll do a few dry runs on the day of the recording, and then he'll cut the final segment. But again, I really need your confession to sound authentic. Then, toward the end, I want you to finish by saying that the reason you've decided to come forward is because you can no longer tolerate or watch any pastor sleeping around on his wife the way Pastor Black has been doing. You can even mention how he's told you a thousand times how awful his wife is in bed and how he basically can't stand the sight of her. Then you can say that your conscience just won't allow you to continue participating in this kind of evil-doing and that you also felt completely violated when Pastor Black asked if you'd be willing to do a threesome with him and one of his other women."

"Wow, you've really got this all figured out, don't you?"

"Pretty much."

"And you're still gonna pay me ten thousand dollars, right?"

"Yep, with fifty percent upfront and fifty percent as soon as we finish recording."

Sasha shook her head. "You must really hate your father."

"I do," Dillon said matter-of-factly. "He's a terrible

person, but once I take his money from him, I'll feel a lot better about everything."

"Well, to each his own, I guess. And as long as I get my payment, that's all that matters to me."

"Good. I'm glad to hear that."

"Well, if that's all," she said, "then I'll see you Wednesday?"

"Wednesday it is."

Dillon watched her walking across the street and into the brick apartment complex. He laughed when he thought about how brilliant his plan was. He almost felt like taking that finished video and uploading it to YouTube and then sitting back, relishing in his dad's destruction. But if he did that, he knew he wouldn't get any money, so it was better to stick with his original strategy: good ol' blackmail. He would play the video for his father and name his price. Ten million dollars. He wasn't sure how much his dad earned or how much he'd saved, but Dillon knew ten million was a good number to start with. He also knew that since his dad had recently returned to the church as senior pastor, professing his newfound relationship with God, he would never want to chance dealing with another scandal. He wouldn't want his members or the public questioning his integrity or envisioning him buying and sleeping with a prostitute. His parishioners had forgiven him before, but they wouldn't likely do it again—not when his father had promised them that there were no more secrets about his past or current life.

Dillon drove away from Brockton Street with a crafty

smile on his face, picturing the downfall of his famous father and church. A year ago, Dillon had been happy just getting the half-million dollars Curtis had given him, which had been more money than he'd ever imagined. But now his financial status was about to change drastically because once he carried out this scheme of his, he'd be a full-fledged millionaire. He'd be filthy rich, and he'd never have to see his cold-hearted father or stepmother again. He wouldn't need anyone, period.

Chapter 42

For hours, Matthew had debated calling Racquel's mom, Vanessa, wondering if he should inform her about yesterday morning. Shortly after Racquel had threatened both him and Nicole and then flew out of the parking lot like some psycho, he'd gone into the bank and called Alicia. He wasn't sure why he'd chosen to contact his sister, although, truthfully, he still didn't feel comfortable discussing his marital problems with his parents. His mother regularly hinted around about his filing for a divorce, and his father supported him either way, but he still didn't want to involve them if he didn't have to. As it was, he'd been forced to move back in with them, and that was enough.

He glanced at his watch and saw that it was four-forty. He only had twenty minutes to go at work and since he didn't have any customers waiting, he dialed Vanessa.

"Hello?"

"Hey, how are you?" he asked.

"Hi, son. I'm good. What about you?"

"I'm okay, but I wanted to tell you about Racquel."

"Did something happen?"

"Yeah. She showed up at my job yesterday morning, screaming and yelling and then she accused me of sleeping with one of my coworkers."

"Oh no. What time was that?"

"Just before eight. I hadn't even gone inside the bank yet."

"I am so, so sorry, Matt."

"Is she still taking her medication?"

"As far as I know."

"I don't think she is," he said.

"Well, she seemed fine this morning and also this afternoon in court."

Matthew was starting to wonder if his mother-in-law was truly that naïve or whether she was wallowing in permanent denial. "Maybe she took it because she knew she had a court date."

"I don't think so, because she's been pretty happy for days now. In a lot of ways, she's like her old self again."

Matthew didn't bother responding, because it was obvious he was wasting his breath.

"I really wish you'd sit down and talk to her, Matt. I wish you'd help her through this court situation. Then maybe the two of you can see a marriage counselor."

"I can't talk to Racquel. She's too angry and violent all the time. Who she needs to talk to is her psychiatrist."

"But it's like I told you before, she's hurt. She's only acting like this because she wants you back."

"Does it sound like she's going to jail?" he asked.

"We hope not."

"What about a mental facility? She really needs help."

"Her doctor believes she'll be fine as long as she continues outpatient treatment."

Matthew listened as his mother-in-law gave one excuse after another, but all she'd done was confirm his decision. He was finally contacting his dad's attorney first thing tomorrow morning, and he was also filing for full custody. If Racquel showed up threatening him again, he would file for an order of protection, too.

When Matthew ended the call, he dialed Stacey.

"Hey you," she said.

"Hey, what's up? You outside yet?"

"Yep. Just got here."

"I'm glad you came," he told her.

"I am, too. You still wanna pick up some food from that little Mexican restaurant?"

"Yeah, and then we can head out to the forest preserve."

"Okay, well, you only have about ten minutes left, so I'll just wait for you."

"I'll be out as soon as I can."

"I love you," she said.

"I love you, too, Stacey."

No matter how many days passed or how badly Matthew wanted to spend time with Stacey, the guilt still ate him alive. He'd thought he might feel better about seeing her, especially since Racquel had shown her behind yesterday, but his love for God and knowledge of the Word wouldn't let him. He remembered how years ago his father had compared himself to Paul in the Book of Romans. He would tell the congregation how Paul hadn't wanted to sin, but he sinned anyway, and he couldn't seem to help it. Paul also hadn't understood why he did some of the terrible things he did and then did them over again. As a child, Matthew hadn't fully comprehended that kind of thinking, but now he understood it very well. He didn't want to sin, but he also didn't want to stop being with Stacey, and for that reason he tried not to think about what he was doing.

Matthew cleared off his desk, but then someone knocked at his door.

"Come in."

Nicole eased his door open, smiling nervously. She'd sort of been avoiding him ever since Racquel had shown up yesterday morning, acting a stone fool, and Matthew didn't blame her.

"Can I chat with you for a few minutes?"

"Yeah, have a seat."

Nicole closed the door and sat in front of him. "I really do like you, Matt, but after seeing your wife yesterday, I agree that this isn't the time for you to be seeing someone else. Still, I hope things won't be awkward between us and that we can go back to being strictly friends and coworkers."

Matthew was relieved. "As far as I'm concerned, nothing's changed. Everything's fine."

"I'm glad you feel that way. And who knows, maybe things will be better down the road."

They chatted for another five minutes and walked outside to the parking lot. But to their great disappointment, they saw Racquel parking next to Matthew. She quickly jumped out, ready to confront them again.

"Maybe I should go back inside the bank," Nicole whispered but kept looking ahead.

"Just get in your car and leave."

"Well, well, well," Racquel said. "I see you're still hanging out with this skank of yours." Then she glared directly at Nicole. "You do know he's married, right?"

Nicole walked a little faster, and Matthew looked over at Stacey, who didn't move. He was glad Racquel hadn't spotted her, because if she did, she might realize that she'd been accusing the wrong woman. She still didn't know Matthew was seeing Stacey, but she would certainly recognize her from high school.

Nicole finally opened her car door, but as soon as Racquel noticed it, she jetted between cars with a knife. Matthew yelled out Nicole's name, but before she could turn around, Racquel slashed her across her back.

Matthew rushed toward them. "Oh my God. What have you done?"

Racquel raised the knife again, charged at Matthew, and slashed him across his arm. Still, he grabbed her wrist and shook the knife out of her hand.

"Let me go! Leave me alone, Matt!"

"Hey, hey, hey," a fifty-something, muscular security guard yelled, rushing toward them. "What's going on?"

Racquel yanked away from Matt, dashed to her car, started it up, and raced into the street. Screeching sounds could still be heard even after she was out of sight.

Matthew knelt down to help Nicole, and Stacey got out of her car to help also. Soon, other employees gathered around, and squad cars and sirens approached them.

Matthew removed his blazer and covered Nicole up with it, and Stacey held her hand. She was clearly in excruciating pain, and Matthew couldn't help thinking about how when Nicole had first seen Racquel, she'd asked if she should go back inside the bank. Now he wished he'd advised her differently, and he would never forgive himself for not doing so. It had just been earlier when he'd realized his mother-in-law was in denial about Racquel, but this proved that he was as well. She'd already stabbed him multiple times two weeks ago, so why hadn't he thought she might try this again? Why had he trusted her to do the right thing when he knew what she was capable of? Maybe a part of him still loved her, or maybe he just didn't want to think the worst of his own wife. He wasn't sure, but either way, he knew Racquel needed to be locked up before she killed someone.

Chapter 43

After meeting Racquel at their usual Chicago-area spot last night, Dillon wasn't sure why she was so adamant about meeting him at a local truck stop, specifically on the outskirts of town. She'd also wanted to leave her car there and ride with him to a hotel on the other side of Mitchell. Actually, he hadn't seen her car, because right when he'd pulled up, she'd been coming out of the truck stop. But when he'd asked her about it, she'd told him she parked it in the back. She'd also told him that she just hadn't felt like driving nearly an hour just to be with him, and that she didn't see a reason for them to keep hiding. Dillon didn't see a reason to either, and to be honest, he'd only hidden their affair for her sake and also because when they'd first started seeing each other, he hadn't wanted his father to find out about them. But both of those reasons were a moot point, and he was glad to not have to drive toward Chicago any longer.

"Can we just spend the night here?" she asked, wrapping her arms around his neck, wreaking of alcohol, the same as always.

"If you want."

"I do."

"Are you okay? You seem a little different."

"I'm fine. I could definitely use a drink, though," she said, slurring her words.

Dillon wasn't surprised that she was already asking for more liquor, but he still wondered why she seemed a little strange, and nervous even. He also couldn't help asking himself why he was so attracted to an alcoholic. This wasn't normal for him, but it was just that he loved the fire and boldness about her.

Racquel gazed into Dillon's eyes, and he kissed her.

"I'm so in love with you," she said, "and I want us to leave here. Let's go away together."

"I'm already planning for that, and we will, just as soon as I get that money from my dad."

"So you really think he's gonna do it?" she asked. "Give you millions just to keep quiet?"

Dillon had told her the details of his plan last night at the hotel, but he could tell Racquel seemed a bit worried about the outcome.

"He doesn't want any more trouble. Plus, all he has to do is write a few more books and travel around to a lot more speaking engagements. He'll have his ten mill back in no time."

"I really want you," Racquel said, not paying much attention to what he'd just told her. She kissed him wildly and heatedly and tore his V-neck shirt over his head so roughly that it ripped in two places. He didn't complain, though, because he loved the way she took control.

Finally, she pushed Dillon onto the bed, but just as she reached for his zipper, there was forceful pounding on the door.

"Police! Open up!"

Dillon sat up, and Racquel backed away toward the wall. "Baby, please don't open that."

"Why?"

"Just don't. Just ignore it." There was more loud beating against the door, and Racquel looked terrified. "I'm not going to jail."

"Baby, what did you do?" he asked.

"I'm not going back to jail" was all she said again.

Dillon stared at her, but then he looked toward the door when he heard a key being inserted.

Racquel hurried over to her purse and pulled out a handgun.

Dillon bucked his eyes. "What're you doing?"

"I told you I'm not going to jail."

Dillon felt like he was in the Twilight Zone. He couldn't speak if he wanted to.

He didn't have to, though, because barely a second later, two detectives and two officers stormed into the room, pointing their weapons.

Dillon raised his hands and surrendered without being told, but Racquel cocked her gun. "Don't come any closer," she instructed them.

Dillon wondered what was wrong with her, and regardless of all the startling commotion happening at the moment, he thought back to that day she'd admitted to not taking her pills. Had he been that blind? Had he pretended nothing was mentally wrong with her? Had he wanted to be loved by someone so much that he'd been willing to ignore her emotional issues?

"Please put the gun down!" the female detective demanded. "Drop it now!"

Racquel stared the woman down and then looked back and forth between the others, and suddenly, she seemed as calm as a country road. It was as if she no longer had any feelings, one way or the other, and Dillon couldn't see how this would end well.

And it didn't. Racquel fired the gun and hit one of the male officers, and the two detectives fired back at her. Racquel's gun fell to the ground, and she dropped to the floor beside it.

Chapter 44

What a night. Dillon parked his SUV inside the garage, but when he turned off the ignition, he sat there. The officers had asked him to come to the station for questioning, but he was still in a total state of shock. What he was more astonished to learn was the fact that Racquel had stabbed a woman whom Matthew worked with, and then she'd hit a car and run. The passengers in the other vehicle had been rushed to the hospital and were in stable condition, but Dillon knew Racquel was in a lot of trouble. Aggravated assault, along with aggravated assault with a deadly weapon against a police officer, was bad enough, but now she was facing felony DUI and possession of a firearm charges—and that was in addition to the felony assault charges she was already dealing with for stabbing Matthew. The good news, though, was that the officer she'd shot had been wearing a bulletproof vest, and she was alive. Racquel had been categorized as being in fair condition, but Dillon saw that as great news, considering she could have been killed.

Dillon leaned his head against the backrest and took a deep breath. He felt sorry for Racquel, but he also couldn't lose sight of his own plans, so he pulled himself together. The videographer would be recording Sasha's confession tomorrow, and he needed to get some rest so he'd be ready.

He got out of the car and went inside. He frowned when he saw that no lights were on, because normally when he stayed out late, Melissa never turned them off. Maybe she'd thought he was going to be home a lot earlier. Who knew when it came to Melissa, though? It wasn't as if she was the brightest scholar in the bunch.

Dillon turned on the lights, but when he did, he saw a garment bag and an overnight suitcase. Maybe she'd taken him seriously and had decided to move out tonight instead of waiting until the end of the month. He hoped so, because that suited him fine. He would no longer be seeing Racquel, but he still wanted nothing else to do with Melissa, so the sooner she left the better.

Dillon walked farther into the hallway leading into the family room, but as he turned to walk up the stairway, Melissa flipped on the light and snaggletoothed Roger walked down in front of her, holding a gun. Dillon knew he had to dreaming.

"Back up!" Roger yelled when he landed at the bottom of the stairs. Then he turned Dillon's body around with his other hand and pushed him into the kitchen.

"You'd better get your country hands off of me," Dillon said.

There was no way this bumpkin was going to do anything. He and Melissa were simply playing some childish, knucklehead game, and when it was over, Dillon would punish both of them.

"Sit down and shut up," Melissa said curtly, and Roger pushed Dillon into the chair and pointed the gun at his head.

"All I did was try to love you," Melissa said. "All I ever did was try to be here for you, even when no one else cared anything about you."

"Melissa, I'm not playin' with you. You'd better call off this country dimwit before I snap on both of you."

Melissa laughed. "Still talkin' crazy, even with a gun to your head. But the thing is, Dillon, you're gonna listen to everything I have to say."

Dillon wanted to protest, but this fool Roger seemed a bit fidgety, so Dillon kept quiet. He was going to beat the mess out of Roger, though, when he got the chance.

"It was one thing when you started talking to me like I was some idiot, but when you started putting your hands on me and hurting me, that was something different. Then all those times you forced me to have sex when I didn't want to. Then all those times you called me dumb and stupid and told me you never loved me. Well, that was way too much, Dillon. But none of that compared to when you started sleeping around with your brother's wife. Only a dog would do something like that. But even so, after all I've done for you... after all I've gone through with you... after all the verbal and physical abuse I've taken from you... you still decided it was okay to sleep with another woman behind my back? I was pretty much done with you then, but the icing on the cake was when you admitted to my face that you'd been sleeping with my best friend. I don't think I've ever been more hurt in my life. I loved Venus like a sister."

Dillon rolled his eyes, but he did wonder how she knew about his sleeping with Racquel. She wasn't smart enough to find out something like that on her own, so he wondered who'd told her.

"Venus was everything to me," she continued. "And now I know why she rarely called me after we left Atlanta, and then when I would call her, she was always busy. You're such a snake, Dillon, and so is she, and I hope I never see you again. Oh and for the record, whether you think so or not, I *can* do a lot of things right. I hired that private investigator just like you wanted... one of the best in the business... but instead of having him follow Charlotte, I had him follow you. Instead of him digging up dirt on her, I had him find out where all your bank accounts were. Then, while you were out sleeping around all night, I found two of your checkbooks."

Dillon tossed Melissa a dirty look. "All my money better be right where I left it."

"Yeah, okay. Whatever you say."

"I'm not playin' with you, Melissa."

"I left you a few dollars, but the other four hundred fifty thousand has already been deposited into another account. And, of course, you put down a hundred thousand on this condo, remember, and then you used the other hundred on living expenses. What you should've done was get a job the way your father told you. But nooooo," she sang, "you were too good for that, *remember*?"

Dillon wanted to strangle Melissa. She'd taken the money his father had given him and also the proceeds from the insurance policies his aunt Susan had left him. He would never let Melissa get away with this harebrained scheme of hers, though, and she had to know that. He also still couldn't get over Country Roger, who had the nerve to be standing there holding a gun to his head. This whole travesty was ludicrous.

"Are you ready, Roger?"

"Oh, so I guess you're sleepin' with this country clown, huh, Melissa?" Dillon laughed out loud, knowing that wasn't true, but he couldn't help joking about it. Then he turned his attention to Roger. "So is this the reason you're suddenly tryin' to work on that raggedy mouth of yours? Tryin' to impress this dumb chick?"

Melissa leaned against the wall and folded her arms. "As a matter of fact I am impressed. When you went to Atlanta, Roger gave me more love and intimacy than any man has. Especially that night you called here. Remember when I didn't answer the phone at first, and you had to call back? And I hadn't even heard about your brother being stabbed? Well, that's because Roger and I had been together all that day....right here in bed. And you know what else, Dillon, you're nothing compared to Roger. Not in bed, not with anything."

If only this nut wasn't holding a gun to Dillon's head, he would beat Melissa into oblivion.

"You thought you were so smart, but Roger always knew how awful you were to me, and he kept telling me I deserved so much better. You just never realized it, because he was always so polite to you. I guess he wasn't as country and as dumb as you thought, now was he?"

If Dillon could murder Melissa and get away with it, he would. "You do know you're going to jail for stealing my money, though, right?"

"I doubt it. Not when Sasha has already given me the tape she used to record your conversation."

Dillon swallowed the colossal lump in his throat.

Melissa's eyes turned cold. "Yeah, that's right. The investigator saw you sitting in the car talking to her on Sunday night, but when you left, he had his own conversation with Sasha. It didn't take much at all to get her to tell what you wanted, and when I promised her twenty-five thousand, that was the end of it. She recorded everything you said on Monday."

Dillon was speechless. What was he going to do without any money?

"Let's go, Roger," she said and they both backed away from him, picked up the two pieces of luggage sitting in the middle of the kitchen floor, and headed toward the garage.

But then Melissa stopped. "Oh, and one last thing. Your father already has a copy. I gave it to him a couple of hours ago, and if you try to come after me, he's giving that tape to the police. You'll be arrested on extortion charges. He also said he was fine with me keeping that money he gave you. I told him everything, and he couldn't believe how much you'd been abusing me."

Now Dillon knew the reason Curtis had been calling him. He'd been told about Dillon's blackmail plot, and he wanted to confront him. It was a good thing Dillon didn't have access to his own gun, because if he had, Melissa and Country Roger would be dead.

But more than anything, Dillon thought about the fact that he'd lost everything. His mother, his aunt, his father, Racquel, and all his money. He had absolutely nothing. Not even the words to explain it.

Epilogue

Three Months Later

Matthew tossed his son into the air, and he squealed with total joy. MJ was such a happy baby, and Matthew was grateful for that. He was thankful for his son and glad MJ was loved by so many.

Although there were times when no matter how wonderful things seemed, Matthew still thought heavily about Racquel. Their entire marriage had been a disaster, but not ever in his most extreme imagination would he have believed she was capable of causing so much tragedy and pain. From neglecting MJ to frequently getting drunk to stabbing Matthew to sleeping with his brother, it had been one horrible incident after another. On top of that, she'd also stabbed Nicole, who thankfully had recovered fine but had left town because of how devastating her experience had been. Then, as if that hadn't been enough, Racquel had hurt two people in a car accident and shot a police officer.

Racquel had done things that Matthew hadn't thought she or most people he knew were capable of doing, and although three months had passed since she'd been hospitalized for two gunshot wounds, he still found himself feeling sorry for her. Of course, not everyone understood why he had so much sympathy for her, but he knew it was partly because she was MJ's mother, and partly because his own mother had taken MJ away from Racquel barely weeks after he was born. Racquel clearly had some issues, but there was no denying the fact that her real troubles hadn't begun until that day child protective services had picked up MJ. She'd cried and suffered in such a grave way that by the time he'd been returned to her, she'd evolved into a completely different person. But what bothered him more than anything else was that no one had paid enough attention or done anything to help her. Here he'd lived in the house with her, yet the most he'd done was hope and pray that she'd get better. Then, when he'd told Racquel's parents that she seriously needed help, they hadn't done a whole lot to get her help either. It had been as if they'd all decided that Racquel was just being mean, lazy, and unsocial, and that eventually she'd return to being her old self. Sadly, though, it hadn't happened, and her illness and unstable mind had only escalated into something disastrous.

On a more positive note, however—that is, if a person wanted to view it that way—a judge had finally sentenced her to a psychiatric hospital. She'd fully recovered from her gunshot wounds, but instead of sending her to prison, the judge had accepted her plea of not guilty by reason of insanity. She would remain there for a few years, but there was hope that she would one day be well enough to be released. Matthew hadn't gone to see her more than a couple of times, but when he had, she'd appeared to be doing a lot better. He also received updates from his former in-laws as well as from Racquel's best friend, Jasmine. Matthew had even offered to bring MJ for a short visit, but Racquel had told him she wanted to spend a little more time getting well. She wanted to be the best she could be before her little boy saw her again. Matthew understood the reason she felt that way, and he respected her wishes.

The one thing he didn't understand, however, was why she'd gotten mixed up with Dillon and how Dillon could have no problem sleeping with his own brother's wife. Matthew knew he and Dillon had never been close—actually, they'd never actually gotten to know each other at all—but he still couldn't fathom any man sleeping with his sister-in-law. There were just certain moral and family lines most human beings didn't cross. It was the kind of unwritten rule that never had to be discussed, but for some reason, Dillon hadn't seen anything wrong with it. In fact, had it not been for Melissa, Matthew might never have found out about the affair taking place between his brother and his wife. Melissa had called Matthew and told him everything. As fate would have it, Melissa had seen a breaking news report on the local six o'clock news about Nicole's stabbing, and this was when she'd realized the police were looking for Racquel. It was then that she'd contacted the investigator to determine Dillon's whereabouts. She'd had a feeling Racquel might be locked away in some hotel with him, what with her having been with him two nights in a row before that. Then, shortly after notifying the police, she'd called Matthew.

But sleeping with his sister-in-law wasn't the only vile thing Dillon had been capable of. He'd actually plotted some crooked scheme and tried to blackmail their father. Thankfully, Melissa was the reason Dillon hadn't gotten away with that either, and right after draining his bank accounts, she'd moved back to the South. Dillon, on the other hand, was still there living in Mitchell, but none of them had anything to do with him or ever saw him. Matthew's dad had immediately confronted him, though, about his extortion plans—wanting to know why Dillon would do something like that—but all Dillon had told him was that he never wanted to see him or any other member of the Black family again. So that had been that, and everyone had moved on.

Now, things were starting to look up, at least in some respects, anyway, because not only was Matthew's divorce just about final, his parents had encouraged him to return to Harvard. They'd almost insisted that he reenroll, not in a controlling way, but in a loving one, and Matthew was grateful to them. He had, of course, lost his academic scholarship, but his parents had offered to pay his expenses, and classes had begun two weeks ago. As a matter of fact, the only reason he was able to have such a great time with MJ at the moment was because his parents had brought MJ out to Boston for the weekend. They'd also brought Stacey along, something Matthew couldn't believe, since his mother had never liked any girl he'd dated. But for some reason, she seemed fine with his current choice. Stacey was still attending college in Illinois, but she and Matthew had promised to try and see each other every chance they got. It was true that they did miss each other terribly, but so far, it hadn't affected the special love they shared. They were committed to their relationship, and Matthew believed they would be fine. There was no denying that he hadn't remained faithful to Racquel, something he still felt pretty badly about, but he'd repented, asked God to forgive him, and he was doing his best to live his life right. He'd made a lot of mistakes, but what he'd promised himself and God was that he wouldn't keep repeating them—it was hard, but he'd even told Stacey that they could no longer have sex.

There was no way he'd ever be perfect, because no one was, but he could certainly try to do the right thing as much as possible. And he would—for himself and for his son. Matthew would live the way God wanted him to live, and life would be good. He would obey all the commandments, and he'd be fine. He knew this because God never went back on His Word. God was the same, yesterday, today, and tomorrow, and just knowing that gave Matthew peace. It made him smile and thankful just to be alive. And to him, that meant everything.

Discussion Questions for

The Prodigal Son

1. Given his personal history, are Dillon's feelings of jealousy toward his siblings justified? What would you advise him to do to get his feelings under control? What could Curtis, Matthew, and Alicia do to help Dillon—or should they not have to?

2. Have you ever experienced sibling rivalry? If so, how did you cope with it?

3. Should Matthew have been more willing to forgive his parents sooner? Was he right to walk away from Racquel when she was in need of help? Can all breaks be mended, or are some actions simply unforgivable?

4. Was it okay for Matthew to talk to another woman about the problems in his marriage? How would you feel if your spouse opened up to a coworker or neighbor rather than a counselor, minister, or family member? Who do you turn to when you have problems you need to discuss?

5. Is Racquel responsible for the problems in her marriage? If so, why? Is she still a victim of Charlotte's action from a year ago? Is she a victim of mental illness? Is there anything Racquel could have done to help heal herself before things got out of hand? If so, what exactly? Should her family have done more to help her? If so, what steps could they have taken to assist her?

6. Should Matthew and Racquel have gotten married at all? Why or why not? Would they have been better off to have waited? Would little MJ have been better off? Can young marriages ever work? What advice would you give a young couple about marriage?

7. Did Vanessa and Neil make the right decision by not telling the judge Racquel's full backstory? What would you have done in their position?

8. Do you believe Dillon really regrets how he treated his aunt, or is he just feeling sorry for himself? Can bonds with friends be just as strong—or stronger—than bonds with relatives? Do you have an Aunt Susan in your life? If so, please describe her.

9. Why do you think Melissa stayed with Dillon for so long? Did she truly love him or truly fear him? Do you know women like Melissa?

10. Both Melissa and Matthew try to hide the abuse they suffer. Does spousal abuse carry a social stigma? Does it matter who is doing the abuse and who is the victim? What advice would you give someone who you knew or suspected was being abused?